One Red Bastard

Also by Ed Lin

Snakes Can't Run
This Is a Bust
Waylaid

One Red Bastard

ED LIN

WITNESS
IMPULSE
An Imprint of HarperCollinsPublishers

One Red Bastard was originally published in 2012 by Minotaur Books, an imprint of St. Martin's Publishing Group.

Digital Edition NOVEMBER 2017 ISBN: 978-0-06-244420-2

Print Edition ISBN: 978-0-06-244421-9

Cover design and art by spoon+fork

17 18 19 20 21 LSC 10 9 8 7 6 5 4 3 2 1

For Cindy

If a daughter turns out badly, she'll go to another family anyway; but having a bad son is serious.

—FROM *A DREAM OF RED MANSIONS* BY
TSAO HSUEH-CHIN AND KAO HGO

October 18, 1976

OF COURSE, THE GRAND STREET subway station was out of commission but luckily the uptown 103 bus on the Bowery was right there. I told Paul to get on it.

"But I don't have any change," he said, frowning at me. He's a bright kid, but he's book-smart, not street-smart. I worry about him sometimes.

"Will you just get in there? I'll take care of this," I said. He should have known by now that his elders would always pay for him.

I pushed Paul ahead of me. I boarded the bus and flashed my shield at the driver.

"That's for me. I'm going to pay for the boy," I said.

"Don't worry about it," said the driver.

"No, I have it."

"You're not taking your whole family out for a day trip in the country. This is a city bus."

I crossed my arms and studied the driver. He was a white male, probably pushing sixty, possibly five feet eight standing, and weighed about one hundred seventy. His face was as worn out as his uniform and his dead eyes told me he didn't care about anything or anyone anymore.

I reached into my pocket and pulled only thirty-five cents in change. Dammit, fifteen cents short. If I hadn't bought these newspapers, I would have had enough.

The pupil fare was eliminated by the Board of Education last month, and Paul would cost the full adult fare. That decision made a lot of sense if we were looking for one more way to encourage our kids to ditch school.

Knowing enough not to bother asking the driver, I turned to the passengers sitting in the front.

"Do any of you have four quarters for a dollar?" I asked.

Two men ignored me completely. One woman shook her head.

"If you're going to insist on paying, just put in whatever change you have on you," said the driver. "We have to get moving now." He slammed shut the door and we swerved away from the curb. I grabbed for the nearest pole and looked back at the corner deli.

I had been ready to step off, get a cup of coffee for the extra change, and wait another year for the next bus.

"You can pay the pupil's fare for the boy," said the driver. "They'll probably change it back, anyway."

I dropped in the change.

"There's something wrong with you people," said the driver.

"Us people?"

"Yeah. You cops always want to be the heroes."

"We aren't heroes. We play by the book. That's all."

"It's because of Serpico, isn't it?"

"No, it's not. He made it seem like everyone with a badge was crooked, but that's not true at all."

"Well then, I salute you, sir." He pulled in at the next bus stop and threw open the door.

"Thank you very much," I told the driver. He nodded, pulled shut the door, and pulled away from the curb. "Would you happen to be going all the way up to Columbia University?"

He continued looking straight ahead and said, "Naw, you're going to transfer to the 104 at Forty-second. That'll take you up there." He tore off two transfers and handed them to me.

"Thanks, again."

"This country has a lot of heart, doesn't it, pal?"

I looked over at Paul. He was holding a hand strap halfway down the bus. There weren't any free seats, so I stumbled through the moving bus and stood by him.

"What's wrong?" asked Paul.

"Oh, nothing," I said.

"You have this pissed-off look on your face."

"Just something the driver said."

"What did he say?"

"It's not what he said, exactly. It was what he meant."

"What are you talking about?"

I didn't answer Paul and swung through some empty hand straps to get fairly close again to the driver.

"Hey," I told him. "I was born in this country."

"So was I. What's your point?"

"I just wanted to make sure that you knew."

"Then how come you were speaking a different language with the boy?"

"It's Chinese. Cantonese, actually."

"How come he doesn't speak English like you?"

"He does!"

We pulled up to a red light and the driver turned to me.

"I don't even know what the hell we're talking about now," he said. I turned and saw two seats open up near the rear exit of the bus.

"Well, that figures," I said, about to walk away. Paul was already heading for the seats. The driver shared a meaningful shake of the head with an old woman up at the front.

Paul and I managed to grab the two seats just before the light changed. We came up to the next stop and the bus driver put on the brakes too hard.

"What are you trying to do, Robert?" asked Paul.

"I don't know," I admitted. "I guess I wanted to let him know that people who look like us are Americans, too. Something to that effect."

"Does it really matter what he thinks?"

"It matters what he thinks because it means he'll treat the next Asian passengers differently."

"You mean he won't try to give them a break on the fare?"

"Agh," I said, unfolding the pro-Kuomintang Chinese newspaper.

A Taiwanese official had opened up a letter bomb that blew off a hand and an eye. Somehow they caught the guy. He was an anti-Kuomintang activist who wanted to have native Taiwanese rule the island, not families from the mainland who were on the losing side of the Chinese civil war.

The Kuomintang, or KMT, hadn't lived up to its noble beginnings. They were also known as the Nationalists, the party founded by Sun Yat-sen, the father of the revolution that ended dynastic rule in China. If it hadn't been for him, we'd still be wearing queues down our backs to show subservience to the Manchus who ran China at the time.

But tragically, Sun died prematurely and the KMT and the Communists stopped working together. After the bloody split, Chiang Kai-shek and Mao Tse-tung rose to power in the KMT and Chinese Communist Party, and there was little for the average Chinese person to do for more than two decades but fight, suffer, and die.

I put away the pro-KMT paper and flipped open the pro-Communist one. The lead story was a feature on Hua Kuo-feng, who was named as Mao's successor as chairman of the Chinese Communist Party. He had already been premier since Chou En-lai's death in January. It was a typical snow-job write-up. His latest and greatest act was signing the order to arrest Mao's widow and the rest of the Gang of Four, who were set on sabotaging the Permanent Revolution.

The Hong Kong–owned newspaper was the editorial lightweight among the three, but it sold the most copies. Some days, half the paper was celebrity news: who was playing patty-cake with whom. But the newspaper was also fanatically pro-business and for free trade, with extensive global-market coverage and analysis of foreign-exchange rates. I guess they expected couples to buy the newspaper and split up the sections between businessman and wife.

I tore through the pages, indifferent to numbers and diet tips. The best section, in my opinion, was the movie listings. The family that owned the paper also owned the film-distribution company that brought in movies from Hong Kong to Chinatown's four theaters. The theaters weren't allowed to advertise in the other papers or else they would get cut off.

I folded up the paper and checked my watch.

"Anything good in the papers?" asked Paul.

"No," I said. I looked out the window. We were only at Houston Street; we had traveled a grand total of six blocks. "I've forgotten how slow buses are."

"We should have just walked up to Prince," Paul whined.

"What if that station was closed, too?"

"Then we would walk up to the next one until we got to one that was open."

"Great, so by the time we get there, we're all sweaty and grimy for your interview. We might as well have gone through the scummy subway. You have to think about presentation, Paul." I pointed at my face. "I don't do this for just anybody or anything."

"Thanks for shaving, Robert."

"I'd do anything to help you. Hell, I even bled a little for you."

"It's all for a worthy cause. If I'm admitted to this precollege project, it could help me get into Columbia as an undergrad."

I smiled, but inside I was worried. Not about Paul. I was sure he was going to get pretty much anything he ever applied to, no sweat. What bothered me was that I was going to be even more in debt with Barbara. I had grown up with her in Chinatown and we even had a little thing going before I got into a relationship with Lonnie, Paul's half sister. It was a tiny thing, even microscopic.

Barbara had gotten Lonnie a job at the United Nations office of a newswire service. Now, through another connection of hers, Barbara arranged an "in" for Paul at Columbia.

I guess that when you go to Harvard, as Barbara did, you tend to pick up connections. When you don't go to college, like me, you end up with a dumb government job that no Chinese kid wants while growing up. I sure didn't want to be a cop, but not because I was opposed to it. I didn't know what the hell I was going to be. Then the draft came to Chinatown and it didn't matter if I had made up my mind or not.

I looked over at Paul. He was reading a paperback book he was holding with one hand. Now, *that* kid had a mind and a future. I like to think that I set him straight when he was hanging out with wannabe gangsters. He lives with me now and I'm comfortable with saying that I'm the brawn of the operation.

He was growing out his bangs too long in my opinion, but what the hell, I wasn't his father. I sure didn't beat him like his father used to. He was Lonnie's father, too, but she insists he never laid a finger on her.

Paul looked up, turned to me, and said, "Please stop staring at me. You're making me feel uncomfortable."

"I ran out of stuff to read."

"You didn't read the entertainment sections. You never do."

"I don't have time for fun. I'm an officer of the law. I'm always on the job." I straightened out my collar to prove it. I nodded to his book and asked, "What are you reading there?"

"Sherlock Holmes stories."

"Are they good?"

"You've never read them?"

"Why would I read them?"

"Because he solves crimes!"

"Those stories are old, Paul! What do you get out of them?"

"I like them."

"I thought you were smart."

He shook his head and went back to reading. I looked out the window. We were stopped at a green light for some reason. I watched an elderly man in a heavy camel coat walking with a cane. He passed the bus as we remained stationary.

I picked up the entertainment section from the Hong Kong newspaper. The Rosemary Theater on Canal was going to have a bunch of old Angela Mao films, so there was an interview with the woman herself next to a page-length picture of her in a typical stance with her elbows up at right angles, hands poised to chop.

The interviewer told her that she was still beautiful even though she had just had a baby and wondered when Angela was going to leave films to take care of her new family.

I folded up the paper, crossed my arms, and waited for something to happen. I watched an open can of Coke roll diagonally down the aisle, hit something, and leak out on the floor right where people walk through when they board.

I couldn't ignore it. I guess that made me a good cop.

I walked over and picked it up. Some drivers have a garbage pail near the front but not this one. I turned back to my seat.

"Thanks, buddy!" said the driver.

I sat down again and held the sticky can as far away from me as I could. As an added bonus, there was a big wad of chewing gum stuck near the mouth of the can.

"That's disgusting, Robert!" said Paul. "You should have just left it on the floor."

"So it can pour out even more crap?"

"Forget it."

"Hey, Paul, are you thirsty?" I pushed the can toward his face.

"Get away from me!" I saw him smile for the first time today. I knew he was worried about the interview.

At Forty-second Street, I shoved the rear-exit doors open and held them for people getting off. I let them go and they closed crookedly. The exhaust pipe blew out an evil black puff as the bus pulled away.

As we waited for the transfer, I asked Paul if he wanted me to throw him some sample interview questions. He said sure.

"Well, Paul, I'm glad you could make this appointment today."

"Thank you for having me."

"Well, yeah, tell me which project you would wish to work on."

"I'm interested in studying the deep-sea sediment cores with Lamont-Doherty."

"And what are those?"

"The core samples. From the sea floor."

"Oh, and why do you want to study those things?"

"Because I feel that environmental studies are going to become more of a pressing need, especially if there's a Democratic administration in place next year. By looking at the fossils in the sediment, we can see what kind of life existed under varying climates over the centuries."

"Are you sure?"

"Yes."

There was a pause because I didn't know what to say.

"How familiar are you with Mr. Lamont Doherty?"

"Lamont-Doherty is the name of your geological studies extension. It's in Palisades, across the Hudson."

"And how do you plan to get there?"

"You have a free shuttle bus that goes there a few times every day."

"Oh, we do?"

"Yeah, you do."

I threw my hands up. "Okay, you did real good, Paul. One thing I have to tell you, though, is you slouch too much. Make sure you've got your back against your chair. Also, you don't want to look too anxious. If they think you're too interested, it's a turnoff. You have to make them want you."

The 104 came and we got on. I fell asleep early on and Paul had to shake me awake at 116th Street.

Columbia University looked like a fortress built to keep out the surrounding blocks of the city. Paul seemed to know where to go, so I followed him to the office that was handling his thing, but I let him go in alone.

I threw out the Chinese papers and picked up a student newspaper. I sat in the hallway and read it. What a rag. These pampered rich kids saw injustice everywhere and were looking for excuses to cut classes and to burn their bras over nearly anything. Even the student cartoon was too liberal to be really funny.

After about fifteen minutes, Paul came out, his face neutral. He walked down the hall toward the exit.

"Well, that was quick," I said as I followed him. "It's either very good or very bad."

Coolly, he said, "I got it."

I hugged him.

THAT NIGHT I hopped up the front steps of the Fifth Precinct, an old brick building on the west side of Elizabeth Street between traffic-heavy Canal Street and tourist-clogged Bayard Street. The Five was built in 1881, and is about as well maintained as any tenement-era building. It looked great from the outside, though.

I sauntered into the squad room with a smile on my face.

"Celebrating already, huh?" English asked me. English, whose real name was Detective First Grade Thomas Sanchez, was the head of the detective squad of the Fifth Precinct. He was a light-skinned Latino with a face that was so pockmarked it looked like it had been pounded by a meat tenderizer. English had gotten his name from not knowing Spanish.

"You know about Paul?" I asked him.

"What about him?"

"He got into that program at Columbia."

"What program?"

"The precollege thing. I might have mentioned it to you."

"If you did, I don't remember. Well, good for him, I guess. I thought you were celebrating for the overtime coming up."

"I didn't hear about this."

"You're not going to like where it is."

"Why not?"

"There's going to be a State Department–level meeting happening at the Jade Palace. It's confidential, but they're worried that word is getting around. Mao Tse-tung's daughter, Li Na, is putting out feelers to seek asylum here."

"Wow!" Even the suggestion was explosive to the community. The KMT supporters would be rabidly opposed to a relative of Mao's entering the United States. They would interpret it as another step in the United States switching diplomatic recognition to the People's Republic from the KMT's Republic of China on Taiwan.

People's Republic backers in Chinatown would find something to be angry about. They always did.

"Do they really have to have the meeting here? In Chinatown?" I asked. "It seems like they're just begging for a riot."

"It can't be held on federal property because it's not an official meeting. Willie Gee offered his place because he had some connection to someone who knew Li Na. Hell, he may have even suggested that she seek asylum in this country. She's having a hard time now, as I understand it."

Li Na was the only child of Mao's with Jiang Qing. It was like being half divine and half demon. Mao was the leader of the

Revolution and the country. Jiang Qing was the head of the hated Gang of Four. Now Dad was dead and Mom was in jail. There was no one left to look out for Li Na and, considering the political environment in China, she wasn't safe. Nobody with a high profile was.

Chinese people hate change because there are gaps of uncertainty that come with it. Not knowing an outcome was terrible.

For all Li Na knew, a faction who wanted to wipe out Mao's legacy could rise up and accuse her of being a rightist, a leftist, or, worst of all, an *adventurist*. She could end up locked in jail for years on no charges, and when she proclaimed her innocence, the guards would laugh and ask, "Then why are you here?"

Chinese people aren't good at comforting each other. Our idioms and morality tales were all about dire warnings and blaming the victims. You can sum up all of them as, "It's your own fault! You should have known better!"

If you had lost all your money or your right arm, it was because of something you had done, possibly years ago. If your marriage didn't work out, then you should have been with someone else back at the start.

I NODDED TO English and then looked around for John Vandyne, my old partner when we were both rookies and now my best friend among the detectives. Vandyne had an actual gold shield while I was still trying to win one. I was on what was known as the detective track—working on investigative assignments while still officially a rank-and-file cop.

I found him in the kitchenette making another bland pot of coffee. I was spoiled by the sweet and syrupy condensed milk that

Chinatown bakeries liked to mix into their coffees, basically rendering the drink as a hot, liquid 3 Musketeers bar.

Vandyne was a dark-skinned black man of medium build who used to be slightly taller than me. He had been slumping down to my height in the last several weeks, starting when his wife moved out on him.

"Chow," he said, as we clapped each other on the back.

"Vandyne," I said. "Your hands are wet, man." I pulled at my shirt to move the wet spot on my back off of my shoulder blade.

"Sorry about that. We don't have any damn towels in here." He wiped his hands off on his slacks.

"That Willie Gee asshole . . ." I started.

Vandyne chuckled and shook his head. He knew all about the contentious history between me and the Chinese guy who looked like an evil Roy Orbison.

"C'mon, partner, he's giving us overtime. You can't hate Willie for that."

"It just bothers me that he's probably getting way more out of this thing with Mao's daughter than us. Think of all the publicity Jade Palace will have once word leaks out. He's exploiting a Communist for the sake of capitalism!"

"Aren't you blowing this out of proportion? People might not even find out about the meeting."

"You know how thin the walls are in Chinatown, don't you? Secrets in the Chinese community get passed around like a jar of hot sauce at dinner, and there's no way word won't get out about this. Willie will make sure of it."

Vandyne sighed and turned to pour a cup of coffee, his first for the night.

"Well," said Vandyne, "if he does, he'll realize later when there's hell to pay that he should have kept his mouth shut."

"How long have you been studying Chinese idioms, Vandyne?"

IT DIDN'T TAKE too long for the story to get out. The next day it ran on the front pages of the papers backed by money from the KMT, the Communists, and Hong Kong. The news had broken so close to printing deadlines, the editorial boards of the papers had no time to weigh in.

Just to make sure that even the tourists knew about it, the American-born Chinese guy who published *Inside Chinatown*, a paper in English, also had it out that day.

All the papers sold out immediately.

KMT supporters put signs in their store windows, reiterating the three No's of their political party regarding the Communists on the mainland: "No compromise, no negotiation, no contact!"

The signage among Communists quoted one of Mao's many dramatic sayings that were wide open to interpretation: "It's always right to rebel against reactionaries!"

I LIVE AWAY from the commotion and, in fact, outside of Chinatown itself. My apartment is in a Spanish-dominated neighborhood to the east of the Communist section of Chinatown. It's on the fourth floor of a slouching walkup just past the southeast corner of Seward Park.

Cops don't live in the boundaries of the precincts we serve in, to prevent potential conflicts of interest.

It's a fairly big apartment for a one-bedroom. It gets hot in the summer and even hotter in the winter so by around later this month, I'll prop open one of the windows in the living room where Paul sleeps on a convertible couch.

Even though we were far enough from Chinatown, I could still hear some ruckus being stirred up. I did the smart thing and put in earplugs.

Paul woke me up that night because I hadn't heard the phone.

The offices of the American-born Chinese guy were on fire. Luckily, the building was empty and everything was under control. Even though the guy was a native speaker of English, the detectives down there wanted me on the scene, too, in case the extreme mental anguish would drive him to seek solace in a Chinese face.

For kicks, I could just tell the guy that he should have known that Chinese people don't want outsiders to be kept abreast of community politics, and that the fire was his own fault.

THE EDITOR AND PUBLISHER of *Inside Chinatown* was a guy named Artie Yee. I had seen him around before. He was an obese man in his fifties who stood at about five nine and weighed maybe 260 pounds. Artie's black hair was thinning and he combed it tight, making his head look like a spool of thread running low. He had some day job and did the newspaper on his own time, publishing once or twice a month.

Somehow, a fire truck had managed to wedge itself into the intersection of Henry and Catherine streets. The fire was now completely out and some kids who clearly lacked a minimum of parental supervision had come out to stomp around in the water on the sidewalk. Why not? It was only two in the morning.

"It wasn't a bad fire," said English. "It's the water damage you have to worry about." He put his hands in his pockets. "I'd really like a smoke now, but it wouldn't look good, considering."

"That's right," I said. "Is that the guy over there?" I pointed over to two big legs wrapped in tight denim hanging out of the open back door of a squad car.

"Yeah. We've already talked to him, but you should go over and do your thing. He says he knows you."

I walked over to Artie and when he saw me coming he rocked his body back and forth. He managed to get to his feet but he almost knocked me down with the forward momentum.

"Hey, Officer Chow!" he said, shaking my hand.

"You're pretty happy for a guy whose business just burned down!"

He smiled hard, pushing his face into a big, lumpy pork chop with two raisin eyes. It was a little chilly out, but he glistened all over with beady sweat. I unzipped my field coat because I was feeling hot from fast-walking all the way over from home.

"I'm insured," he said, "and I moved out my jazz records last month, so I'm all right. How are you, though?"

"I'm doing all right, too."

"Your girlfriend, Lonnie, is beautiful, by the way. I'm so envious. But I think the last time we talked you were going through a little bit of a rough patch."

"I don't remember, Artie."

"I interviewed you about two years ago, for our community profile section."

"It sounds possible."

"I took you out for some beers and we talked until you fell asleep on the table."

"That was a bad time for me, Artie. I'm in recovery now. Anyway, let's talk about who could have done this to you."

"Oh, I . . . I get it! Well, about the fire, I told the other cops, I'm not sure who in particular would have done this to me. A lot of people don't like what I do. The right-wingers say I'm a social-ist and the left-wingers say I'm a fascist. I'm a middle-of-the-road guy, just trying to be objective."

"When you're in the middle of the road, you can get hit by traf-fic going either way."

"That's a good point. I should be on the shoulder."

"Artie, this paper isn't your livelihood, is it?"

"It makes money, but I work full-time at night managing an offset-printing plant in Long Island City. I get a break on printing my newspaper there."

"You work at a place that prints the Chinese papers?"

"Not only that. We do a lot of corporate literature. I write a lot of it, too. Shareholder communications sort of stuff. Lot of money in that."

"Okay," I said. I had no interest in asking more about his job. It sounded boring as hell. We watched the firemen gather up their hose and shake hands with the kids.

"Boy, this is really something," said Artie, wiping his face with his hands.

I wondered why a newspaper guy didn't have anything more interesting to say.

"This isn't the end of the paper, is it?"

"Well, when I get the insurance money, I'll be back at it. They can't keep this fatso down. I actually have a very intriguing inter-view set up for the next issue," he said. "But the time factor on it is pretty immediate. It'd be a shame to cancel it. Unless . . ."

"Unless what?"

"Unless your lovely little lady Lonnie wants to do the interview."

"But your newspaper's torched."

"Not for me! She can do it for her newswire."

"How did you know she worked at a newswire?"

"Everybody in the media business knows everybody else. Of course, we all know where the chicks are."

"Artie," I said as I smiled, "are you trying to get a rise out of me?"

"Robert, you should be proud. You're with this girl that all these other guys have the hots for. And not just the few Asian guys, you know."

"If anyone gets any ideas . . ."

"They have ideas, but they'll never try anything. Journalists cover things, they don't make things happen. Look at the women they end up with!"

"Who are you with?"

"I'm still working on it," he said, rubbing his stomach. "I need to get back down to my college weight, and then I'll see what comes my way. Problem is, I work at night and women don't like lunch dates because they think you're trying to be cheap." He looked up at his dripping, burned-out office and folded his hands over his crotch.

"Anyway, Artie, who is this interview with?"

"Oh, well, get this, it's with the representative for Mao's daughter. He's not related to Li Na, but he has had a long association with her. His name is Chen Xiaochuan. He is willing to speak after the meeting at Jade Palace."

"Long association? Chen is Li Na's boyfriend?"

"Oh, no! I think she's married," he said, winking at me. "She's very ugly! Terribly so! Like Mao in a skirt."

"Wow."

"I'll bet that Chen likes beautiful girls. He'll definitely want to talk to Lonnie."

"How do you know him?"

He shuffled his feet.

"I can't disclose my sources," said Artie.

"It's Willie Gee, isn't it?"

"I'm not telling you anything."

"It is, isn't it? Jade Palace advertises in your paper."

"Look, do you not want Lonnie to do this? I can find a lot of other people who would want to break an exclusive interview!"

"Okay, fine. I don't care who your connection is. I'm sure she'll be thrilled to do this."

He nodded, turned his head, and spat into a puddle.

"Robert, do you think they're going to find out who did this? I know what the answer probably is, but I was just wondering, for my sake."

"You already know that nobody testifies in Chinatown, right? They'll more likely talk to reporters than they'll talk to cops."

Artie nodded. He pulled out a stick of gum and slapped my arm.

"No, thanks," I said.

"I'm going to call Lonnie at work," he said.

"You need her number?"

"I have it already. See you, Robert."

I watched him leave and then walked back to English, zipping up my field coat.

"What did he tell you?" he asked me.

"Not too much."

"What did you tell him?"

"That we're working on it."

Imitating Richard Dawson on *Family Feud*, English said, "That's our number one answer!"

I MET UP with Vandyne in the lobby of a Catherine Street apartment building. We had both come in through a rear entrance so that nobody on the street would see us enter the building. We each grabbed a plastic bucket from the refuse left under the stairs and walked up to a landing between the fourth and fifth floors.

The window to the street had been painted over. I turned my bucket upside down and took a seat as Vandyne worked the window open.

"What . . . kind of . . . idiot . . . would paint . . . over . . . a window?" he grunted as he pounded away at the frame.

"Careful, partner, don't smash the glass there."

He gave a final shove and asked, "Is that good enough?"

"One more. Another one. Okay, that's it."

Vandyne rubbed his hands together and sat on his bucket next to me. We had a great view of the sun setting behind the burned-out building that housed Artie Yee's newspaper office. It looked like a giant gray skull, the headquarters for a bad guy in a comic book.

Vandyne took a hard look at the building. "Dammit, Chow, you made me do all that extra shoving for nothing! Look at all this viewing space I made."

"Come on, you have a lot of stress to work out. If you ever want fifteen seconds of my time, they're yours."

"Hey, I'm going to take more than fifteen seconds. In fact, I want you to check out these Eddie Gale records I've been getting into."

"Who's Eddie Gale?"

"He's a horn player. A jazz guy who's trying to open the boundaries of the form."

I began to feel apprehensive. Jazz wasn't my kind of thing. I thought the two of us had that common disinterest.

"Jazz? I thought you hated jazz, Vandyne."

"I don't like the traditional jazz, but this guy Gale has really done something to the whole feel of the music. When you don't have a woman in the house, you have some extra time and a lot of extra money, so I stopped by a jazz records store and asked what was good. I wanted to hear something new."

"When you say that, you're telling the guy, 'Sell me something you're trying hard to get rid of.'"

"You're wrong and I'm going to prove it to you. I'm going to borrow your ears one of these nights and play you those albums."

"Sure, man," I said, hoping it was going to be one of those guy promises that never happen and are never referred to again by either party.

He shifted around, and the sound was amplified by the mouth of the bucket slapping against the floor.

"I think you can make more noise if you pound it like a drum," I said.

"I can't get comfortable on this thing! It's all sharp and pointy. You have a nice one."

"This is a piece of crap! I'll prove it. You want to trade?"

"Okay."

We switched places. Vandyne's bucket hurt in all the wrong places, but I gave a big smile.

"Nothing wrong with this one here," I said.

"Give it a minute," said Vandyne. He brought a pair of binoculars to his face and played with the adjustment. I took a newspaper from inside my jacket and shoved it between the bucket and me.

"Any criminal who comes back the night after," Vandyne said in a distracted voice, "is one stupid jackass."

"We're not dealing with Mensa members here. Setting a building on fire isn't exactly a plan that comes from a sophisticated mind. You don't even get anything out of it."

"What could you steal from a little newspaper?"

"Well, I'd back up a moving van there and take all the desks, chairs, shelves, and maybe even the sink and toilet. You can resell all that stuff pretty easily. You can make more money than you'd think from used furniture and they don't exactly have identifying marks."

Vandyne put down his binoculars.

"Hmmm," he said. "I gotta keep an eye on you, partner. If my wallet disappears one day, I'm coming after you."

Outside, the neighborhood was now bathed in the yellow light of the setting sun. It would be dark in about an hour.

We didn't know what to expect, but if there was one thing you could count on, it was criminals fucking up sooner or later. I think it's a part of human nature to expect to be caught and punished for a misdeed. Even if criminals managed to pull off a clean job, they would loop back and linger in the general area. On the next job, they might intentionally get sloppy to see if they could get the sirens to come.

I saw someone peel off from the crowd, step over the yellow warning tape, and walk close to the charred walls of the building.

"Vandyne, can I see those binoculars?" I asked dimly, not taking my eyes off the figure.

He handed them over without a word. I looked through them at the figure.

"It's a woman," I said.

"You know her?"

"Yeah."

THE WOMAN WAS standing in a pool of wet ashes, her hands at her sides. She was about five seven but that was with heels on. Her thick black hair cascaded over her ears and shoulders, and she did something to it to make it shiny. A light brown coat stopped above a skirt that stopped midway down two taut thighs in stockings with a dull glow.

I smirked because I was sure that she had spent some time thinking about how she wanted to look from the rear. To men.

But this was no time for amusement. I came in close to her forehead and growled under my breath, "Barbara, what the hell are you doing here!"

When she turned around I saw my head and torso in her two black, sparkling eyes. Her face was long and not too narrow and came down to a chin that fairy princesses had. Her red lips, usually curved like a little blossom, were pulled taut into a wide smile.

She grabbed my arm and said, "Robert!"

"This is a crime scene! Now let's get out of this thing!"

"I'm so sorry!"

She continued to hold on to me as we stepped over the tape together, matching leg for leg. I had lost part of my mind in Nam, but she had lost a lot more. Barbara used to be the prettiest girl in Chinatown. Now she was its prettiest widow.

"You know anything about the fire, Barbara?" I looked into her face. There was lightning behind her dark eyes.

"No. I don't. Can we stop whispering now?"

"Well, I guess it doesn't matter at this point," I said in full voice.

"Look, I didn't mean any harm. I just had to see the place up close. Artie Yee published my first story, back when I was in grade school."

"I didn't know about that."

"I brought it into school to show everybody. Don't you remember?"

"How am I supposed to remember that one thing? You always had something to show off in school. If it wasn't a story you wrote, it'd be a story about you."

She snorted.

"Did you stay in touch with Artie over the years?" I asked.

"I'd run into him from time to time."

"Were the two of you friends?"

"Oh, no, no. I learned to keep my distance from that one. Did you know that he asked me to marry him when I turned eighteen?"

"He wasn't much better looking back then, was he?"

"He looked like a younger walrus."

"You're not enemies with Artie, though, are you?"

"I'm not one of them, but he has many enemies, you know that," she said.

"He did his part in pissing off all areas of Chinatown."

"Artie doesn't respect authority. That's a good thing for a journalist."

"Then how come you didn't keep writing for him?"

"Artie doesn't respect women." She shivered and then slapped my arm. "I heard Paul got into that program at Columbia."

"Thanks to you," I said.

"Thanks in part to me, anyway." She pouted. "Doesn't that mean you'll take me to dinner?"

"Maybe Paul should."

"Get serious. Actually, maybe Paul should come and meet my youngest sister. You know she's up at Columbia because she got into Barnard early. Maybe she should stick to Chinatown boys, like I should have."

"Hey, Barbara, let's talk about this later. I have to get back to work here."

"You're going to call me?"

"I'll get in touch."

She walked off and I returned to my post.

Years ago, Barbara and her three younger sisters were the four little princesses of Chinatown. She liked to say that her parents never did get that son, but the truth was her parents learned to love all their daughters to death. They all had beauty and smarts, and because of that you knew they'd get out of Chinatown and never come back.

But Barbara did return after her husband was killed in Khe Sanh. The oldest, the prettiest, and the smartest of the sisters, she moved back alone into their old family home to find some comfort, I guess.

There was a brief period when I thought she was the love of my life, but it was a while ago and it ended embarrassingly enough. Thinking about it again put me in a bad mood.

"Hello, Sunshine," said Vandyne.

"It was Barbara," I said.

"Oh! What the hell was she doing there?"

"She wanted to see the place up close. Artie published one of her stories back when she was a smart, little girl."

"Seriously, though, could she have had anything at all to do with this?"

"Her? No way, man!"

"Do you know that for sure?"

"Yes," I said. "I would bet my soul on it."

"That's a trick answer. Chinese people don't believe in souls, right?"

"We believe in many things, Vandyne. But eating good food is at the top, not this afterlife nonsense."

I folded my newspaper seat over again to make it thicker and resumed my spot on the bucket.

"Speaking of getting fed, are you anywhere near hungry?" Vandyne asked in a voice that told me he was.

"Not yet."

"We'll just wait a little bit, see if anything starts developing."

Nothing happened except it got colder and harder to see. I went back down to a small noodle dive off of Henry Street and brought back two containers of lo mein, chicken for me and beef for Vandyne.

He ate a few bites and then he gave me a funny look.

"What's the problem?" I asked.

"Are you eating with a fork just to show solidarity with me?"

"Chopsticks aren't even an option at this place. Their biggest business is from the jerks on jury duty out for lunch."

"I could've handled chopsticks in this situation. From the container, I can do it."

"I'll test you next time."

We finished up and shoved all the garbage under our buckets.

Around 10 P.M., people came back from their night shifts in the restaurants and passed us in the stairwell. I saw one older man eyeing us on the way up. When he got to his apartment, he loudly warned someone to stay away from the homeless men in the building.

"He's telling everyone there's a black man out on the stairs, right?" asked Vandyne.

"Actually, he said 'homeless.'"

"Yeah, but they think a black man sitting on a bucket is homeless, right?"

I could only shrug.

"Next time, we bring chairs," grunted Vandyne. "With cushions!"

"MY BOSS IS really excited that we have this interview with Chen Xiaochuan!" Lonnie told me.

We were having breakfast in a place on the Bowery that steamed everything. It was convenient because she could see the bus approaching from downtown. Traffic was usually so bad Lonnie had time to cross the street before the bus made it to the Canal Street stop.

"That's great," I said. "How does Artie Yee happen to know your phone number at work?"

"It's a 1-800 number, Robert. You can be patched in to any of Presswire's staff through it. Do you think Artie and I are dear friends?"

"He's your old boyfriend, isn't he?"

She threw a used napkin at my face.

I reached to the table behind us for an open jar of hot chili sauce. It had been emptied and refilled so many times the threads for the lid to screw onto were covered by a hardened black crust.

"Do you really need hot sauce in the morning?" she asked me.

"These rice-noodle rolls have no taste. They're just mushy."

I really missed eating pastries in the mornings. In fact, Lonnie used to work behind the counter at Martha's, one of the most popular bakeries in Chinatown. They made a lot of really nice sponge cakes and stuffed buns there. In particular, I liked the hot-dog pastries, the things that look like Viking helmets with the two ends of the hot dogs sticking out.

But after she stopped working there, she forced me to stop eating them, telling me how bad they were for me and how everything else there was unhealthy. She could have told me before, right? I don't see why she had to wait.

Well, I guess she wanted me to keep going there to see her. I glanced across the table at her and noticed she looked a little annoyed.

"Are you listening?" she asked.

"I am now."

"Paul is doing the project at Columbia."

"He sure is!"

"Is it going to be easier for him to get into the college later on?"

"Probably. Assuming he doesn't screw it all up."

"Do you think they'll give him financial aid? It's a very expensive school."

"I'm sure Paul's going to get scholarships and grants. They love a story like his. Poor little immigrant boy pulling himself up by the bootstraps."

"Borough of Manhattan Community College gave me hardly anything, and now NYU isn't much better."

"I hate to say it, Lonnie, but Paul is a little smarter than you, isn't he?"

She laughed and kicked me hard under the table.

"Don't tell a woman that!" she said.

I grabbed her hands loosely. "You're beautiful. You're very, very beautiful." She broke free, crossed her arms, and grunted. "Maybe too beautiful."

"What?" she asked.

"This Mr. Chen that you're going to interview, I understand he has a thing for pretty girls."

"So do you."

"Lonnie, the fact that he's coming over must mean that he's a powerful man. Politically, not physically. He probably has the body of one of those eighty-year-olds running the country. He might be like the Blob in a suit. He might ooze all over you if you get too close."

"No matter what kind of shape he's in, I can handle it."

I drummed my fingers on the table.

"Wait a minute," I said. "Someone torched Artie's newspaper to stop this interview. Maybe it's not safe for you to talk to Mr. Chen."

"Why not?"

"Someone might try to hurt you!"

"Look, Robert. Artie has been making people angry for years with his little newspaper. Whoever's responsible for the fire has probably been mad at him for a long time."

"Lonnie, you're thinking again. Don't do my job for me."

She continued anyway.

"So they probably weren't trying to stop the interview with Mr. Chen in particular. It was about stopping Artie." She picked up her bag. "I see my bus!" She stood up and patted my shoulder. I rubbed her arm.

Chinatown couples aren't openly affectionate, partly because of societal restrictions and partly because the sidewalks are too narrow and busy to accommodate hugging or kissing.

I watched Lonnie cross the street, walking away from me. She was a beautiful sight even in her thick wool coat.

Lonnie was right. The fire couldn't have been to prevent the interview. The guy would have had to know that the interview was being set up.

I chuckled at the very thought and sipped some tea.

I checked my watch. It was time to get out of this place and get something good to eat.

THE ONLY REASON Paul, the midget, Vandyne, and I watched game four of the World Series together on my television was because the Yankees were already down by three games. I wanted to watch them play like men without hope like the Mets.

This year the Mets had managed to finish above .500, and that was about as close to the pennant as they could come.

Vandyne went back and forth between the two New York teams and in truth, I was only a mild Mets fan. I saved the soft part of my heart for the Rangers to shit on. I saw fewer hockey games this season on TV because of the detective-track assignments. It was probably for the better that I missed them.

Nevertheless, I didn't want to miss a chance to see two big Yanks fans get an idea of the pain we felt in 1973, when the Mets lost to the A's. But at least that year we had beaten the Reds and pushed the World Series to seven games.

The midget had closed his toy store early. He wasn't going to lose any business because every kid in Chinatown, even the stupid gang kids, was in front of a TV.

The game had been set for Wednesday but was rain-delayed to Thursday. Being a polite host, I took a folding chair and let my guests have the couch. I had a selection of soda cans lined up on the coffee table and bags of chips. I took a handful of Doritos and then spun the opened part of the bag away from me.

I waited until the first half of the first inning was over, and the Reds were held scoreless, before dipping back into the Doritos.

When I was done chewing and swallowing, I said, "I'm so ready for this game."

"How come Lonnie's not here?" asked Vandyne.

"She's studying for that interview with the Chinese guy. What sucks is that Presswire isn't going to pay for an interpreter, so she's getting a friend who's fluent in Mandarin to come along with her. It's probably safer. These Chinese fat cats, I don't care if they're Communists or KMT, they treat women like they're objects."

"Not Madame Chiang Kai-shek. She had the Generalissimo by the balls."

The midget slapped his knee and pointed at me. He said in English, "Same thing with him!"

The midget was one of those Chinese guys with extra fat layers in the eyelids. I think it's a Mongolian gene that pops up every now and then. Those heavy half-opened lids suited him well because he was the funniest, most sarcastic man in the world.

"Lonnie and I are equal partners in this relationship," I said.

"Aw, come on," said Vandyne. "The only reason we're here and you're here is because Lonnie is busy. Otherwise you'd be off with her, eating something healthy for dinner."

I smiled. It was fine for Vandyne to rip on me if it made my old partner feel better. I'd punch myself in the eye if it would help, but that wouldn't bring Rose back to him from her sister's apartment.

"You're wrong," said Paul. "They would be here and they wouldn't let any of us come over because they'd be busy together. I'd have to spend the night somewhere else."

"The kid's right," I said to the grunts from Vandyne and the midget. Thurman Munson, the Yankees catcher, stepped up to the plate with two outs. "Three for three. Let's go." The son of a bitch singled. Then Munson scored when Chris Chambliss doubled. The midget slapped hands with Vandyne and Paul. I crossed my arms and squirmed. "If the Reds don't come back in the second, I'm gonna go read my evening Chinese newspapers."

The Reds promptly went down, with a man caught trying to steal second.

I stood up and said, "I'm getting a bad feeling about this."

"Sit down and watch," said Vandyne. "You don't know what's going to happen."

"I'm cutting my losses for now. I'll check back on the situation if I hear the enthusiasm die down." I picked up my newspapers and retreated to the bedroom.

The Communist-backed paper called for unnamed people to seriously reconsider their follies that were reactionary in nature. "A child, female or male, should carry on the great struggle of the parents," read the editorial, an obvious dig at Li Na. I was amused at how Communists were apparently paraphrasing Confucius, whom they had once pilloried.

The KMT-backed paper hailed Li Na as a hero of the Chinese people for apparently rejecting Communism. The story took up the entire front cover, both above and below the fold. There weren't many pictures of Li Na in existence and certainly none that the mainland would make available to the KMT, but that didn't stop the paper from placing an altered picture of Taiwanese film star

Hsu Feng next to the story. "If Miss Li finds that the U.S. is not to her liking, we would be proud to have her as a citizen of Free China," the report concluded.

But there was also an editorial about how President Ford and the U.S. State Department should reaffirm the strength of America's political ties to Taiwan before even considering Li Na's case.

The Hong Kong–backed paper threw cold water on the entire controversy. "How do we know that Mr. Chen legitimately represents Li Na? He seems to be getting a free trip to New York City while also unnecessarily fanning the flames of supporters of both sides of the Taiwan Strait."

I found myself in the odd position of agreeing with the editorial, or at least not agreeing with the other two.

I heard my houseguests start up a "Let's go Yankees" chant. It was going to be a long night.

I WENT TO see the midget the next day at his toy store on Mulberry. He was sitting on a stool behind the counter. His head was down, sipping the last of an herb-tea drink through a straw. His combed black hair was so shiny it looked white where the sunlight hit it.

He glanced up at me quickly and turned away.

"That was a tough loss, huh?" I said. "I think that's the first time I've ever seen you on the losing side of something."

It was well known throughout Chinatown that the midget had never lost at any game ever. He could whip you at chess, American chess, checkers, and Sorry! Monopoly, too, if you had the time.

"You want something fun to play?" he asked. "I think we just got some new four-piece puzzles. You can handle that, right, Officer?"

"Yeah, I think I can handle that," I said. "Hey, I just wanted to come by to say sorry about Paul getting that research spot up at Columbia." The midget looked directly in my face and raised an eyebrow.

"What are you trying to do to me? I'm running a business here! You can't take my best people away and expect me to like it. I was supposed to get him back in the evenings and weekends after his summer internship."

"You know he'll get more experience there. More *useful* experience."

"Are you trying to say that working in a toy store is easy? You used to work here and it kicked your ass!"

It was true. I spent my lost years after coming back from Nam working in that same store under the previous owner.

"Paul was my best worker," the midget went on. "He showed no emotion, worked hard, and ate shit without complaint. He would have made a fine Chinaman one day, and now you've shoved him through the door of an Ivy League school."

"I thought you'd be happy for him. . . ."

"Oh, I am," said the midget, dropping his faked annoyance. He pitched the empty drink container into the garbage can. "But, really, I don't know how I'm going to get someone to replace him here."

"How about hiring an illegal? They work cheap."

"No way. Too many cops come in here. I wouldn't be comfortable with it. Anyway, I'm sort of training a new guy today." He smacked a pencil a few times against the countertop. "Hey, Drew! Come up here! I want you to meet someone!"

I heard a broomstick drop to the floor and a skinny kid came out from the back. He was about five three and maybe ten pounds too light. At some point Drew had had some bad acne on his forehead; he still had pimples across his cheeks and chin.

"Yes, sir?" he asked the midget.

"This is Officer Chow, a personal and professional friend of mine."

"Hello, Officer Chow. My name is Drew."

"Drew what?" I asked.

"Drew Bai."

"Were you born over here?"

"Yes. Actually in Queens. We live in Confucius Plaza now." Confucius Plaza was a new government-subsidized housing project over on Bowery that had just opened.

"If you were born here, then how come you can speak Chinese so well?"

"I learned it. My parents forced me to go to Chinese school."

"Yeah, but where did you learn Cantonese from?" Chinese schools, even the ones in the heart of Cantonese-speaking Chinatown, taught Mandarin, the language of the educated.

"I just picked it up hanging around the neighborhood."

"Are you in a gang?"

"No, I'm not."

"You're about that age. Fourteen? Fifteen?"

"Fifteen. You sure ask a lot of questions. Am I a suspect for something?"

"Officer Chow's just a very inquisitive fellow," said the midget. "He can't help but make you uncomfortable. It's his job."

"I didn't mean to interrogate you, Drew, at least not yet. I just want to know who's working in my pal's store. That's all."

"That's all right. If there's nothing else, I have more work to do in the back." The midget waved him off and Drew withdrew.

"Wow," I told the midget. "Where do you find these guys who work so hard?"

"He was a store regular. I noticed that he would reshelve toys that were lying around and I said to myself, 'Hire that kid someday. He cares about this place.' So when I heard about Paul, I did a favor for myself and a favor for him."

"At some point, Drew is going to finish high school, too, you know."

"I'll bet you, though," said the midget, crossing his arms, "if he goes to college in the city, he'll beg me to let him keep working here."

"I'm sure you'll accommodate him."

"Hey, I'm a generous guy!"

IT WAS COLD, crisp day and there was just something in the air—mostly yelling and screaming.

Two different groups of idiots who thought that their shouts and sign-waving were going to convert the masses were crammed on either side of Jade Palace. In my experience, the only thing you can convince passersby of is that you have time on your hands or that you're crazy, or both.

The younger, hairier side supported the People's Republic of China. The people with better coats backed the KMT. They were united in opposing the meeting with Li Na's envoy, although for different reasons.

The KMT side had convinced itself that despite Li Na's noble stand against Communism, the meeting itself was another step in the United States phasing out diplomatic ties with the Republic of China on Taiwan in favor of the mainland. The United Nations had voted to expel Taiwan and seat the

People's Republic in 1971, and the United States hadn't been able to stop it. Maybe the Americans were losing resolve to stand with Taiwan.

The Commies were opposed to allowing Li Na political asylum in the States—an act of treason against Mao and the Revolution from Mao's daughter herself.

Strangely enough, this particular group of Reds was also opposed to diplomatic ties between the People's Republic and the United States. It was seen as a "sell-out" move.

Both groups had permits and the Boy Scouts, the auxiliary police, were out to make sure everyone stayed within their blockades. A Chinese auxiliary policeman came up to me and said, "Robert, how are you doing?"

He was about the same height as me, though a few years older with a little less in the girth department. His face was fatter, though. I knew I'd met him before, but I'd forgotten his name. "Hey, man," I said. "How are you doing, buddy?"

He looked behind him before saying, "I'm good. Say, do you know how I might get an offer to get on the job for real?"

"It's tough, man. First priority is rehiring the cops who got laid off in the financial crisis. There's still quite a few."

"I know all that, but hey, I'm a minority!"

"I hear ya, I know there aren't a lot of cops who look like me. Or you. But you gotta pay your dues. Right now, it's a pretty high price. You're doing the right thing. Auxiliary's probably the best way to go now."

"C'mon, man, don't give me that!" He pulled his mouth to one side of his face. "Didn't you get your post as a minority hire?"

"That's not the whole story. I was hired because of the need for a Chinese cop in Chinatown."

"For the newspaper pictures."

"Yes, for the newspaper pictures. But I've moved on. I'm detective track now. Don't forget, I had seniority over other people out of the academy because of my military service."

"I don't see why that should count. Being a soldier is completely different training from being a cop. I have college credit from criminal justice—that's relevant."

I leaned into his face and said in a low voice, "I never spent a day in college and look at me now." He shrank back but I gave him a firm slap on the shoulder to let him know I didn't hate him too much.

I walked over to the Commie protesters to look them over for future reference. A mentor of mine told me to observe the crowds and to become accustomed to faces. Although New York was a huge city, you saw the same people over and over again within five square blocks. Nearly all the crime committed in that area was by only a few individuals. Try to pick out the ones who look too self-conscious.

If nobody sticks out, just have someone in the squad car crank up the siren for a few rounds and see who jumps the highest and who runs.

It wasn't necessary to resort to that measure here, though. I made a careful note of the people holding up signs and the rooster-looking boy on the megaphone hollering, "Crush Li Na and the Gang of Four!"

Megaphones weren't permitted.

"You're not allowed to use that!" I shouted at the guy.

He lowered the megaphone and I saw that he had a soft, thin face that contrasted with his angry black eyes. He was about six feet tall and weighed about 160 pounds. The guy might have long hair, but it was tucked up into his Mao cap. His vest was covered with Cultural Revolution propaganda badges.

"What?" he asked me.

"Asshole. You're not allowed to use that thing here. Put it away or I'll take it from you."

In English he said, "I have a right to be addressed in English."

I accommodated him and asked, "What's your problem? You memorize slogans in Cantonese but you can't speak it?"

"I don't let language become a barrier between me and the people." He crossed his arms and made a face as if he were trying to bend me like a spoon using his mind.

"I know your kind," I said. "You went to college, got your head stuck in some pseudo-socialism, and then you came down here to take a stand with 'your people.' Let me tell you something, pal, you didn't grow up here and you don't know anybody here. Do yourself a favor. Go back home to the suburbs and study up for law school."

"I live here now, so this is my home. These people are my friends and neighbors. We all support the People's Republic over the puppet state of Taiwan and we're not going to stay quiet over the issue! Our voices will never be silenced!"

"See? You don't need the megaphone!"

He looked at the instrument in his hand and I could see he didn't have the guts to raise it again. I was walking away to the KMT side when he yelled after me, "I studied Mandarin in school! And my girlfriend speaks Mandarin!"

"So have some fucking oranges!" I muttered. The usual suspects were here among the KMT protesters: local business-men, cranky and retired association members, and conservative students.

One clean-cut kid was holding a sign that simply had a cross on it. I recognized him from the membership-drive parades that Lonnie's church staged from time to time in Chinatown. He was the one swinging the incense vessel around on a chain. I guess that Chinese Catholics knew they had that in common with Chinese Buddhists.

When he saw me, he came over and waved at me.

"Hello," I said.

"Robert, I've been asking Lonnie why we haven't been seeing you in church."

I looked down at his black Play-Doh hair. "I've been busy with things like this. Every day I have to be on my toes so the bad guys don't win."

"Some things are more important than our daily routines."

"Some things are more important than eating wafers."

He made a face like I had cursed. "I will pray for you," he said.

A kindly old man with more spots on his head than hair handed me a flyer with a smile. It read, "Boycott Jade Palace and traitor of the Chinese People Willie Gee. Beat the Red Bandits into their graves. Support Righteousness."

It was wrong for me to take the flyer, but he had caught me off-guard. I handed it back to him and said in English, "I can't read Chinese." I put both hands in my coat pockets so I couldn't get suckered again.

At the street corner, I connected with Vandyne who was wearing a leather jacket to fight the cold. He looked upon the twin protests with amusement. "Seems like old times, eh, brother?"

"That's right," I said. Less than a year ago, Jade Palace was swarmed with ex-waiters decrying the management's practice of taking a percentage out of the tips. "These protests attract so much attention to the restaurant, I can't help but feel that Willie's still the one pulling the strings."

"That may be so, but he is making some sacrifices," said Vandyne. "I understand that Golden Peace, the association that Willie formerly headed, has canceled his membership."

"That's a loss for the association, as well. Willie was their superstar. He was the golden boy of Golden Peace."

"Golden Piss," said Vandyne.

We both laughed. "So, everything's okay, right?" I asked.

"Oh, yeah, everybody's already in there."

The protesters had naïvely expected all the dignitaries to enter from the front. In fact, Li Na's man and the State Department brass had entered the restaurant from the storage area of a corner store down the block. Willie Gee himself operated the freight elevator that took them up to a private room that had commanding views of the Manhattan Bridge and none of the protests below.

Lonnie and her interpreter friend had been snuck into the restaurant also. I wondered how her interview would go.

Some jerk walking by yelled, "Death to Mao!" and threw a bucket of water on the Communists. He practically ran into me.

"Mao's already dead, idiot," I told him.

He was a wiry guy, practically part spider. "I hate all Communists!" he yelled. Vandyne went to check on the wet protesters as the KMT side jeered.

"I'm taking you into the precinct for assault," I said. I cuffed him and his arms were like twist ties.

"I'm proud of what I did!"

I saw Vandyne and, although people were screaming at him, I knew that none of them would follow through and press charges.

I knew taking this guy in would just result in paperwork for me but it was worth it to stick a fine on him. I just wanted to try to make everything as much of a pain in the ass for Spider-Man as it was for me. He shouldn't be able to throw freezing water on people with impunity.

I walked him into a fire hydrant, knees first, and watched him stumble. I pulled him back upright by the handcuffs and said, "Oopsie."

I looked back at the crowd as I pushed my guy onward and caught a mean look from the auxiliary cop who had buttonholed me earlier. I also saw rooster boy yelling at his girlfriend even as she helped him take off his soaked vest. What a jerk.

I WAS TYPING away at my desk in the detective squad room. To my left was Detective Second Grade Stuart "Bad Boy" Piccolo, who looked like Lou Costello gone gray, but he was quiet and never made anybody laugh.

To my right was Detective Second Grade Anthony "Pete" Risso. "Pete" was short for "Pizza Man." His light brown hair went down to his shoulders. Pete had an amazing memory and his unblinking eyes recorded everything.

He got the name Pizza Man because it was a character he played back in his old Brooklyn precinct when they knew where a bunch of drug dealers were holed up. Pete would knock on the front door with a pizza. Whoever was closest to the door wouldn't be that suspicious because he figured that even if he didn't order it, someone else might have. A look through the peephole would have shown a skinny white guy with a thick mustache. Pete would lift up the lid of the box to show the hot pizza. It was tough for a hungry idiot to resist.

When the drug dealer opened the door, four guys with guns would swing in. The bit worked for years before all the criminals figured it out.

I'm not sure why Pete ended up as a precinct detective in Chinatown. He cleared a lot of cases and should have been with a prestigious spot maybe with Manhattan South. I asked him about it once and he just said that he had gotten fucked over. It might have been a political thing, or maybe he had been caught doing something he shouldn't have.

Both Bad Boy and Pete had been tied up earlier in the year with a bomb the FALN had set off near Police Headquarters. The Puerto Rican militant group wanted complete independence from the United States, but their methods were repugnant and, worst of all, their spokesman had the same name as Thomas "English" Sanchez, our top precinct detective.

The FBI did the heavy lifting on the investigation but they still wanted Manhattan South and local detectives working with them. The bombing did occur within our precinct boundary, after all.

Now that the media hype was dying down on the case, Bad Boy and Pete were released back to the precinct.

Bad Boy was probably a decade older than English and he spent most of the day chain-smoking with one hand and writing with the other with the phone wedged between a shoulder and an ear. Supposedly Bad Boy was coordinating with cops in other cities who dealt with tax scams and pirated goods. It was tough to tell. His voice was so soft it was impossible to eavesdrop.

Last year, Bad Boy took down an entire block of merchants for charging tourists sales tax that they never reported. The stores settled quickly with the Internal Revenue Service and the state

and local tax offices. The stores were closed over only one weekend. Maybe justice wasn't truly served, but what the hell, it made
the city money.

Pete's caseload was packed with stupid gang kids shooting or
beating or vehicular-assaulting each other with zero witnesses.
Ever since I picked up investigative assignments, he'd been pushing them on to me.

About a year ago, a carload of kids was kidnapped by a rival
gang. One of them managed to sneak out and called Pete for help.
He got a few collars out of it because some of the kidnappers were
over twenty-one. It's tough to build a case against a teen when
the system is always bent toward sparing the rod and spoiling the
child.

Vandyne had helped Pete nail some over-twenty-ones while
busting a heroin ring that had operations in the United States,
Canada, and Mexico.

But apart from that it was tough to say how effective Pete and
Bad Boy were. They didn't seem to be doing anything day to day or
night to night. I'm not saying Vandyne and I were any better. We
were just four guys at our desks, trying to get through the shift and
through the shit, and seemingly getting nothing done. The only
times I felt like I was finishing anything was at the end of meals.

If you manage to close down some crooked stores, they reopen
almost immediately. If you sweep up some of those stupid gang
kids in a heroin bust, they're back on the street within hours. If
you manage to help stop a human-smuggling ring, like I did, you
get a Meritorious Police Duty bar, but no gold shield.

This day was no different. After releasing the water-bucket jerk
with a fine and warning, I had to type up the day's proceedings
and make it look like I was earning my pay.

I walked over to an empty desk that was the unofficial library and condiment station. The desk had belonged to a guy named Lumpy who had retired early two years ago in a voluntary buy-out during the city's financial crunch. The drawers were crammed with salt, pepper, duck sauce, and hot mustard packets. Outdated *World Book Encyclopedia* volumes protected the desk surface from getting dusty.

I opened the bottom drawer for my jar of Jif peanut butter but it was scraped completely transparent. Now I had to get by on some steamed rice buns with nothing on them. Each bite sucked all the saliva out of my mouth and they didn't even taste like anything. But they were healthier to eat than my old standby, the hot-dog pastries. I was hungry a while ago but the rice buns didn't sound appetizing until I was nearly doubled over in pain from not eating. I took one out of the bag and felt despair.

Vandyne was already gone and Pete was on his way out. Bad Boy was on the phone and in no rush to leave. He never was. I wanted to go meet Lonnie and see how that interview went.

My phone rang.

"Detective," I said.

"Robert!" said Lonnie.

"Yeah!"

"I can't meet you for dinner tonight. I didn't get a chance to really talk with Chen Xiaochuan. Willie Gee wanted to give us a private room for the interview but the FBI guys insisted that we leave. Mr. Chen went back to his hotel."

"That's not surprising. It's a security issue."

"Well, Mr. Chen asked me to have dinner with him. At his hotel. In his hotel room."

I switched the phone to my other ear. "Oh, he did, huh?"

"I know what you might be thinking and I was cautious, too. But he said his security detail would be right there. We're not going to be alone."

"Well, I guess that sounds okay. I can't possibly object to that."

"The best thing is he can speak Cantonese pretty well. Far better than my Mandarin. I would have never guessed."

"He probably learned it to meet Cantonese mistresses."

"He's not like that at all, Robert. He is a perfect gentleman. You'll be all right eating by yourself?"

"Of course!"

"Make sure you eat vegetables, too. Don't just get some over-rice pork dish."

"I won't. Do a good interview, Lonnie. Make sure you stick him with hard questions, too. Otherwise you're just his publicist spreading propaganda. We already have Chinese newspapers that do that."

"Oh, I know. I've been prepped by the managing editor of Presswire. I'm going to have follow-up questions and everything."

"You call me when you get back to your parents' place," I told her.

We said good-bye. When I was done for the day, I decided to swing by the toy store to see if the midget would eat with me.

IT WAS ALMOST half an hour before the toy store would close, so I went to Columbus Park to kill some time. The sun had already gone down and everything was a different shade of blue. A few solitary people perched on the wooden benches, staring at their own cold breath in the air. Anybody who had someone to talk to was already eating with that person.

I took a walk around the handball court near the south end. That place used to be a battlefield, in the playful sense. I remember watching the older kids running around, slapping that rubber ball. The air and the asphalt seemed almost to burst into flames in the summer heat. The boys would roll off their shirts and tank tops, and I remember being surprised at how different their skin tones were even though they were all Chinese.

Some had pretty bad scars on their backs, chests, and necks. These were the guys who acted friendly to me and made me feel I was cool when I was a little nobody. They made it real easy for me to join their gang.

Now the handball court was all broken up, like a team of treasure hunters had taken pickaxes to it. What was left of the chain-link fence around the baseball diamond was rusted and curled, looking like the burned edge of a plate of pan-fried noodles. Yum. That sounded good.

Even though the city's funds were as strapped as ever, some of it could be allocated to Columbus Park if the residents made a big enough issue out of it. But Chinese people like to complain only to fellow family members or close friends. Taking your criticism to the authorities was useless at best, and at worst you and your family could be singled out for harassment. If there was something you didn't like about your neighborhood, then save money and move out.

"It's a shame, isn't it?"

Startled, I turned around and saw an elderly Chinese man standing behind me. He was wearing a Yankees cap, a dirty white sweater, and jeans. I was surprised more by the fact that he was speaking to me in unaccented English than how he had sneaked up on me.

"Sure," I said. "They really ought to fix this park up. I'm sorry for your loss." I pointed at his cap.

"Well, there's always next year for the Yankees and I'm feeling good about Billy Martin. He's been good for the team. But this poor handball court may be finished for good. Problem is, apart from the Department of Parks, the associations don't want to deal with it."

"What do you mean?"

"The associations could go to the city government and demand they make repairs and renovations, but they're too concerned with fighting out the civil war all over again. The Communist associations are trying to get the U.S. to sever ties with the Republic of China on Taiwan. The nationalist associations are trying to sabotage warming ties between the U.S. and the People's Republic. It's the poor kids who suffer. They don't get to have a decent playground."

"I think you're right."

"Damn right I'm right! Throughout the long history of the Chinese people, we've always been our worst enemy. Right now it's KMT versus Communists. Used to be Confucianism versus Taoism. Before that it was Three Kingdoms and all the other states in the periods when China was divided. If you ask me, we should have never united. We should have just left well enough alone and stayed separate countries like Europe. Would have been better for all of us!"

"That sounds kind of anti-Chinese to me."

"I'm the anti-Chinese Chinaman. I grew up here and then I committed the ultimate disgrace to my ancestors." He chuckled a little bit. "I married a white girl."

"At least she wasn't Japanese."

"Ah, ah, you're right! Ha-ha!"

"You still live here?"

"No, we left this neighborhood a while ago before my kids became teenagers. I don't know if you're old enough to remember this but there was a budding gang problem here."

"Oh, really?"

"Yeah, believe it or not. They called themselves the Continentals. These little bastards would break off the metal emblems from cars. I caught some kids going after my car and I chased them off. The next night they came back and smashed my windshield. That was when I said we had to leave."

I had been in the Continentals, but I got my emblems from tourist cars in a parking garage. "Did you tell the cops?" I asked.

"No. What was the use? They couldn't do anything."

"They can't do anything when crimes aren't reported. But maybe I'm biased." I handed him my card.

"I should have known who you are, Officer Chow. I will come directly to you if I see anything out of the ordinary. I'm not here that often, though. I'm a widower now. I move back and forth between the kids, New Jersey and Massachusetts. One boy and one girl I had. They both ended up marrying Chinese. Can you beat that? After all my warnings to them."

"Maybe you kind of drove them to it."

A sedan at the edge of the park honked its horn.

"That's my boy. We're going to eat Chinese tonight. Care to join us?"

"Sorry, I have plans already, but I appreciate the invitation. What's your name, sir?"

He shook hands with me. "Byron Su. That's my name. I'm sorry you're busy. Why is it so hard for Chinamen to just get together?"

I gave him a nod and started for the toy store.

THE MIDGET WAS pulling the metal gate across his storefront. "Oh, Robert, I was wondering if you were going to show up for dinner with me."

"What made you think I was going to?"

"I knew that Lonnie had that interview with the Chinese official guy today. I figured that when he got a look at her, he'd make some excuse to have dinner with her tonight."

"They're not eating alone. His guards will be right there."

Talking to himself the midget said, "They can't eat in the hotel's restaurant for security concerns, so they have to eat in his room. He'll find some way to get his guards to leave. . . ."

"What are you talking about, man?"

"Aw, nothing, I'm just trying to annoy you. Next time just give me a ring when you want to do dinner. It will make me feel less like a backup plan."

"I wanted to be spontaneous. I mean, we're close enough friends that we know we don't take each other for granted at all."

The midget flexed his arms and snapped two large padlocks into place. "I might already be busy tonight, you know."

"Please have dinner with me. I turned down another invite tonight to eat with you."

The midget smiled. "Sure, in that case, let's go."

We went to a noodle-soup shop below the street level at the southern end of Mott. He made sure to order two vegetable dishes on the side. I think Lonnie had gotten to him about my diet.

"How's Paul doing with that Columbia thing?" asked the midget.

"Seems all right. He never tells me too much about it, and honestly I wouldn't understand what he's researching."

"Ever thought about going back to school part-time?"

"Sure, I've thought about it. In the end, though, I don't think it's a good idea. I've been out for too long and I was always a crappy student anyway."

He sucked down a mouthful of soup. "Would probably help with promotions, job security, and better assignments."

"It might."

"Would probably help you and Lonnie have a better future together."

"I'll light up some incense at the Buddhist temple and pray for that."

"God helps those who help themselves. Besides, libraries don't smell nearly as bad as those temples."

"You ever use the bathroom at the library?"

The midget put his elbows up on the table. "I never tell you to do anything, right, Robert?"

"Sure."

"Go to college and get a degree. This GI bill isn't good forever."

"I'll think about it."

"Think about what school and what major."

"I will."

I WENT BACK to my apartment and Paul showed me a bulletin from NYU. The descriptions of the classes all sounded interesting, but so did food on a menu, and I wasn't sure that I could eat the same meal for an entire semester.

"What do you think I should study?" I asked Paul.

"That depends," he said. "Are you going to stay a cop or going to get a different job?"

"I'm in for the twenty years, Paul. I made a commitment to the city."

"In that case, you should probably enroll at John Jay and get a degree in criminalistics."

"I don't know about that. I met this guy who studied criminal justice and he's doing worse than me. He's not even a real cop."

"How about studying business and leaving the force? You could make a lot more money and not have to put your life on the line."

I laughed all the way to the refrigerator. I popped open a Yoo-hoo and drank some. "I like my pretty little gun too much, Paul. I also like Vandyne too much to leave." I could quit the NYPD, no problem, but I could never let my old partner down. If anything ever happened to him on or off duty, I could never forgive myself for it.

I finished the Yoo-hoo and then hooked it into the garbage can in the kitchen. "Oh, did you see that?" I asked Paul.

"I did." He was trying to read something now and I was bothering him.

"What did you do today?"

"I cataloged some more core samples."

"What kind of job can you get after you study these things?"

"I can go work for an oil-exploration company and make a whole lotta money."

"Like how much money?"

"I don't want to think about it."

"Just give me a rough idea." It was going to be so embarrassing when Paul starting making more than me, and it wouldn't be that long from now.

The phone rang and Paul told the ceiling, "Thank you!"

I checked the time. Twenty-two minutes after ten. It was safe to answer the phone.

When people have something bad or negative to tell you, they tend to wait until the hour or the half-hour as a deadline to help force themselves to make the call. I don't answer the phone on the hour or half-hour.

Anyway, I knew who it was calling me. "Lonnie," I asked, "how did it go?"

"Oh, it was very interesting! The Plaza is an unbelievably beautiful hotel! It's right out of a Cinderella story."

"Tell me about Mr. Chen."

"Mr. Chen likes to joke around a lot. He's very funny."

"Did he try anything with you?"

"Oh no, his guards were there most of the time. They left near the end. He was sort of touchy-feely. Nothing bad. You know those kind of men? They like to grab you to make a point."

I gritted my teeth and tried to chuckle. "Does it look like Li Na is going to be allowed over?"

"He thinks the chances are pretty good. You wouldn't believe how things are in China now. The political environment is absolutely poisonous. But, Robert, I should go now."

"What? We just started talking."

"Yes, but I have to transcribe my tape. Usually we have people doing transcriptions at work, but because this is in Cantonese and not English, I have to do it myself."

"I see. Well, make sure they count this as your work hours."

"They're not going to do that, of course."

"That's not fair at all."

"I know, I know. Robert, I have to get to work now."

"Okay, Lonnie. Don't work too hard."

"I already am!"

I didn't go to sleep too late. I let Paul beat me at two games of Quickopoly. That's when you deal out the properties to Monopoly at the beginning of the game to make sure that things keep moving. I let him beat me because if I actually tried to win, I know I would have ended up so frustrated I'd be up all night.

At some point in the morning the phone rang and I picked it up, although I wasn't awake until the receiver hit my ear. Body. Older Chinese man. Possible mug victim. Eastern part of Chinatown.

"I'm coming," I croaked.

MY HEAD WAS freezing from the cold morning and my inability to dry my hair properly. My ears were numb by the time I had walked the few blocks from my apartment to where Hester Street ran across Chrystie Street into Sara D. Roosevelt Park. The man's body was curled on one of the park's splintered benches. He was wearing a collared dress shirt and wool slacks. His socks and shoes were gone and his bare feet looked waxy.

The caved-in part of his skull was most likely the cause of death, though it was always dangerous to assume anything. Hell, he might have been poisoned and dumped, and then had his head caved in by someone testing out a sledgehammer.

It was 0700 and English was already smoking.

I came up and touched his shoulder. "I thought you were going to quit, man," I told him.

He folded his arms and puffed out his cheeks before exhaling. "Whenever I get enough willpower together to stop, some bullshit like this happens," he said. "I'm probably going to go through two, three packs today. There really should be a law against murder."

"Who found him?"

"Don't know. Phone tip. Probably gonna be a pain in the ass to identify, as well."

"Let me get a good look at the face."

"That's the spirit, Chow."

After enough pictures were taken and the man was officially declared dead, the paramedics rolled the body away with the same casual disregard they would have with a securely packed side of beef.

"Just a second," I told them. I craned my neck and stared hard. There was a very strong resemblance between the victim's blood-colored face and Chen Xiaochuan, aka Mr. Chen, Li Na's representative from the People's Republic. I wasn't sure. I hadn't met the man in person. But Lonnie had.

I went back to English. "I think I know who that is," I said.

He glared at me. "I'm in no mood," he warned.

"That's the envoy from Mao's daughter."

"You sure?"

"Pretty sure. Won't be too hard to find someone to positive ID him. Lonnie just interviewed him yesterday."

His cigarette wagged in his left hand. "Can you have her at the Bellevue morgue this afternoon?"

"She'll be there."

We watched the medics lift the man's body into the wagon.

"Say, Chow," asked English.

"Yeah?"

"What time did Lonnie interview him last night?"

"They had a late dinner."

"What restaurant they go to? Right around here?"

"No, they actually ate up at his hotel in Midtown. Um, in his hotel room."

"Oh, okay."

I gave him a hard look. "She had nothing to do with this."

"Didn't say she did."

"Even if that is him, I'm ruling her out as a suspect."

"Whatever you say. Just make sure she IDs the body today."

"She will."

"And I hope you know that if it is in fact the guy, we're going to have to take down a statement from her."

"Wait, let's have an idiot test right now. Someone should call the hotel and see if he's there."

"Assumed name."

"Ask the FBI."

"You have a contact there?"

"No."

"Does Lonnie know?"

"I'll see."

I WENT BACK to my apartment to call Lonnie. It was almost time for her to get up, anyway.

She answered the phone, talking slowly like she was underwater. "I was up all night, Robert. I can't believe it takes so long to transcribe and then translate."

"Are you finished?"

"I think I am. I have to read it one more time. There may be some more corrections I have to make."

"Well, make sure you get it right. That interview may be pretty damned important. I think Mr. Chen's been murdered."

She dropped her receiver on the floor, sending a hard clunk into my ear. "What!" I heard her yell. Then she picked up the receiver and yelled "What!" again.

"Yeah, we had a body down here. I think it's him, but you would know for sure. Do you happen to know the name that Mr. Chen was staying under?"

"I don't know. One of his security guards met me in the lobby."

"What room number was it?"

"I don't remember, I was so nervous."

"What floor was it on?"

"Ten. No, wait, twelve, I think."

"Lonnie! Do you realize what kind of fix you could be in?"

"Don't yell at me, Robert! If Mr. Chen is really dead, that would really terrify me!"

"If we can't figure this out, you could be the main suspect, Lonnie!" I blurted out.

When I got into the squad room, I called The Plaza and bullied the manager. After waiting a while I learned that Mr. Chen wasn't in his room although his belongings were. If he was at breakfast, that son of a bitch better choke down his oatmeal and come back to the hotel.

BECAUSE I AM usually right in being paranoid, I met Lonnie in the anteroom of the Bellevue morgue.

"Robert," she asked, "why are you here?"

"I just want to make sure you're going to be all right."

"I'll be okay."

"You're okay with seeing a dead body?"

"Sure I am. I mean, I have to see one sooner or later, right? I'm a journalist."

We walked through the doors and nearly ran into English.

"Hello, Chow," he said, smoke rolling out of his nose. He tossed his cigarette into a metal ashtray stand that looked like it had been pulled from a serious house fire. He turned to Lonnie and said, "As I mentioned, we would have been happy to pick you up and escort you here, but we're glad you made it just the same."

"Thank you very much, Detective Sanchez," said Lonnie. "We are actually very close to my office, so it was no problem. I didn't know Robert would be here waiting for me."

English smirked. "I didn't know, either, Lonnie."

He stepped back and then I noticed two guys from Manhattan South, one black and one white. I studied them and we all nodded to each other. Two lamps hanging from the ceiling illuminated the dust in the air and a body under a sheet.

I touched Lonnie's shoulder. "Are you ready?" I asked. She nodded.

The mortician, a husky young white man, stretched his fingers in his gloves and gently lifted the sheet and folded it below the shoulders.

Lonnie came around to the other side and gasped. "It's him," was all she could say.

I pulled her back and pressed her to me. "It's all right," I said.

"Hey," she said as she pushed gently away from me. "I'm okay. I told you I'd be okay."

"You got that?" I asked English.

"Oh, we already know it's him. The Chinese U.N. delegation already identified him." English grimaced. "Now we just need to follow up with Lonnie."

"What do you mean, 'follow up'?"

"She's the last one who's seen Mr. Chen alive."

"One of his security guards saw him after!"

"That's not what we heard."

"Lonnie, didn't his men come back into his room?"

She looked at me and then English. "I assume they did."

"They say they didn't," said English. "Lonnie, I'm going to ask you to come down to Manhattan South and tell us what happened. Don't worry. You're not a suspect, all right?"

"She came here voluntarily!" I said, glaring at English.

"We appreciate volunteerism. It's the spirit of America."

Lonnie looked worried. "I need to be back for the edits to my interview, and I guess to write about this. Will I be out by three?"

English smiled. "You'll be out by one thirty at the latest, I promise. This is just a formality in a murder investigation." Looking at me, English added, "You'd be doing the same thing if it wasn't her."

"Do I need a lawyer, Robert?"

"I don't think so, Lonnie. They know better than to mess with a reporter!" I yelled the last word loud enough to make the Manhattan South guys wince.

THE LATER EDITIONS of the Chinese newspapers reported Mr. Chen's death. The Taiwan-biased paper declared that Communist agents had gotten to him. The Hong Kong–biased rag lamented how unsafe Chinatown had become ever since those lowlifes from Fujian province started coming into the country.

The pro-Communist paper did not say one word directly about Mr. Chen. The People's Republic had likely imposed a news blackout on him. But there was yet another article criticizing the Gang of Four, noting that counterrevolutionaries sow the seeds of their own demise.

I came home with all three papers folded under my right arm. I was surprised to find Paul. "What are you doing here? What about your job at Columbia?"

"How many times do I have to tell you?" he asked. "Wednesdays and Saturdays. Wednesdays and Saturdays. Two days a week!"

"I've got bigger things on my mind!"

"Then get a bigger mind."

I noticed there was a wave of static coming out from my stereo. "If you don't know how to use my equipment, ask me how or don't turn it on. You left the receiver between stations, that's why all we have is noise."

"It's not noise. I'm playing an album."

"This is a record? What is this crap?"

He showed me the record cover. The Ramones. They looked like four white dirtbags who should have their hands against the wall and their legs spread out.

"Who the hell gave you this, Paul? A drug dealer?"

"My boss at Columbia lent it to me. She wanted me to hear it."

"Your boss?"

"Yeah!"

"Does she look like the tall one on the cover here?"

"Let me know when you're ready to talk about something serious."

"Actually, I am, Paul. Have you heard from Lonnie?"

"No. Is there something wrong?"

"There could be."

"What did you do?"

"I didn't do anything!"

"Then what did you forget to do?"

"Paul, did you hear about that older man that was found dead in Roosevelt Park?"

"Sure I did. A homeless guy, right?"

"He wasn't a homeless guy. That was a brief we put out to mislead the American press until we were sure. It didn't work with the Chinese press, though. The dead man was the guy from the People's Republic—the one Lonnie interviewed!"

"Was he murdered?"

"Yes. Lonnie may have been the last one to see him alive."

Paul got up and took the needle off the awful record. He turned to me and asked, "Can she prove she's innocent?"

"Not yet."

"Can you?"

"I need time."

"You do believe she's innocent, right?"

"No, I think she actually interviewed the guy, killed him, and then dumped his body in the park."

"The Mr. Chen interview was Lonnie's big coup. It could really help her career, and his murder will only raise the profile of this piece."

"Your sister has to prove she's innocent first!"

"How hard could that be?"

"You never know. Manhattan South took her in for questioning and then let her go back to work."

"Why is Manhattan South involved?"

"Because this could be a politically sensitive case."

"Did you talk to Lonnie after she got out?"

"I did, but not for long. I didn't want to take up too much of her time because she had to finish a story."

"If they had any evidence, they would just plain arrest her, right?"

"Yeah, but she's the leading candidate for the murderer."

"I remember reading this story about a reporter who went around killing people to get exclusives on the serial murders going on around town."

"She's your sister, man! Don't talk about her like that!"

"Fine. So then, how are you going to prove she's innocent?"

"I'm not a lawyer! Damn, maybe she needs one."

ARTIE YEE, THE GUY whose newspaper office burned down, came by the precinct to see me.

"My insurance company is giving me a hard time, Robert," he said.

"Why? I thought it was ruled an accidental fire."

"The FDNY has determined that it was an electrical fire. A wire in the wall I couldn't have known about. But my insurers have hired a private investigator to see if I could have possibly set it off. Can you help me out on this one?"

"That's a tough break, Artie, but I don't see what I could do," I said.

"Oh, I get it. You're blaming me for that trouble that Lonnie's in because I got her the interview."

"I'm not blaming you for anything. You actually gave her a big break, but maybe you can help her out of the jam she's in now. Just tell me who killed Mr. Chen."

Artie laughed and looked around the squad room nervously. "Jesus, I don't know, Robert. How could I know?"

"Don't worry, Artie. We're the only ones here who know Cantonese. Now tell me who got you in touch with Mr. Chen to begin with."

He put his hands in his pockets. "I came in here looking for help and now I'm being interrogated!"

"Would you feel more comfortable talking outside?" Not waiting for an answer, I stood up and put an arm on him. "Let's go to Hop Won."

"Only tourists go there!"

"That's the point."

Hop Won on Lafayette Street is the kind of place you've seen in every television show when they need a Chinese restaurant. It's got bowing, smiling waiters in silk outfits, and paper lanterns everywhere—even on top of the tables. The numerous gaudy paintings of rivers and mountains on the walls were mirrored in the free-flowing duck sauce and mounds of crispy noodles. Hop Won's menus were in English with marked-up prices that only a tourist would pay. And Hop Won actually took credit cards.

Most important, the restaurant kept up a din of piped-in cymbals, drums, and flutes that foiled eavesdropping waiters.

"Hullo and welcome!" the restaurant greeter chimed as we walked in the door. He was a thin man about five feet tall and probably got his job because of his light-colored skin and cheek-to-cheek smile. When he saw Artie and me up close, his forehead creased and his eyebrows puffed out with worry.

In English I said, "How about that table by the speaker?"

Without a word he yanked out two menus and stomped over to the booth. Before we took our seats, he swatted the table with the menus and left without looking at us.

See, the only reason we were there, he thought, was to mock the décor, the food, and the greeter himself.

We flipped open the heavy menus. They were thicker than usual because every item was accompanied with a picture, requiring more pages.

"They shouldn't have used a flash," Artie remarked. "It makes everything look even more greasy."

"It gives the pineapple chunks a nice sheen, though."

Our waiter approached our table with much trepidation. He'd already been forewarned. "You want forks or chopsticks?" he asked in Cantonese.

"Chopsticks are fine," I said.

"You want tea or water?"

"Tea."

"I want a Coke," said Artie.

"You want a Coke, huh?" said the waiter. He was only slightly less contentious when we ordered. For four-dollar dishes in this economy, he should've been giving us shoulder massages. Instead, we only got silence and sugar-laden sauce.

While we ate, I asked, "Artie, who hooked you up with Mr. Chen?"

He wiped his mouth with his fingers, smearing a dab of orange gunk across his bottom lip, leaving a thin streak. "It was this girl who used to work for me. I think you know her, too."

"Wait, not Barbara."

"Yeah, her! Apparently she had contacts with the Republic of China who put her in touch with him. I was glad she thought of my paper first, even though it didn't turn out that way."

"Her Taiwan contacts put you in touch with Mr. Chen from mainland China?"

"See, it's an embarrassing story to the People's Republic, that some private citizens in Taiwan were quietly sponsoring some of Li Na's efforts. They took care of Mr. Chen's airfare from Hong Kong and put him up in a hotel here." Artie looked thoughtful for a moment. "The FBI took care of his security, though."

"What a nice job they did, too."

Maybe the Taiwanese had flown in Mr. Chen to kill him and embarrass the Communists. I played around with my rice. The rice grains weren't sticky at all—in other words, not chopstick-friendly. I picked up the bowl, put it to my lips, and shoveled some of it in. What was this? Minute Rice?

"Who were the people that Barbara talked to?"

He shook his head. "You have to ask her. She gave Mr. Chen my info and he called me." Artie took a swig of tea and shrugged. "Well, that's not terrible."

"I'm not even going to try," I said.

"She doesn't know it, but I've known Barbara her entire life. My dad used to own this little grocery store on Mott Street just below Canal. I worked there until my early thirties. You remember that place, right, Robert? It was called Ginny's."

I rubbed my chin. That was the place all the kids in my gang, the Continentals, used to boost stuff from. I picked up chocolate bars there like my coat sleeve was a vacuum cleaner hose.

"I'm sorry, I don't remember it all that well," I said.

"My dad died pretty early on. He was a hardworking guy who put his shoulder to the wheel every morning. The results were definitely on the moderate side but nobody put in more effort than him. His problem was that he was too honest. All the other grocers were pushing their suppliers for kickbacks and other discounts, but not my dad. They all told me he was stupid for not asking for it."

"Getting a discount isn't illegal."

"When you don't report it on your income, it is."

So Artie's dad instilled a principled foundation in him. They had probably spent a lot of time together in the store. My father didn't try to instill much in me, apart from the idea that being a cop was stupid, and I would find that out on my own soon enough. But we hadn't had as much money as Artie's family, and Dad certainly wasn't very good with the money that passed through his fingers.

"So," I said, "your family had the money to put up a store."

"No, not exactly. I know what you're thinking," said Artie. He pushed back in his seat and leaned his face into mine. "We didn't have very much money at all. Tell you the truth, Dad's brothers and sisters all put their money together for us to run the store. We made money, plenty of money, but not enough to keep my uncles and aunts from accusing us of skimming from the top. They said that what I ate alone was costing twenty dollars a day." He patted his gut. "I was always big, but that was a hell of an exaggeration."

I cringed. The Continentals would easily sweep out twenty dollars' worth of merchandise on a regular basis from Ginny's. I nodded and let him continue.

"In the end, they came down on us and forced my dad to sell the store to get their money back. It killed him, you know. He was a man of honor, but he was also too proud to go work for someone else. He wasn't much older than me now when he had a heart attack and passed away.

"But believe it or not, I remember only good things about the store. All the customers who would come in and the stories they would tell. I remember when Barbara's dad brought her in, she was this little baby girl all wrapped up like a little squash. He was showing her off like he was taking bids."

"I'll bet he became less and less enthusiastic with each baby girl."

"You can say that again! He didn't even bring the fourth girl in when she was a baby! Of course, it wasn't much longer after that when we lost the store. But didn't Barbara turn out nice?"

"Sure, she did."

"You two were together for a little while, right?"

"Sure."

"Didn't work out, huh?"

"No."

"You're still friends, right?"

"Oh, yeah, of course! We're just both really busy people. We don't see each other much."

"Were you two ever in love? I mean, ever serious about getting married?"

"You don't have to fish for anything anymore, Artie. Your newspaper's gone so there's nothing to report."

"Hey, you don't have to get like that. I'm just saying, you know, as men, we can agree that Barbara is very attractive, right?"

"We can agree on a lot of things, I guess."

"I don't know if I should tell you this, but a number of years ago, I could have made a play for her."

"I didn't know that."

"Oh, I don't like to brag. But, anyway, have you heard anything about the second sister?"

"She's in medical school somewhere in California, I think."

"That's so far away," Artie said. "She is a real looker, too."

"They all are beautiful women."

"Do you think I should try calling the second sister? Do you think she'd remember me? With my paper gone, I could be free to move out there and settle down."

I wasn't comfortable with the way the conversation was bending. I did a drumroll on the table with both hands and said, "How about we get that check now?"

I nodded. Our keenly attuned waiter took that as a cue to come over.

"Everything all right?"

"Not really," I said. "But we got what we expected."

The waiter tore off our check and placed it on the table. "Next time, don't go where you're not wanted," he said with a big smile.

LONNIE CALLED ME late that night. She assured me that Presswire had its own legal team and that they would protect her legal rights.

Meanwhile, her interview with Mr. Chen was making the rounds. She had scooped the Associated Press, and newspapers all around the country were running the interview with a sidebar she had written about his untimely death. The top editor of Presswire had embarrassed her by making everyone in the newsroom stand up and clap.

The guys at Manhattan South hadn't given her a hard time. They had only asked a few questions and then let her go.

Lonnie was going to be working overtime the next few days to write follow-ups, but we made plans for the weekend. Nothing big. Just dinner and a movie.

After hanging up, I put on my coat and pulled a rain hat low over my face. I went by Lonnie's apartment and walked around the block.

VANDYNE CAME BACK from time off and we met up early in the morning to eat in a crappy diner by my apartment. I caught him up on the murder and Lonnie's situation.

"I saw two Manhattan South motherfuckers parked outside Lonnie's apartment last night," I said. "I could hear them eating even with the windows up."

Vandyne shook hot sauce all over his eggs. "Don't get too worked up about it. They're just doing their jobs. They think it's bullshit, too."

"You think?"

"Yeah, man. I bet if there wasn't someone checking up on them, you would've heard them snoring." Vandyne pulled his mouth to the left and looked out the window at nothing.

"You all right?"

"I'm better now. Had a long talk with Rose."

"How did it go?"

"Honestly? It was infinitely depressing."

"I am really sorry to hear that."

"Just to think that this woman you've already promised to spend the rest of your life with is like a stranger again. Actually, worse than a stranger, because a stranger doesn't expect anything from you. I feel like I have something to prove to her."

"You don't have anything to prove to anybody."

"I know. I have half a mind to just let it all go."

"But you don't want to."

"I don't know." He put more hot sauce on his eggs.

"Vandyne, you're going to set your plate on fire there."

"Oh, shit," he muttered. "How am I supposed to eat this now?"

"Don't worry about it. You can have half of my pancakes."

"You sure?"

"Of course, man!" I took the saucer from under my coffee cup and dragged two pancakes onto it.

"Look, you and Lonnie, whatever happens, remember to stay young."

" 'Young'?"

"Yeah, man, 'young'! When you get older, you forget how to forgive."

"You're scaring me."

"I'm just trying to share knowledge with you."

"I ever do anything to piss you off?"

"All the time."

"You forgive me, though, right?"

"How could I hold anything against you, Chow?" he said, smiling for the first time in a while. "Just keep the pancakes coming."

"Take the rest of my butter, too."

IN THE SQUAD ROOM, I went over to English. "I see that Manhattan South is staking out Lonnie."

"So what?"

"She's not the murderer."

"Prove it."

"I can't."

He looked at me and shrugged.

"Thanks," I said.

"You can have an attitude as long as you don't stop working. Check in with Pizza Man. I'm sure he's got something to keep you busy."

I grumbled and shuffled over to my desk. When I was walking a foot-post, I was really envious of Vandyne because he had picked up investigative assignments. When he got the gold shield and the official promotion to detective, that old green devil hardened into jade.

Now that I was trudging through investigative assignments that ranged from hopeless to thankless, I found that maybe a beat cop didn't have it so bad.

When I helped put an end to that human-smuggling ring a few months ago, I think I would've gotten more official credit for stopping a purse-snatcher. I did get a Meritorious Police Duty bar and a nice letter from Mayor Abe Beame, though. It seemed to be actually signed, too.

Maybe things got better with that gold shield.

"Chow," said Pete. He held out a manila folder to me. "Maybe I have something for you to check out."

"Something good I hope."

"I save all the good ones just for you, man." He chuckled, assaulting me with coffee breath. "Three guns found in an apartment mailbox on Henry Street two days ago by the building super. Two were cheap Saturday night specials but one was a nice .32 revolver with a fancy walnut handle. I'm surprised nobody's come up to claim them."

"A thirty-two's not a big gun," I said.

"Yeah, but the great thing about the gun is that the shell casings don't pop out when you fire from it. I guess that makes it environmentally friendly, in addition to not leaving evidence. You don't have to clean up after it."

"How come City Wide Anti-Crime isn't handling this?"

"These guns weren't recovered at a crime scene. Might not even have been involved in a crime yet. They're at ballistics now, but they're not on the priority list. There are pictures of the guns in the folder."

"You want me to frame them or something?"

"C'mon, Chow! Just go to the address on Henry and talk to people and figure out who left the guns."

"You're giving me another dead-end assignment here."

"It was a dead-end for me, but I think people will be more amenable to talking to you because you know the language."

"I'll understand what they're saying when they're cursing me."

English called over, "Just give it your best shot, Chow. Let's see what happens."

I took in a breath and held it.

This is what you wanted, I thought to myself. Show them you're not going to let the bullshit get to you.

"Hot dog," I said.

I WAS ABOUT a block away from the precinct when my newfound spirit slipped away, probably off to cheer up some sick kid in a hospital bed.

I put my hands in my coat pockets and kept walking. It all seemed like a funny joke. Send the Chinese cop on a wild goose chase while you try to pin a murder on his girlfriend.

When I hit Bowery, the sunlight hit me full in the face, bright white and warm. I shaded my eyes but I couldn't help smiling.

Lonnie would be exonerated, eventually. Maybe she was even getting something out of being followed—a sharpened reporting instinct.

The man who had found the guns had either given his name only as Mr. Wing or the responding officer hadn't been able to write down the rest of his name. I guessed the latter happened because there was a question mark written after the name. But the apartment number was clearly marked 5F.

I didn't have to buzz his apartment because the building's front door was unlocked and the foyer door was propped open with a splintered wood wedge. Hopefully he was home. Maybe he would talk to me. It's harder to ignore a knock at the door than a buzz from downstairs.

I started up the stairs and cursed the fact that apparently nobody ever lives in the ground-floor apartments. The corners of each landing were filthy. I'd like to see them shoot a commercial for one of those tile-and-grout cleaners here. Goddamn sponge would probably dissolve.

Mr. Wing's door had several Wacky Packs stickers slapped on it. Some were ripped in half while most were merely torn at the edges. I heard a radio through the door.

I knocked lightly by the bolt.

"Uh?" called someone inside.

"I'm looking for Mr. Wing," I said.

Someone came shuffling to the door and asked, "Who are you?"

"It's the police," I said. "My name's Robert Chow."

He sighed in response and then unlocked the door. He swung open the door and pointed at it. "I call you for this," he started, "and you don't come. When I find guns, you're here in five minutes. Why?"

Mr. Wing was in his mid-sixties and stood at about five feet two. He had withered a bit to about 140 pounds or so. His silver-rimmed glasses were lopsided.

"Finding guns is a big problem, Mr. Wing. I actually have some more questions about them."

"Just a minute. It's not a problem when my personal property is defaced?"

"These stickers aren't that big a problem. They probably aren't that hard to get off."

On cue, he reached behind the door and handed me a paint scraper, its wood handle blackened with years of sweat. "Not that hard to get off, huh? Well, put some muscle into it, pal. I'm not talking to you until that door is clean."

I looked into his eyes. He wasn't fooling. How hard could this be, anyway? This may very well be my good deed for the day. I crouched slightly and scraped away.

I was right. It actually was sort of easy, but I still broke a sweat. Five minutes was all it took. "At your service," I said as I handed the scraper back.

"I think I have some more odd jobs around the apartment for you," Mr. Wing mumbled. He took off his glasses and wiped them on his shirt. With his head still down he asked, "You wanted to ask me something?"

"About the guns. How did you find them?"

He slid on his glasses and scowled at me. "I told my whole story to the cop, already. White people never listen, never give respect to Chinese people! You know that, right?"

"Whatever you say, Mr. Wing. So what happened?"

"Well, I was opening my mailbox downstairs. I saw that my neighbor's box was broken into. The metal door was all bent back, like someone had pried it open.

"I opened the mailbox because I thought I could be helpful and bend the door back the right way. Then I saw a brown bag in there, all wrinkled up. Of course, I had to take a look. There were three guns in there! I called the cops right away!"

"You did the right thing, Mr. Wing. Tell me, do you have a lot of teenagers hanging out in this building? Especially ones who don't live here?"

He looked at me hard. "Who do you think put all those stickers on my door! Everybody who lives in this building is old. Nobody under fifty, I guarantee!"

"Then where are all these kids coming from?"

"Where do you think? Stupid kids! They're a part of those Fukienese Commie groups that are infiltrating our country."

I already knew the answer but I had to ask. "Mr. Wing, would you be willing to come to the precinct and look over some pictures to see if you recognize any of these possible gang members?"

"No way in hell. I would be seen going to the precinct and then those same kids will come back and harass me. I'll ask you for help and then you'll say there's nothing you can do because they haven't actually killed me yet."

"I think you're exaggerating quite a bit, Mr. Wing."

"No, I'm not! Everybody here has eyes. Word gets around. I don't have to tell you. At least I shouldn't have to tell you."

"Well, enjoy your new clean door, now. I worked hard on it."

"And you enjoy your new sobriety, Mr. Chow." He closed the door in my face.

I WENT THROUGH the photo albums of Polaroids that we kept of suspected gang members. "My Beautiful Vacation" had photos shot secretly from Columbus Park. "Happy Memories" covered Bayard Street, East Broadway, and part of Pell. "Those Were the Days" covered Mott. We were supposed to pretend that these were the individual detective's personal photo albums on our desks.

If the D.A.'s office had ever gotten wind of these books, our asses would be on the line because they were illegal. Something about the presumption of innocence until proven guilty and how these binders amounted to unofficial "mug" books of innocent kids being treated as convicted criminals.

Yet, there was no other way we could keep tabs on the young wildlife that some of Chinatown's youths had become. Sure, a lot of good kids were mixed up in there, too. I made a conscious effort to weed them out. A few months ago, I tore out a picture of Paul because he didn't belong there.

Honestly, if the department had been equipped with Polaroid instant cameras back when I was a teen, my picture should have been in the photo albums.

I flipped through "Live, Laugh, Love" as I sipped from my dirty coffee mug.

"How's it going, there?" asked English.

"It's all right," I said. "Any word on those guns?"

"Check in with Pete when he's in. He was keeping tabs on them. Knows someone at ballistics, so he can get a priority review. Won't matter, though, if we can't figure out whose they are."

I stopped on a page with two photos that were sloppily shoved under the plastic cover sheet at jaunty angles. "I've seen that guy." I pointed at a guy in his twenties who was shot from the side.

"Not him!" exclaimed English.

"You know him?"

"No, I don't. I was just messing with you. Where did you see him?"

"That's rooster boy. He was a jerk who had a megaphone during the protest in front of Jade Palace."

"Photographed on Henry Street, too, huh? He might know the kids that dick around there."

IT WAS NO wonder that the guy was photographed on Henry Street. The permit for the Commies to assemble was in the name of the Union of the Three Armies, which had a below-sidewalk-level address right next to Mr. Wing's apartment.

I leaned over the railing and tried to look in, but the windows were covered with blinds and even though they were crooked there weren't any gaps. I could tell the lights were on and not much else.

The last step on the wooden stairs down to the office door was broken in half and rotting. The steel door itself was bland corporate gray. I tried the handle and found it open.

I went in and immediately a loud and continuous whistle went off. A middle-aged woman came into the room with her hands over her ears.

She jumped when she saw me and screamed something. I screamed back that I couldn't hear her. She shook her head and went behind an office desk and ducked down behind it. The alarm suddenly stopped.

"I thought the alarm had malfunctioned again," she said, smiling. "We have a doorbell for a reason. You really shouldn't go barging into places."

"You shouldn't leave your door unlocked," I said.

"Well, Officer, my name is Sunny Chu. How can I help you?"

I chuckled. "My fame precedes me."

"I know you're the guy who stopped that smuggling ring. That was terrible what those people did."

"It sure was. Right now, though, I'm looking for the guy who had the bullhorn at your protest at Jade Palace."

"Our protest?"

"Yeah, this is the Union of the Three Armies, right?"

"Oh," she said, rolling her eyes. "You must mean Lincoln."

"Who?"

"Lincoln Chin. He's supposed to be our English coordinator."

"What is this place?"

"This is the BDC After-School Program. We're a quasi-government agency that provides programming and services for kids through high school."

"So you guys basically babysit."

"Sometimes, yes, it does come down to that. I also like to think that we keep our kids out of trouble."

"This place doesn't have room to hold that many kids."

"This is just our administrative office. We operate facilities in the schools themselves when the day is over and let them do arts and crafts in a cafeteria or dance around in a gym."

"What does BDC stand for?"

She blinked and tilted her head. "It's the initials of someone who gave a lot of money."

"What do you do here, Ms. Chu?"

"I'm the Chinese coordinator. I schedule the directors—that's what we call our teachers—and make sure they continue to perform well."

"What does Lincoln do?"

"Well, he's *supposed* to be writing grant applications and being the liaison with the city agencies."

"What does he actually do, then?"

"Not too much. I have half a mind to complain to our board of directors but they wouldn't do anything about it. Besides, I do like him. He has a good heart."

On the wall above Sunny's head hung a picture taken in the 1950s, judging by the clothes. A younger version of her stood in the middle, in front of a crowd, handing a trophy down to a smiling kid with a bow tie.

"Is Lincoln supposed to be here now?" I asked.

"He went to lunch a while ago. Sometimes he doesn't bother to come back. It's supposed to be the two of us here, but since I end up alone in the office so much my brother installed the security alarm. You know that son of a gun has a master's degree?"

"Figures. You spend that much time in college it'll make you a Communist."

"Ha, you know what the Union of the Three Armies is, right?"

"That was when the Communists regrouped after the Long March."

"So you know your history! So nice to see that in a young man. Maybe you should replace Lincoln here. All he does is loaf around. What he does work hard at is trying to get the high-school students to come to his socialist meetings and events."

"I didn't see any kids at the protest at Jade Palace."

"Even young children are too smart to follow an idealistic daydreamer like Lincoln. But would you believe that some of the girls think he's cute and dashing?" Sunny dropped her voice. "You know something? He treats his girlfriend like dirt. Who does he think he is? Chairman Mao?"

"I don't think so. He told me he knows how to speak Mandarin." I saw Sunny laugh. The Chairman had spoken his native Hunanese and butchered the national language when he tried to speak it.

"People from Hunan!" she said knowingly. "You know what they're like. Hot-tempered and impulsive. Communist or not, he was the wrong guy to lead China."

"What kind of Chinese is Lincoln?"

"From Jersey. So he's got a chip on his shoulder."

"Should I wait here for him?"

"You could go to OK Noodle over on Division Street. At least that's where he told me he was going."

"I know where that is. Thanks, Sunny."

"Are you married, Officer Chow?" she asked.

"Girlfriend. Do you have kids?"

"No, I haven't got anybody," she said, trying to smile.

ONLY TWO OF OK Noodle's tables in the front were occupied. The back was completely empty. Lincoln wasn't around.

There isn't really a lunch rush in Chinatown in the restaurants that are far from the crowds stuck in jury duty. The good restaurants always had fairly steady traffic throughout the day. The bad ones struggled. OK Noodle, as a merely decent place, was appropriately named.

It had launched fairly recently. The press-on tiles hadn't been scuffed too badly yet and the manager didn't know who I was. Also, the ceiling above the Guan Gong shrine high up on the wall wasn't stained yet by constantly burning incense sticks.

Yes, Lincoln was there earlier but he had left about an hour ago. They called him "that foreign Chinese guy" because he couldn't speak Cantonese, couldn't really speak Mandarin, and couldn't eat organ meats. I handed my card to the manager and when he read my name he mentioned that someone had come looking for me there, a certain Mr. Song.

I played with my collar and bought a Coke on the way out.

Mr. Song had had it in for me because he thought I was after his college-aged daughter back in the summer. More like the opposite was true, but fathers don't know their daughters any more than men know women, so there was no use in arguing it.

In fact, there hadn't been any use in me even seeing Mr. Song. I had been sort of dodging him and the front door of his umbrella group, Together Chinese Kinship, for the past few months. Mr. Song, as chair of the organization, lobbied on behalf of and mediated among Together Chinese's dozen members, which were all associations aligned with the People's Republic.

Mr. Song had landed in hot water for being suspected of aiding the smuggling ring that I had stopped. I had never said anything about him. But someone had shown the INS my notes and they pulled a full-on daylight raid on Together Chinese. The only illicit material they uncovered was pirated volumes of Lin Piao's works that were now banned by the People's Republic.

The INS had issued a press release that exonerated Together Chinese, but the Chinese papers didn't bother running it to counter their dramatic photographs of white and black agents carrying out boxes from the group's office. There were shots of Mr. Song being restrained by two agents, his face wild and rabid like Old Yeller near the end of the movie.

I chucked the empty Coke can and headed for Together Chinese's office on East Broadway with leaden feet. I wondered why he would want to talk to me, after he thought I had tried to stick it to his group and his daughter. It must be something serious that required a lot of help.

Maybe it had something to do with Mr. Chen's murder. Something that would prove Lonnie innocent.

I took my hands out of my pockets and picked up the pace. Despite everything, Mr. Song and I did have a common denominator in that we were both alcoholics and that he had been in recovery far longer than me. Would our mutual condition be enough to turn him back into a friendly acquaintance, if not a friend?

Together Chinese's office building was made of brown crumbling brick that would probably get soggy in milk. A blackened scar two floors up marked where some KMT supporters allegedly tried to burn the flag of the People's Republic.

Two thin guys shivered on either side of Together Chinese's front door. One was in a tan sports jacket while the other one, a real youngster, wore an unzipped black padded coat and had spiky hair.

"You looking for something?" the tan-jacketed man asked me in Mandarin.

Spiky Hair cut him off. "That's the cop, asshole!"

"I'm sorry! So sorry!" said the first man. "Mr. Song's been looking for you! Please come in!"

"No offense taken," I said as they opened the doors for me. I stood in the middle of Together Chinese's modest foyer. Before the doors were closed behind me, I heard thumping footsteps on the stairs. I took a deep breath and decided to let him do as much of the talking as possible.

I watched a man step down the last flight. He wore eggshell-blue twill slacks and a white, buttoned shirt with a jacket that matched his slacks. His hair was parted like Richie Cunningham's.

"Robert," he said, pronouncing my name like he was giving me detention. We always spoke in English because my Mandarin wasn't great and he didn't know Cantonese.

"Mr. Song," I said. "I understand that you're looking for me."

"Yes, you've heard right. The truth is . . ." he paused to cross the floor and shake my outstretched hand. "The truth is that I need your help."

"I'm glad to offer it. Assuming that I am able to."

He motioned that we enter a side room. We had sat in that room when we first met. We went in and took adjacent seats at a round table.

He rubbed his mouth vigorously with both hands before talking. "Robert, I have to say that I've unfairly blamed you for a number of woes."

"I've already forgotten what's happened."

"I haven't, of course. I know what happened was completely not your fault." Mr. Song was doing that old Chinese trick of a too-humble apology to get me to meet him nearly halfway in the blame game.

I was supposed to say, "I was also wrong," or something like that. Instead, I said, "That's all right."

He narrowed his eyes and smiled at my snub. A young man with a tea tray came into the room. As Mr. Song and I looked at each other in silence, the man set two green ceramic cups and filled them with jasmine tea.

"Mr. Chow," said Mr. Song, "this is our intern, Daniel. He goes to Hunter College in Midtown."

I turned to get a good look at Daniel. Seemed like your average kid with limp black hair and instinctive shyness. "Hello, Mr. Chow," he said.

"Call me Robert, Daniel. I feel old when people call me Mr. Chow." He nodded. "What are you majoring in, Daniel?"

He opened his eyes wide. "I haven't declared one yet. I'm only a freshman."

"Daniel, don't worry about it," said Mr. Song.

"I didn't go to college, myself," I offered.

"You don't have to go to college to become a policeman?" asked Daniel. "How is that possible?"

"Mr. Chow is gifted in many other ways," Mr. Song said curtly. He tilted his head to the door.

Daniel placed the pot on the table, nodded to both of us, and left.

Mr. Song sipped his tea and swallowed hard. "He's a very curious boy," he said. "Daniel didn't mean to question your intelligence."

"I didn't take it that way. He asked about college, not about my brain."

"Sure. Anyway, I do have a rather urgent matter that you could help me with."

"Those two guards at the door sort of tipped me off that it was urgent. They're armed, right?"

"They are contractors trained and licensed to carry firearms, just as I am." Mr. Song had received death threats for his Communist affiliation. "They're just a precaution for now, in the wake of this latest news." He brought his teacup to cover his lips. "You know those KMT bastards are already claiming that Communist agents killed Mr. Chen?"

"That seems like the logical thing to think. Someone trying to flee the country probably isn't a friend of the regime."

"It's a setup!" growled Mr. Song. "In fact, we had nothing to do with the protest of Li Na at Jade Palace. Together Chinese is the only organization in Chinatown that has official ties with Beijing. That group that supposedly represented the People's Republic was a sham, a front, and did nothing but embarrass our political cause."

"What is the position by the People's Republic on Li Na?"

"We have no position and no comment, whatsoever."

"How do you feel about the death of Mr. Chen?"

"It's tragic but not to be unexpected in a dangerous town like New York. He probably shouldn't have been out unescorted so late at night."

"How do you know he was out late at night?"

"Why, he was being interviewed by your girlfriend until late that evening. I assumed he went out after it was over. That is, if I remember the interview I read correctly."

"Yeah, that's right."

"That interview really got around. It was a coup for Lonnie. You're very proud of her, I'm sure. The timing of it was unfortunate, though. I'm sure she hadn't planned to capture his last interview."

"The whole thing is a mixed blessing for Lonnie," I said. "But, wait, are you familiar with the Union of the Three Armies?"

He sat back and crossed his arms. "You want to test *my* knowledge of Chinese history?"

"Let me clarify. It's sort of a made-up group based here. They were the ones protesting at Jade Palace."

"For a group to name themselves that is an insult to the sacrifices made by the men and women of the People's Liberation Army. I wouldn't be surprised if this wasn't some puppet group of the KMT to make us look bad. Does anybody seriously think we would give any publicity to Li Na and her counterrevolutionary clique?"

"People only know what they see. And they saw Commies protesting Li Na."

"Robert, you've got to sort this out. Consider it a personal favor to me. Beijing has been a little distant from me after the whole goddamned INS debacle but now that the leadership seems solidified after Mao, they've asked me to quiet down this whole mess."

" 'Quiet down?'"

"You know what I mean, give it a lower news profile. What would really help is if you could discover that it was a common mugging gone wrong. At least you could help defuse the political implications of the case."

"How am I supposed to do that?"

"Tell me more about this fake Communist group. I can pass on the details to contacts at the newspaper backed by the People's Republic. They'll take it from there."

"I'm looking for the guy in charge of it, myself."

"What's his name?"

"I can't tell you that."

Mr. Song smiled. "You've already told me the name of the group. Wasn't that a little unscrupulous of you?"

"Not at all. It's a matter of public record. Look it up if you want more information. One of the best things about a *democracy* is that our government is accessible and accountable to the people."

"Don't forget, Robert, that this little democracy of yours killed Mr. Chen. But let's not argue about the merits of one system against another."

"Good, because I didn't go to college."

"I also realize there's little you can do but pursue this case to your fullest powers."

"Actually, Manhattan South is handling the case."

Mr. Song covered one hand with the other. "So this case really is a big deal?"

"It could be." In actuality, Manhattan South handled thousands of murders that were off the press radar.

"But you could still contribute any findings you make, right?"

"They sure wouldn't turn away help."

"Am I right in assuming that your girlfriend is a natural suspect?"

"No, you're wrong."

"It's just that based on television shows, they always go after the people who last saw the victim." He smiled. "Aw, don't listen to me, I watch too much TV."

I sipped at my tea for the first time. It had a light, elusive taste, which meant that it was probably pretty good.

"Drink up that tea," said Mr. Song. "It's not expensive, but it is difficult to get."

"I can't have that much. I've just had a Coke."

"What a shame. Well, that's more for me. Are you drinking, um, anything else?"

"No. I've been sober the whole time."

"I'm glad to hear that. I was actually worried about you."

"You could have dropped me a line."

"You could have, too."

"You were mad at me."

"Yes, I was. But, still, I was worried."

"How is Stephanie doing up at Yale?"

Mr. Song gave a hard half smile. "Oh, she's doing well. And her male roommate is doing well, too."

I knew better than to ask any more about his daughter.

ASSOCIATIONS AND GROUPS loyal to the KMT and the Communists were in general under the respective umbrella groups of the Greater China Association and Together Chinese Kinship. Each umbrella group lobbied local city politicians for their own political causes as well as mediated disputes among members.

Together Chinese Kinship was far smaller than the Greater China Association, but it was riding a wave of momentum. The People's Republic had displaced Taiwan from the United

Nations. High-profile visits of the mainland by Nixon and Ford had melted down the American public's perception of evil "Red China" into a genuine curiosity. Once they found the mainland on the map and traced their finger around its grilled-pork-chop shape, Americans could see for themselves how insignificant the "Free China" of Taiwan was. It wasn't even a French fry next to that pork chop.

Every October 1, the national day of the Communists, Together Chinese Kinship held a parade in its section of Chinatown. The celebration was undeniably growing in size and area with each year.

On October 10, the national day of the KMT, the Greater China Association held its parade. In recent years the umbrella group had boosted the number of flags that were waved. It even regularly flew in from Taiwan thousands of cheap plastic flags of the Republic of China to hand out to the sightseers snapping pictures. These Americans would examine the flags with quizzical looks on their faces. "What flag is this?" they would ask each other. "Doesn't the flag of China have five stars on it?"

Despite the apparently fervent rivalry between Together Chinese Kinship and the Greater China Association, there were unofficial fringe groups on both sides of the divide that saw the two umbrella groups as secret collaborators. In this scenario, representatives of the two umbrella groups met in secret to carve up Chinatown according to their own business interests while setting fixed prices for wages, restaurants, and even the Bruce Lee memorabilia for sale on both sides of Bowery.

Rumors of these secret meetings were completely unsubstantiated by evidence, but both sides did, after all, maintain that there is one China and that Taiwan is a part of China. It was in the interests of both umbrellas groups to have open communication lines should the People's Republic of China and the Republic of China someday reunite, even if such an idea was as likely as bitter rivals East and West Germany getting back together.

Of course, there was a small fringe group that was vehemently opposed to Taiwan "reuniting" with the mainland because Taiwan was its own country. After all, before the Qing Dynasty collapsed on the mainland, it had officially ceded Taiwan to Japan in 1895. Taiwan had been a colony of Japan until the end of World War II. When the KMT lost to the Communists in the Chinese civil war, the remnants of those armies retreated to Taiwan and took out their frustrations on the local Taiwanese by imposing martial law and brutally suppressing any dissent. Supposedly. The pro-KMT newspaper reported nothing but a continuing economic miracle on the island.

Lincoln's group, the Union of the Three Armies, didn't qualify as a fringe group. Protesting in public was a stupid idea. Even dumber was having a name and identifiable principals in the group. The underground extreme right and left wings were small, efficient, and operated internationally. They made the triads of old look like a lemonade-stand racket.

When night fell in Chinatown, stupid gang kids did their best to bullet-graze each other's foreheads while trained and disciplined operators walked in the shadows. They apparently broke into offices and stole Rolodexes, and paid homeless people to bring them bags of garbage from businesses and associations. The fringe groups didn't operate gambling dens or pross houses or deal in drugs; their trade was in selling information, blackmail, and, apparently, assassination. When you read about killings or disappearances of right- or left-wing agitators in Taiwan, Singapore, or Chinese communities throughout East Asia, you can bet their hands were in it. Funny how these stories never made the American newspapers.

Even though their reach included North America, they hadn't noticeably killed anyone here until a few months ago. Out in Vancouver's Chinatown they had shot a guy twice in the back of his head. He was an ex-cop from Hong Kong who had freelanced as a security guard for Jade Palace. I had met him and he actually turned out to be a decent guy. They had never found his killers and the story faded away, as according to plan.

These fringe groups, and not the Greater China Association, were what worried Mr. Song.

I CALLED LONNIE from a pay phone at Canal and Eldridge.

"Robert, I can't talk too long now!" she said. "I have to finish another story I'm doing and I'm doing all these interviews on the side."

"What interviews?"

"You know, other news sources from all over the world want to talk to me. My interview has been published by so many newspapers!"

"I'm worried, Lonnie. Manhattan South has been staking out your apartment."

"Don't worry. Our lawyers say that if the police had any evidence at all against me, they would have arrested me already. I'm sure I'm going to be cleared."

"Well, I'm sure they know better than me. I'll let you go now."

She said bye and after we hung up I punched in the number of a guy I knew at Manhattan South.

Inspector Izzy Rosenbaum met me at his office door. He clapped me on the back and said, "Chow."

Izzy was an average-sized man, but there was a gentle menace to his demeanor and his dull brown eyes alone could pin you to the wall. He kept his gray hair in a crew cut so that it looked like a light fungus growing on his muscled and veiny forehead. Izzy hated wasting time and never said more than was necessary.

"Hi, Lefty," I said to Izzy. He had gotten the nickname from punching out a jerk years ago when he was back in the academy. That jerk was now the commander of my precinct.

"Let's talk."

"How can I stop your guys from shadowing Lonnie?"

"You can't."

"Her boyfriend is a cop. Doesn't that give her a pass?"

"Can't trust cops."

"You don't have a single shred of evidence against her. All you have is that she met him for an interview and then she left."

"We heard more."

"How much more?"

"They left together."

"You mean Lonnie and Mr. Chen?"

Izzy nodded. "Uh-huh."

"They left the hotel together?"

"Yup."

"I'm sure she was just going home."

"How about him?"

"He was probably going to get a magazine."

"No."

"Look, you can't honestly believe Lonnie killed him."

"I don't believe anything at this point."

"Who told you they left together, anyway? Some drunk on the street?"

"Lobby cameras."

"Did you ask Lonnie why they walked out the door together?"

Lefty stretched out his jaw and rubbed his chin. "We already did, at the original interview. I guess you didn't know about it."

"Oh, I knew," I said. "He just wanted to see her off."

"How come he didn't come back?"

THAT NIGHT I was on the phone with Lonnie.

"Why the hell didn't you tell me?"

"Don't talk to me that way, Robert!"

"Why?"

"Because it doesn't matter, that's why."

"You told me you left by yourself after the interview!"

"I forgot that Mr. Chen came down after! I was waiting in the lobby for the limo service and he chatted with me for about a minute. He asked me if I wanted a ride from his security detail, but I said no. The car came right after and he walked me outside. I got in, he chatted with the driver in Mandarin, and then he said good night to me."

"He and the driver were chatting in Mandarin? What limo driver speaks Mandarin?"

"Robert, I hired a Chinatown livery car, Heavenly Horse. Presswire was paying for it and I wanted to bring some business to the community."

"You talked to Heavenly Horse on the phone?"

"No, I walked into their office. It's close to home."

"Good. Since they saw you in person, they'd probably remember you. You came home alone, right?"

I heard her sigh. "Yes-ss-s."

"Don't do that. You sound like Paul when you do that."

"Then don't treat me like this. You're meaner than the Manhattan South guys."

"Did you see Mr. Chen go back into the hotel? Maybe through a side door or something?"

"I didn't. When they told me he didn't come back in it was a surprise to me. He wasn't ready to go out. He didn't even have a coat on."

"You told the detectives all this, right?"

"Yes, of course!"

"That's good, then. I'm glad you told them everything."

"Me, too. How are you?"

"Oh, you know me, I'm fine."

"You sound really worried!"

"I am! You don't know how much of a jam you're in!"

"The lawyers say I'm completely in the clear! Please relax, Robert!"

But I knew better than to let up. When you relax they slip the noose over your head and drop the floor.

I HAD A late dinner with Vandyne. We met up at a place downstairs from the sidewalk where Mott runs into Bowery, a busy intersection. Tourists don't go there because the stairs down are usually covered with blown-in trash.

The best thing about the restaurant was that it was one of the few that actually had booths running from the floor to the ceiling. It used to be a speakeasy, according to the midget, but he might have been pulling my leg when he said it.

It was a good thing they no longer served alcohol.

A waiter in his fifties came over, leaned against the booth wall in his black T-shirt, and asked us what we wanted. I ordered greens in garlic sauce and roasted chicken for both of us. The waiter turned to Vandyne and asked in English, "You want tea, Detective?"

Vandyne's eyebrows shot up. "Sure."

The waiter smiled and went away. When he came back he flipped our ceramic cups over and poured tea, Vandyne first. Vandyne rapped his first two knuckles against the tabletop, making the waiter chuckle.

"You know, you know," said the waiter. After he put the teapot down he added, "My first English teacher was black man!" The waiter gave Vandyne a thumbs-up.

Vandyne smiled and said, "I can tell he was a good teacher."

"Very good, very good!"

After he went away, I said, "He had to make it a point with you that he knows another black person."

"So what?"

"That's racism."

"That's not racism, Chow. Racism is coming in and being seated in the back or not being seated at all. He's just trying to reach out across cultures. That's a beautiful thing."

"So is my ass."

"So when I tapped my knuckles when he was pouring the tea, was I being racist or was I sharing some cultural knowledge?"

I grunted and took a sip of my tea. "He poured it too early. It hasn't had time to steep, yet."

"This poor waiter can't do anything right, can he?"

"He can shut up and bring our food without the chitchat."

"It's the Lonnie thing that's bugging you, right?"

"You're goddamned right it is! Am I the only one really worried about the whole thing? She's not even taking it seriously!"

"Just lay off of it, Chow. Let the investigation run its course. The public doesn't trust us but we should at least trust each other."

I looked at him sideways.

"Hey, man," Vandyne continued, "these aren't fuckups handling this. It's Manhattan South. They'll do a good job."

"Izzy wouldn't tell me who was handling the case."

"Good thing, too. You just stay away. How would you like it if you had someone telling you how to investigate those guns in the mailbox? That so-and-so was innocent and that so-and-so was guilty?"

"You're right, Vandyne."

"See? If you try to interfere, you're just going to make things worse. A lot worse."

The waiter swung in with our greens, chicken, and two bowls of rice. He poured us more tea and smiled, which nudged up the bags under his eyes. He wasn't such a bad guy after all.

I FELT RESTLESS at home. Paul played both sides of the Ramones record and the back of my brain was pulsing, the lizard part. I couldn't stop thinking about those two jerks who were tailing Lonnie around town. They were probably parked outside of her apartment now.

There likely wasn't much that I could do about the Manhattan South guys, so I set my mind to other things. I thought about those guns stuffed in the Henry Street apartment mailbox. What if a little girl had opened that box instead of old Mr. Wing?

I zipped up my heavy black coat, the one with the blanket lining. I had to be ready to stay outside for a while.

"Where are you going, Robert?" asked Paul. He was sitting on the couch reading a book, seemingly undisturbed by the racket coming from the stereo.

"You really want to know?" I asked.

He closed the book on his left index finger and stood up. "It's about Lonnie, isn't it?"

I pulled on my gloves and didn't say anything.

"Robert, what are you going to do?"

"Go to sleep."

"You can't just go over to the guys staking her out and start swinging!"

"I am not going there, all right?"

I put on a Rangers cap and pulled the brim low, almost over my eyes. "I'm going out now on official work, if you don't mind."

"I don't mind. I just don't want to see you get hurt doing something stupid."

"I don't do anything stupid. Anymore."

Chinatown is deserted at night for the most part. The halfway decent restaurants start closing at nine at night, creating dim blocks of rolled-down metal grating with garbage bags sagging in the gutters. They never have pictures of Chinatown like this for the tourist pamphlets and postcards.

The rumor was that the restaurants closed that early to avoid roving bands of idiot gang kids looking to score a free meal. What the kids typically do is go into restaurants and eat up complete meals—with alcohol when possible. When the check comes, they sign their gang name on it and split. The nicer gang kids would leave a tip for the waiters, because their parents are waiters. Gang kids typically wake up in the afternoons and wouldn't be set to eat dinner until close to midnight. Restaurants that closed at nine at night didn't have gang kids pawing their lazy Susans.

Another rumor about the early closings was that there was a deal with the Little Italy restaurateurs, just north of Canal, so the Italian places wouldn't have to compete with cheap Chinese food with the late-dining and after-theater crowd.

Maybe they were both true. The only people walking around the neighborhood now were people coming back from work or those going out now to the garment factories.

But at least one restaurant was still open—OK Noodle on Division Street, where Lincoln Chin might be hanging out. The manager there had told me that Lincoln would stay late and not order very much at all.

I walked up to the restaurant and pretended to read the reviews taped to the window. I saw Lincoln, all right. He was sitting at a table with four other Asian guys.

I went to the corner and looked around. Thankfully, on the other side of the street there was a phone booth. Drafty as it probably was, it would be better than standing around in the cold. I went across and shut the door on the booth. The windows were all scratched up but I had a pretty good view of Lincoln and his buddies, at least until a guy walked up and stood in front of the door.

"Are you making a call?" he asked in English. I looked at the man. He was the same guy I had met in Columbus Park the other day, the one who had moved out of Chinatown to get his kids away from the gangs. I hoped his eyes were bad enough so he wouldn't recognize me.

He cupped a hand to the glass. "Hey, you're Officer Chow, right?"

I smiled and waved. "Yes, that's me!"

"It's me. Byron from the park, remember?"

"I remember."

"Well, officer, I hate to be rude, but are you done with this phone? I need to place a call and I had to walk all the way here from Bowery to find a pay phone that works."

We were still talking through the glass because I didn't want to give up the spot.

"I'm actually waiting for a call," I said.

"You expect it soon?"

"Could be soon."

"Would you mind if I waited here until you get the call?"

"See, the thing is, I have an informant who's going to be calling and it has to be a private conversation. No offense."

"I do apologize, Officer Chow! I'm interfering with police business now." He moved away and I saw Lincoln and his friends were now standing outside the restaurant. "I'll see you again, huh?"

I swept the phone-booth door aside and said, "On the other hand, I need to respect my elders. Here you go!"

"Are you sure?" he asked me.

I kept my eyes on the back of Lincoln's army surplus jacket. "Yeah, I'll catch up with him and see where he goes," I said absently. I watched across the street as I followed a parallel path.

"Hey, Officer Chow!" the man called to me. "There's no mouth-piece on this phone!"

"Yes!" I said, not breaking my stride. Lincoln turned a corner onto Henry and I jogged across the street. He was a fast walker.

I made it around the corner and saw him talking with someone on the sidewalk. I bent down and pretended to tie my shoes. As their conversation dragged out, I stood up and leaned against the low stone fence by some garbage cans as if I were waiting for someone. I looked up to watch the D train rattle by on the Manhattan Bridge overpass. It slowed to an unscheduled stop and I could almost hear the collective groan of the passengers.

The conversation ended and the guy who had been talking to Lincoln passed me on the other side of the street. I recognized him as a former associate with some gang kids. Somehow he had managed to save himself. I think he ended up going to college.

I turned and saw Lincoln jog up the steps to a building near the end of the block. I walked toward it slowly until he went into the building's front door. I continued at the same pace and walked by, noting that it was number 91. I cursed the fact that I had left my radio at home.

I made a left when I went around the block and I wrote the street address in my notes. I also took off a glove and wrote it in permanent pen on the back of my hand. Just in case my body was found, I wanted to leave a clue. If only all our corpses were so considerate.

I went to Lincoln's building. It wasn't tough to find his apartment. There was only one Chin in the building, at 2R, and the nameplate was split with someone named Lee who didn't bother to write an English translation for the Chinese character. That had to be his girlfriend's name. I added the apartment number to the back of my hand.

I rang the buzzer.

"Hello?" a man asked in English.

"It's the police. I'm looking for Lincoln Chin. I just want to ask you a few questions."

"You have a warrant?"

"I don't want to search your place. I just want to talk. You can come down if you don't want to let me in."

"It's pretty goddamned late, don't you think?"

"Sure, but we're both up, anyway."

He made a growling sound and then buzzed the building door open. I went up one flight and knocked on the door.

Two locks clicked and a chain rattled. The door opened and I was staring into the face of a woman who had full chipmunk cheeks, thick black hair, and dark eyes. Although she wasn't pretty, she looked well fed and healthy. I pictured her on a Communist propaganda poster with her fist in the air, one arm holding a bushel of bitter melons with a speech bubble reading, "Let's have a bountiful harvest to feed the never-ending revolution!" She was Lincoln's girlfriend, all right, the woman he was yelling at back at the protest.

"Hello," I said to her.

"Hi," she said.

Suddenly Lincoln shouted from somewhere in the apartment, "Teresa! Don't say anything to that goddamned cop!" He came up and shoved himself in front of the woman. "I remember you from back at the rally!"

"I'm Robert Chow," I said. "Still playing with your megaphone?"

He smirked and moved to block my view of the apartment. "Well, what'd you come up here for?"

"I wanted to know a little bit more about the Union of the Three Armies, an organization that apparently only exists in your mind."

"We are a real group!"

"You're not registered as an organization, business, or charity."

"We don't need the recognition of the capitalist establishment. We only need to declare that we exist! Anyway, if it's a question of being a legitimate group, then why did the NYPD cash our money order and give us a permit?"

"That was a matter of poor oversight on our part."

"As usual."

I managed a little laugh and showed him my teeth. "Well, Lincoln, the reason why I wanted to see you was that I was wondering if you knew anything about a small cache of guns that were found in a building on Henry."

His face crumpled a little. Was it from guilt or confusion? "I don't know what you're talking about."

"The Union of the Three Armies must have guns, right? That was one of your little stashes of handguns in that apartment mailbox next door, wasn't it?"

"No! We are unarmed but well informed. We seek change through education and demonstrations."

"If you let me in, we can sit down and talk. Like real Chinese people."

Lincoln gave a slight nod and opened the door. "No tricks, now."

"Don't worry about me, I've got slow hands," I said, stepping in. "Is this a shoes-off kind of place?" I asked, looking around the living room. Mr. Revolution actually had a nice TV, a nice stereo system, and even a nice coffee table. Nary a hammer-and-sickle icon in sight.

"No, don't worry about it," he said. Teresa stood by, apparently awaiting instructions.

"Are you Teresa Lee?" I asked her.

"Yes."

"Teresa," said Lincoln, "why don't you go in the bedroom while we talk?" She did what he said and shut the door.

"Can I take your coat, Robert?"

"I like it on. I won't be long."

We sat down on the far ends of the couch, which was nicer and bigger than mine. There was enough room for both of us to swing our legs up onto the cushions.

"Lincoln," I said, "you've been seen associating with known gang members on Henry Street. That's where you work and that's also where a cache of guns was found."

"Did you say 'associating'?"

"Yeah. It's polite for 'engaging in criminal planning and activity with.'"

"Look here, cop. You know what my job is?"

"I know what it's supposed to be. You're apparently a big no-show at the after-school program offices."

"I'm having a tough time adjusting. Do you know what it's like working with someone who cramps your style just for the hell of it?"

"I actually do, Lincoln."

"I'm there for every important meeting. Haven't missed one yet. You ask any of the kids if Lincoln Chin is there for them and they'll all say yes."

"What'll they say if I ask them where the guns are?"

He smiled. "I doubt they'll tell you. They won't tell me, that's for sure. There are some troubled kids, Robert, but I'm trying to engage them—even more so than the kids that don't give anybody grief. Our programs are meant to keep kids out of trouble and to rope in the ones that have strayed too far."

"I've heard you've been trying to pull the kids into the red and indulge yourself in a Communist fantasy romp."

"A number of boys and girls have expressed interest in the Chinese Communist Party, but I'm trying to show them the true path. You know, with Mao dead and Deng Xiaoping back in power, China's moving towards a market economy. The party itself is in danger of becoming as Communist as West Germany."

"Why do you care what happens in China? You're an American."

"I guess you don't get it, Robert."

"What?"

"You've seen what a failure capitalism's been for America, and now China wants to follow in those same footsteps! They're going to be Communist in name only. Just like that Together Chinese Kinship. More like Together Chinese Bullshit. They're only about money.

"I'll tell you something else, too! That traitor of the people, Li Na, disgraced her father and now her nation. She was looking for asylum here but I will never stay silent on that issue!"

"You would even kill her representative to stop her from coming over, wouldn't you?"

"I get it. Trying to get me to incriminate myself. Nice. It would be funny if it weren't so obvious."

I shifted in my seat, turning to face him dead-on. "I've been wondering something, Lincoln. You don't really understand spoken Chinese so well and I seriously doubt you can read characters, so how do you know what's going on in China?"

"I read the newspapers for him." We both turned to look at Teresa, who was standing in the hallway, leaning against the far wall.

Lincoln stood up with a hurt yet angry look in his eyes but Teresa didn't move.

"I told you you were asking for trouble," she said.

"Go back and stay in the bedroom!" he said.

"Teresa," I said, "how was he asking for trouble?"

"He had to go do his stupid protest!"

Lincoln crossed his arms and didn't say anything. Teresa also fell silent.

I brushed off imaginary dust from my lap and stood up. "You folks look like you want some privacy now. Lincoln, I'll visit you again . . . at work sometime. Be there for a change."

IZZY ASKED TO meet me in a nondescript diner on the West Side the next day.

"You said you had something bad," I said.

"I do. The bill from Lonnie's livery-cab ride. It says two passengers."

"What? No, there's some mistake."

"No mistake. Two passengers from Midtown to Chinatown."

"The Chinese characters for 'one' and 'two' are very similar. 'One' is one horizontal line—"

"And 'two' is two. Like this." He held up a copy of the voucher. "We got the original from Heavenly Horse. There's the 'two' and there's Lonnie's signature."

"The driver probably added the second line later to get more money."

"For two lousy bucks?"

"That's two hours of Chinatown waiter or sweatshop work. Two dollars for just adding a line. I wouldn't be surprised if that happened all the time."

"This little second line also shows Lonnie could be a murderer."

"You know, it's about race. You've singled her out because she's Chinese."

"That's your final argument? Here's mine: She was the last one to see Chen alive."

"He could've been killed by anyone."

"That narrows it down."

"He's the representative of Li Na. She has a number of enemies in the Chinese community and, therefore, so did Mr. Chen. One of these fringe groups could have killed him."

"After Lonnie lured him down to Chinatown."

"Bullshit!"

My outburst cued a big and tired man to refill our coffees without a word.

Izzy stirred sugar into his cup. "We're under a little pressure," he said flatly. "Very light pressure."

"Pressure from whom?"

He licked the spoon dry and balanced it on the saucer. "Republic of China. Taiwan."

"The KMT wants this murder solved?"

Izzy nodded and turned his coffee cup clockwise by fifteen minutes and pointed the handle out the window.

"It's the pressure of an index finger through the State Department. Not bad on the NYPD at all, but it is there. It's strange that a country on the way out is trying to get us to solve the murder of a guy from a country the U.S. doesn't officially recognize as existing."

I poured some milk into my coffee and watched it billow and churn. In the face of overwhelming facts, the U.S. still recognized the KMT on Taiwan as being the legitimate ruler of the Chinese mainland. As such, the Republic of China was pushing for the investigation of the murder of one of its "citizens."

"Have you heard anything from the People's Republic?" I asked Izzy.

"Not a peep. You?"

"Are you going to take the word of the boyfriend of your suspect?"

"What do you have?"

"Maybe nothing."

"Don't withhold evidence. You wouldn't like to see me mad."

"Let's get this straight. You'll take into account anything I give you?"

"Yes."

"I can work on this case, then?"

"I didn't show you this slip so I could get my jollies watching your face. It's obvious to me my boys can't move through China-town as smoothly as you."

"Did something happen?"

"Heavenly Horse wanted them to pay for using their Xerox machine and there was a scuffle. My guys should have paid the lousy nickel. I think they didn't want to give money to a little yellow bastard for something they thought they had a right to."

"Aw, Christ."

"No sense in them going now to apologize, right? It's over now, any potential for a good cooperative relationship."

"Pretty much."

"You might have an easier time moving through this neighborhood. Your manners are better informed."

"You're giving me a green light to work on this case, Izzy?"

"You will work on this case. But not directly. Everything you get goes through me."

"All right."

"If The Brow finds out, he'll have a shit fit."

The Brow was the Fifth Precinct's C.O. The guy Izzy had punched out back at the academy.

I said, "Don't worry about him finding out, Izzy. I have a personal interest in keeping The Brow in the dark."

"Now, what do you have?"

"I understand that the People's Republic wants the murder to be solved to prove that it wasn't one of their agents."

"That's what the KMT wants, too. They swear it's a Commie that did it."

"If he was assassinated by someone who knew what they were doing, then why wasn't he shot? Why would someone get up close enough to bash his head in?"

"Maybe it was a caveman." Izzy slurped some coffee. "You heard about the body?"

"I saw the body. I saw the hole in Mr. Chen's head."

"What did you think of the hand?"

"What about the hand?"

"There's a finger missing. Left index finger. Mean anything?"

"It was chopped off?"

"After death."

"I don't remember hearing about that part."

"Kept it away from the press."

"If I find anything I'll let you know."

He nodded and stood up.

"Izzy, thanks a lot for letting me horn my way onto the case."

"Why not let you? You've got the motivation for solving this murder, not racking up overtime."

WHEN THE LAWYERS at Presswire found out that the voucher from Lonnie's livery-cab ride showed that two people shared a ride to Chinatown, they recommended that she be given a leave of absence.

Her editors had protested and then they reached the compromise that Lonnie would be allowed to continue working but from outside the newsroom.

With such a substantial piece of circumstantial evidence uncovered, Lonnie was, by my guess, a security risk for the organization as a maybe murderer. It wasn't nearly enough evidence to charge Lonnie with anything—the driver himself hadn't even given a statement yet—but those skittish lawyers were always good at saving their own skins. I can't remember the last time one had been shot in the line of duty.

Lonnie swore that the voucher had only one line in the passengers blank for "one" when she signed it.

I visited Lonnie at her temporary desk at the general press office of the United Nations. All the reporters there took turns to type out their stories on three Teletypes that would transmit their stories back to their newsrooms all around the country and the world. Lonnie was the only one submitting a story just two blocks away.

The press office was loud and smoky, like the Off-Track Betting joint on Bowery, only nobody had even a glimmer of hope in his eyes. In fact, their eyes were either on the floor or on Lonnie.

"What a crappy place," I said.

"I'm glad you like it as much as I do," she said.

"Lonnie, I am very uncomfortable with the fact that you're the only woman here." I opened up a paper bag and gave her a tuna on a hard roll that she was craving. "They think you're like this exotic sex doll."

"Don't say that, Robert. Look at all the people here."

"They don't know what the hell we're saying."

"You don't know. They could have studied Chinese in college."

"Yeah, but colleges don't teach Cantonese, they teach Mandarin, the language of the learned."

"You can't be sure until you ask everybody. A good journalist never makes assumptions."

"Well, that's all a cop has. At first, anyway."

"I'm not a cop, Robert."

I nodded and unwrapped my pastrami on rye. I glanced around the room before picking up half of the sandwich. "Which one is the guy who asked you out to lunch?"

"It doesn't matter. Don't make a big deal out of it."

"You think I'm just going to let some asshole ask out my woman?"

She frowned and signaled with her hand that she wanted a drink. I pulled the tab off a 7UP and handed it to her. "You didn't get straws?" she asked.

"I never bother. You can drink faster right from the can."

Lonnie sighed and then drank. "This means I have to reapply my lipstick later."

"You better look good so that guy asks you out to lunch again."

"Will you stop, Robert? I have so many other things to worry about."

"You're right."

"I'm shut out of my own newsroom like I have leprosy, just because of that driver's mistake."

"I was also thinking that the guy did it on purpose so that he could charge your company extra for two passengers."

"All they need to do is ask the driver in and I'm sure he'll clear it up. He'll admit he faked it."

"What did this guy look like?"

"He had an unshaved face, a big mole on the right cheek, had a hat on, and smelled like a cigar."

"That sounds like every Chinese livery-cab driver, Lonnie!"

"Why don't they get his name from Heavenly Horse so they can question him?"

"The cops already have the voucher. They probably won't contact him until they have more evidence or if they don't have any more. Wait, how do you know Manhattan South hasn't talked to the driver yet?"

"The two detectives told me."

"They called you or you called them?"

"I just went up to them this morning when I was leaving for work. They weren't waiting in their car. They were standing on the sidewalk and their badges were out."

I took a big bite of my sandwich. Too big. I took some effort to chew with my mouth closed.

The open-surveillance method by the detectives was an escalation in the pressure they were putting on Lonnie. They didn't have enough to initiate a conversation with her but they were there if she wanted to volunteer new information. Such as a confession.

When I finally got my food down, I said, "Lonnie, don't go up and talk to them. They can twist around what you say and use it against you."

"I just want them to get the story straight."

"What else did you tell them?"

"I told them to ask the driver! That's all! They said they were sorry to hear that I had to work out of the office and then they smiled! What a couple of jerks."

"That's it, that's it," I muttered.

"What, Robert?"

I leaned back and cracked my neck. I finished my sandwich and grabbed Lonnie's hand. "I'm going to fix this."

"Your left eye is all bloodshot!"

I smiled.

I WENT TO bed late but I woke up at six in the morning without the alarm. I took a shower and dressed in ten minutes. I tried not to wake Paul on the way out but he's too sharp. Must've been all that wild-animal alertness he'd gleaned from being in a gang. I had been in a gang, too, but being a punk is a young man's game. I couldn't beat him.

The light from the stairwell came in when I opened the apartment door and I could see his one open eye watching me. I winked at him and stepped out.

I went to the three dispatch-car companies on Allen Street huddled next to each other for maximum customer confusion. They all looked like little lean-to shacks built with cinder blocks. I went to Heavenly Horse in the middle first.

A man behind a glass window had his back turned to me. Two idle drivers behind open newspapers sat on benches to my left and right. I went up to the reader with black herringbone slacks first.

"Pardon me," I said. "Have you got the time?"

"There's a clock on the wall," he said without lowering his paper.

"I have really bad eyes. Could you look at your watch for me?"

"I'm reading a story right now and you're breaking my flow."

"Please, I just need to know the time."

"Then wear a fucking watch."

At that I pulled down the top of the newspaper to get a look at his face. He had a beak like a turtle and looked ready to snap my fingers off. Instead, he folded up his paper and swatted my face. No mole, though.

"Get away from me, you weirdo!" he said.

The man behind the window stood up. He was tall, pushing six feet, and probably weighed 190 pounds, in his late forties and nearly bald. "Officer Chow, right?" he said. I heard him through the wall vents near the ceiling.

"That's right," I said.

"Well what do you want?"

I looked over at the other reader who had also put down his paper. I smiled. There was no mole but it was a mean face, eyes close together, small mouth, and a wrinkled forehead. He scowled at me and picked up his paper again.

He looked familiar, but from where, I wasn't sure.

I went over to the window and asked, "What can you tell me about a driver with a mole on his face?"

He shrugged and stared at the floor. "You want a driver with a mole? That's no problem. Where do you want to go?"

"I don't need a ride."

The man shuffled to the side, took a handful of nuts and shoved them in his mouth. "Then why the hell are you here?"

"You know I'm a cop."

"I know."

"You know I'm Lonnie's boyfriend."

"I know that, too."

"Who was her driver?"

"I don't know. I won't know until I pay him," he said as peanut pieces ricocheted off his side of the glass.

"Calm down, all right? I don't mean to upset you. I'm trying to help Lonnie, you know."

"I know Lonnie very well! I know her parents, too. They are good people."

I nodded. Her dad was so good he couldn't help beating Paul. "Anyway, if you could tell me one thing, anything, that would help Lonnie."

"This is Lonnie's boyfriend?" asked the turtle. "This one?"

"Yeah," I said. The turtle shook his head slowly.

The man behind the window twisted his mouth up and rubbed his forehead. "I'm telling you this because it's for Lonnie, not for you."

"Sure."

"These drivers have no loyalty to me whatsoever. If someone pays them a higher rate, they're gone. If I raise my rate, they come flying back like migrating pigeons."

"Pigeons don't migrate," said the turtle.

"Yeah, but you did. You're lucky I took you back."

"Pardon me, Uncle," I asked the boss. "About Lonnie's driver. The one with a mole. Have you seen that driver around anywhere?"

" 'The one with a mole.' That's a good one. Almost all my drivers have a mole."

"These two don't."

"If they don't already, they will soon. You know where it comes from? Too much smoking and too few girls. That's the life of a driver!"

The turtle coughed while Mean Face wrestled his paper into a pile of crooked folds. In five seconds he was exhaling smoke from a newly lighted cigarette.

"You said you don't know who drove whom until you pay your drivers. How do you assign rides?" I asked.

"I fill out a voucher form and hand it to somebody here."

"I notice the vouchers have one original form and one carbon copy."

"That's right."

"When a driver picks up a voucher, do you keep the original?"

"I don't separate them. I give the whole thing to the driver."

"You don't keep a record of what rides drivers are assigned to?"

"I don't bother because a voucher is worthless until a customer gets a ride. Actually, it's worthless until a company pays for it. When the driver is done for the night, he fills in his name and then I separate the vouchers. I take the originals and he takes the carbon copies."

"When do you pay the drivers?"

"I pay them after the voucher is paid. They come back with the carbon copy and if the check has cleared, then I pay the drivers. I usually get a check within a week and then it takes a few days for the check to clear, so a driver usually gets paid two weeks after the actual ride."

The turtle grunted. "Sometimes it's three weeks or a month. Sometimes not at all."

"Hey," said the boss. "I can't help it when companies pay late or dispute the tab. A lot of times, it's the driver's fault." He pointed at the turtle and said, "Customers don't expect to ride in a car that is filled with trash."

"You should pay the drivers the night they hand in the vouchers," I said. "They shouldn't have to bear the risk of the companies paying up."

"Don't tell me how this business works. If these guys were paid automatically, there would be no incentive to give the customer a decent ride. They would just drive recklessly to get as many vouchers as they could." Again pointing to the turtle, he added, "They also wouldn't bother to clean up the inside of the car between rides!"

"One time!" cried the turtle. "It only happened one time and this guy never shuts up about it."

"If I stopped talking about it, you might forget."

"Well, what's the big deal? I ended up not getting paid. Nothing happened to you."

"The company did pay for the gas," I pointed out.

The turtle blinked. "*We* pay for the gas, Policeman Chow."

"You should pay for it," said the boss. "It's expensive."

"Is each driver assigned a car?" I asked.

"It's first come, first served every day. We have a fleet of about twenty Continentals."

"How do you know someone won't drive off with one of your cars?"

"I'd like to see them try. They wouldn't get too far."

"The cars would probably fall apart before you made it past Jersey," said the turtle.

The boss ignored him and said to me, "We're owned by a very connected individual. It wouldn't be any good crossing him. Believe me."

"Can't this very connected guy find the man with the mole on his face?"

"I am sure the driver will be back with his carbon copy to collect his fee. It should be a few days from now. I'll tell you what. When he shows up, I'll call you."

"Are you sure he's going to show up?"

"He'd be a fool not to. Nobody would work without getting paid."

"I'm not making any money now," muttered the turtle.

"It's slow right now," said the boss. "After the morning rush, business doesn't pick up until night."

"You call that a morning rush?"

"You don't like your job very much, do you?" I asked the turtle.

"No, I don't. It sucks."

"Why don't you do something else?"

"He can't do anything else," said the boss.

"Then why do you keep giving him work?"

The turtle put his newspaper down and crossed his arms. "Because I'm a very connected individual!"

"There are some particular customers who want him as a driver," said the counterman. "Because they like to go to whorehouses and they need the local pimp to point them out."

"You can say anything you want," said the turtle as he leaned forward and rubbed his kneecaps. "I was here before you and I'll be here long after you're gone. The gods give long healthy lives to the just and sickly, phlegm-filled existences to the dissolute."

"You call me when that guy comes in," I said to the boss. "Call me before you pay him." Mean Face looked at me as I left. I didn't like him.

I went to the two other dispatch-car offices to see if they knew anything about Lonnie's driver but had no luck finding the mysterious mole-man. But I made sure to keep an eye on the street in case Mean Face popped out.

Lonnie was right in saying that the businesses were hurting. They were doing their part in keeping air pollution down by not running their cars. Customers don't need to be driven anywhere when they don't have jobs, meetings, or flights to catch.

The drivers used to look down on the waiters, table bussers and dishwashers. The guys in greasy clothes were laughing now. People always have to eat, after all.

I came out on the sidewalk and peered into Heavenly Horse's window.

The turtle was sitting there by himself, picking his nose with his knuckles. Mean Face was gone.

I STOOD ON the curb where Mr. Chen's body had been found and looked at the dirty, twisted warning tape that wound around chain-link fence posts and two dented garbage cans. It was sad. A barren place in Sara D. Roosevelt Park that squirrels avoided.

I wasn't as familiar with this park as I was with Columbus Park. I looked around carefully in all directions.

To the north, someone had raked piles of dead leaves but nobody had bothered to bag them up. Maybe the city had canned that particular person.

To the south, there was a scary little brick building that hummed. I had no idea what was inside, but it was the right size for a witch who liked to eat children. The door had several padlocks on it. I walked around the building to see if there was anything more to it, but the other three sides were sturdy brick walls tagged heavily with spray paint.

To the west, across Chrystie Street, was a short block with three storefront apartment buildings. The southern end of the block housed a Fukienese church that was painted white, which was usually a bad color because Chinese wear white for funerals. But in the context of Christianity being a foreign religion, it was acceptable.

The middle of the block was a small dumpling wholesaler and the north end was occupied with a kitchen-supply store that had chained down samples of its shelving and standing sinks as if they might run away.

I crossed Chrystie to the north side of the block. I examined a metal three-shelf rack. A short, heavyset guy in a gray sweat-suit came out of the store.

"Hi, my friend," he said, tipping me off that he didn't know I was a cop. "I've got everything you need. You like those shelves?"

"They're crooked and dented," I said.

"That's because they're defective. I keep the perfect ones inside. Come in and have a look."

"You should have your best stuff outside."

"Then someone would rip it off."

"Maybe, but I don't understand why you bothered to lock up these ugly shelves."

"People will steal anything and everything! I used to have a broken cinder block to prop open the door and someone stole that. You don't know how it is. I've been in this business almost twenty years. I know this guy who put his scummy fryer outside to air out. It was all covered in clumps of brown and black stuff, looking like someone had diarrhea in it. Somebody stole that, too."

"Unbelievable."

"It is. Say, can I set you up with a new sink? I have to move out last year's model, so I've got my best price for you. You look like a nice and smart guy. I won't waste your time."

"I don't have a restaurant."

"You can install it in your home. It's great. I have one. I live upstairs. You want to see it?"

"You live upstairs?"

"Yeah, second floor."

"Were you here when a body was found across the street?"

"Was I what?"

"Were you here the night before the body was found?"

"I was here," he said, suddenly cautious.

"Do you remember seeing or hearing anything unusual?"

He crossed his arms. "Who are you?"

"I'm sorry, I should have gotten around to this earlier. My name is Robert Chow. I'm with the Fifth Precinct. NYPD."

"I don't remember anything."

"Are you sure? You seem to be a pretty observant guy."

"No. When I sleep I'm a rock. I snore louder than the traffic."

I handed him my card. "In case you remember anything."

He quickly countered with his own card. "I know you're going to need new shelves someday."

I STOOD AT the window to the dumpling wholesaler. Most of the dumplings served in Chinatown restaurants were bought frozen and in bulk from a place like this.

Making dumplings isn't difficult but it is labor-intensive. It also takes up a lot of space to roll out the dough and store the finished dumplings.

Teams of two people were crammed in each of the two back corners, scooping meat filling from plastic tubs and swaddling them in dough. Finished dumplings were set off to the side on a bamboo tray.

The counter was manned by a woman in her fifties wearing a hairnet. Her arms were caked in flour past the elbows. She stood in front of two vertical freezers. As soon as she saw me her eyes narrowed.

"Hi there," I said. "How are you doing?"

"Good."

"I'm Robert Chow with the Fifth Precinct. I was wondering if you or anybody who works here remembers seeing—"

"We don't remember anything."

"I understand that you're open at five in the morning."

"No, we are not."

"That's what it says on your sign."

"It's dark when we come in. We don't see anything."

I didn't bother to leave my card with the flour lady. Nothing good could have come from it. I wondered if I had offended her at some point in the past. Maybe I had ticketed her van. Maybe she had a son who was one of those stupid gang kids and I had taken his picture. Maybe, maybe, maybe. Some people simply don't like cops and that's how it is.

THE FUKIENESE CHURCH had so many coats of white paint over the brick walls it looked like the side of a Carvel ice-cream cake. I stepped through a metal gate to get to the main entrance. A glass-enclosed signboard noted that services were held in Fukienese except for one sermon each in Spanish and English on Sunday afternoons.

It seemed quiet from my side of the wooden door, so I opened it and eased my way in.

I was surprised to find about twenty men crowded in the lobby, wearing cheap sports jackets, and smoking as if they were hanging out at an Off-Track Betting facility.

I walked around to the side and looked up a stairwell. I thought I spotted someone I knew and went upstairs.

"Hello," I said in English.

"Oh, Robert," said Mr. Song. "What are you doing here?"

"I was in the neighborhood, examining recent murder scenes, and figured it was time to get it right with God."

"You mean one murder in particular, right out there."

"Yeah."

"Together Chinese Kinship is conducting English-language classes in partnership with the church. We're just taking a break right now. Let's go into an empty classroom where we can talk."

He led me up another flight and found a small room that had windows only slightly above the floor level. There was still enough sun coming in that we didn't need to turn the light on.

"My contacts with the People's Republic say they're glad the news has died down a bit about Mr. Chen, but they want to know what progress has been made. If it turns out that a KMT-backed person or group was behind this, then I have to warn you that there could be a retaliatory hit. Not anything sanctioned from the mainland, of course, but there are left-wing agents who would take it upon themselves to mete out justice."

"The pro-KMT paper keeps calling for a bigger investigation," I said. "How do you figure that they're behind the murder?"

"Typical dirty Nationalist trick. They know who killed Mr. Chen. They might have even killed the guy to cover their tracks.

This way they can step up the anti-Communist rhetoric in their media and justify their own brutal tactics in Taiwan."

"The last time I checked, the Taiwanese economy was booming."

"For the rich."

"How do you know a Communist didn't kill Mr. Chen? Wouldn't a hard-core Maoist want to strangle him for betraying the motherland?"

"We don't care about people leaving China. If they want to go, they can go. Together Chinese Kinship members all left China, yet we have a dialog with Beijing. They wouldn't bother to talk to us at all if they thought we were traitors."

"Of course they want to be in touch with you. How else could they check the KMT's influence in New York?"

Mr. Song only gave me a tight smile.

"I need to ask you something," I said. "Just on a person-to-person level." I felt like I could ask for a degree of privacy from him because of our common bond.

"What is it?"

"Promise you won't tell anyone."

"I promise."

"Swear to God."

"I swear to God."

"I thought you people didn't believe in God."

"We believe in God to the capacity that the idea embodies the brotherhood of man and the common goal of all workers and the fact that it brings a degree of comfort to the masses. Now, Robert, what is it?"

"Why would someone chop off a man's left index finger?"

"I don't know."

"Mao didn't advocate such a thing?"

"No, never."

"What do Communists do to enemies of the state?"

"We wouldn't cut off fingers. We would send reactionaries to the gallows or to labor camps. We would want to punish the entire body, not just a part. We're Chinese, not Japanese."

"Mr. Chen's finger was cut off. After he died."

"Hmm."

"The press doesn't know."

"They won't find out from me."

"Do you think it's something one of these fringe groups would do?"

"I'm not sure. Do you want me to ask people from the mainland?"

"Oh, no. I want as few people as possible to know."

"All right, Robert." With a meaningful look in his eyes, Mr. Song added, "We also hold open meetings in this church, in the basement. If you're ever interested."

"I'll keep it in mind."

I MET THE midget the next day for lunch. I brought soup noodles from a cart. The extra one was for the kid who worked there, Drew. I unpacked the plastic containers on the counter, away from the register.

Drew pulled up a chair but the midget reached out and touched his arm. "Hey, how about you go eat yours in the back? We have some man talk to do here."

"I'm sorry, I should have realized," said Drew.

"Stop with the sorry! You couldn't have known!" said the midget with exaggerated weariness. The kid smiled. "Now, go!"

When Drew had reached the storage room in the back, the midget said, "How's Lonnie holding up?"

"Fine on the outside, but she has to be worried." I leaned in and said in a low voice, "I'm actually going to be helping out on the case. Just not officially."

The midget nodded and slid out bamboo chopsticks from their paper sheath. He rubbed them together to get rid of the splinters. "Have you thought about hiring a private lawyer for her?"

"It's not going to be cheap," I said. I prepared my chopsticks also and then used them to haul up a tangle of glistening egg noodles into my mouth.

"What's cheap, anyway? How much would you pay to have that open surveillance stopped and get Lonnie's life back to normal?"

I wiped my mouth with the knuckle side of my left thumb and trawled through the soup for a chunk of chicken. "How can I put a price on that?" I asked, sighing. "This stupid system forces us to pay to live our little lives."

"Well spoken, comrade," said the midget. "When we're done eating, let's give three bows to the Chairman's portrait to thank him for helming the nation so well."

I pointed the chopsticks at the midget, sending soup droplets flying. "I fought Communism, pal. I've killed Communists."

"I guess that means you won?"

I shook my head. "Don't joke around about this."

"I kid because I care. Anyway, I can get a lawyer to look at this and maybe take on the entire thing free of charge."

"A real lawyer? I don't want some stuttering kid."

"Yeah, a real lawyer—a *criminal* lawyer. He owes me."

"How did you meet this guy?"

"In the usual way. He saw me in Columbus Park and he wanted to learn how to play Chinese chess."

"What favor did you do him?"

"I don't remember. But I do know that he's a principled kind of guy and helping a beautiful and vulnerable reporter is right up his alley."

The kid called out from the back. "I'm done eating now! Should I just stay here?"

"Yeah, hang out there a few more minutes!" yelled the midget.

"I'm gonna go. I feel bad about making him sit back there."

"Don't feel bad for him, he's getting paid for it."

The midget threw his head back sharply and cracked his neck.

LONNIE CAME OVER to my apartment about three hours later than scheduled. The Teletype was acting up and it took several tries to get her story through. Then she had to wait for the late editor to come back from a meal break to edit her story and ask questions.

"Those detectives are really wearing me down," she said, closing her eyes "They don't even really do anything. They're right behind me whenever I turn around."

I reached out my right hand and rubbed both her temples with my thumb and middle finger.

"I think I might know someone who can help," I said. "The midget told me about this lawyer he knows who will work for free."

"If we don't pay him anything, how hard is he going to work?"

"Lawyers do this all the time, Lonnie. They work to build up their reputation."

"Robert, I don't want to hire a lawyer. Even for free."

"Why not?"

"If I hire a lawyer, the people will think I'm guilty."

"Don't do the stupid, superstitious Chinese thing, Lonnie."

"Don't call me 'stupid'!"

"Do you think you'll get cancer if you see a doctor or that you'll die if you walk into a funeral home?"

"No, I don't. It's my parents, really, not me. If I hired a lawyer do you know what people will say about them?"

"Do you know what could happen to you if you don't have adequate legal representation?"

She counted off points on her fingers. "I am innocent. I have not been charged with anything. I have nothing to hide. The police will find the killer. My parents' reputation must be protected."

"What's so great about your parents that you worry about their reputations?"

"I don't always get along with my dad and my stepmom. But I do believe that children need to respect their elders to a certain degree."

"I don't have to respect them, though."

"You do."

"Why?"

"Robert, how serious are you about us?"

I WENT OVER to see Lonnie at her parents' place on the south side of Bayard Street. The ground-floor storefront sold souvenirs including a fan that folded out to read I LOVE CHINATOWN.

I had brought over those traditional Chinese treats: a bag of oranges, a box of Almond Roca, and a tin of Danish butter cookies.

It was the first time I was meeting her father and stepmother, who was Paul's mother, and the circumstances were far from ideal. But it would have been awkward at any point. One reason why Paul lived with me was the poisonous cycle of his dad beating him and Paul hanging out with wannabe gang kids to get away from him.

I was a little taken aback to find that Lonnie and Paul's dad was a fairly small guy, barely five feet tall. In my imagination, he was a hulking linebacker brandishing a belt. In reality he was a thin man in his late-fifties and his hair had thinned out to black streaks smeared over the top of his head like skid marks. The stepmother was in her early forties and wore too much makeup. It was her perfume that you could smell in the hallway. Lonnie hovered in the background as the hallway was too narrow for her to squeeze through.

"How are you, Mr. Chow?" Lonnie's dad asked as I took off my shoes. "We finally meet."

I shook his hand and it wasn't that strong. I realized then that Paul had taken all those punches and belt whips without fighting back. He could have knocked his old man flat.

"I brought these," I said, transferring my bags from my left hand to him.

"You shouldn't have!" he said, even before he saw what I had brought.

"We have too much food, already," called Lonnie's mother.

"I only brought over a few snacks," I said. "It was the least I could do." All of us were wearing socks on our feet, and we made dull thumping sounds on the hardwood floor while walking to the kitchen.

When I got close enough to Lonnie, I gave her a little half hug and she rubbed my arm. It's a Chinese thing, this restraint from showing affection in front of others. I personally don't really go for it, but I'm always aware of what other people would think. Besides, kissing Lonnie in front of her parents would only convince them that we were sleeping together, and there was no need for them to know that.

Whenever she stayed over with me, she told her parents that she was studying with a female friend. She had to. Lonnie was already a grown woman, but older Chinese people think the "Americanized" younger generations are degenerates who have orgies, shoot up heroin, and, worst of all, don't say "thank you" fast enough to relatives.

Now if we were at my place, Lonnie and I would have been practicing our hand-balancing act about now. We wouldn't have gotten around to eating until much, much later.

Lonnie's stepmother came over and grabbed my shoulder, sticking me with her fingernails. She gave a knowing little smile and said, "I'm so glad my daughter has such a strong and handsome friend!"

"I'm glad, too," I said. We all sat down at the table. Lonnie and her stepmom were on either side of me as I faced off with her dad.

The square table was crammed with a number of dishes, including pork, sautéed spinach, a pile of sticky noodle ovals with bean sprouts, and a crispy fish. Lonnie's father picked up his rice bowl and started piling morsels into it with his chopsticks. Whenever he had gathered five items, he would bring the bowl close to his lips and noisily shovel food into his mouth. He made a sucking sound like an old Hoover. My dad had done the same.

"Lonnie always works too hard," said her stepmom above the din. "I worry about all the hours she puts in. I think it is affecting her looks!"

"Chinese people have to work hard in America," I said. "I have to do twice as much in order to get equal treatment. Look how ugly I'm turning!"

"Don't be so funny," the stepmom said. "Of course you are good-looking. That's why you represented the police department in so many pictures. Lonnie used to show us in the newspapers!"

I smiled. Those were the days when I was little more than a cardboard cutout for the NYPD at various Chinatown functions. I was used by the cops and by the community groups to give each other face. If I had a dollar for every restaurant opening, Boy Scouts of America dinner, and birthday celebration of supposedly important community dignitaries that I had to sit through, Internal Affairs would be on my ass so hard.

"I am not attractive," I told the stepmom. "I was only in the newspapers because I didn't have enough work to do. Lonnie is the one who is beautiful." I had to force myself to smile before adding, "And so are you."

She put her hand to her mouth and giggled. I looked at Lonnie. Her face remained blank but she rubbed her foot against my leg in a gesture that meant "You're scoring points" and "I wish I could go home with you tonight."

Her dad, the steam-shovel operator, continued working away without interruption. "Why did you beat Paul?" I wanted to ask him. "Don't you know your son is a great kid and a genius?"

"This food is incredible," I said. "What amazing restaurant did you get this all from?"

"You're joking!" said Lonnie's stepmom. "You know I cooked with some help from Lonnie!"

"Yes, I only did a little bit," spat Lonnie. "But Mom handled the fish all by herself." I'm sure that Lonnie did at least half of the dinner. I'm also sure that she told her stepmom that I was allergic to seafood, yet it didn't register that she shouldn't prepare a fish.

"Please try the fish," said the stepmom, tapping my arm. "You might not think it's that good, but it is the only specialty I know how to cook! The recipe has been in my family since before the Manchus came down upon us."

"So you mean the Ming Dynasty, right?"

"Yes, yes! You know your history. Young people today, they don't know where they come from. Not only here, but in Hong Kong, too. They don't want to know their own culture and their language. They way they all dress is a disgrace to the Chinese people!"

Lonnie's dad grunted, startling all of us. "Yes," he said. "A big shame."

Knowing her eyes were on me the entire time, I reached out for some more pork while telling the stepmom, "I am so sorry. I can't eat your fish because I'm allergic to seafood."

"Oh my gosh, I didn't know!" she said, trying to magnify the horror quotient. "I had no idea!"

Lonnie nudged me with her toe.

"I know what you need to do," said the stepmom. "You have to eat a lot of fish and then you will be fine." There we go again. The Chinese solution to everything was bringing everything back into some alleged balance.

Allergic to seafood? You're not eating enough of it!

Can't swim? Spend more time in the water!

Is your son running around with wannabe gangsters because he hates you for beating him? You're not beating him enough!

"I'm sorry that I can't eat your fish," I said again. "I'm sure that it's the best and most expensive plate on the table. I really am truly very sorry." One can never apologize enough with Chinese people. Saying it just once meant you weren't sincere.

Still, she looked hurt. Lonnie took it as an opportunity to speak up. "Robert got a promotion recently."

"Not really a promotion," I said. "I was given more responsibilities."

"They pay you more money?" asked the stepmom.

"Just a little bit more," I said. "Not enough to get nice things for Lonnie, I'm afraid."

"Lonnie doesn't need nice things," said the stepmom. "She's not the kind of girl who has expensive tastes. She's a modern girl who wants to do the same work as a man. That's something she's learned from being in America."

"This is a good thing," I said.

"Well, the problem is, if women want to be the same as men, then it means they don't want to be women anymore. They don't even want to have children. Now, who is going to fall in love with them? Who is going to marry them?"

A spitting sound from Lonnie's dad interrupted the discussion and yet articulated my thoughts perfectly. With his chopsticks he scraped fish bones from his tongue and into his bowl and then turned it 180 degrees so he wouldn't sweep the bones back into his mouth.

I started tuning out of the evening. I remember Lonnie pushing an orange onto me and me peeling off its skin. Between the chatty stepmom and noisy dad, Lonnie didn't say very much and I felt annoyed at her for being so quiet.

Yet this was the fate of Chinese kids. At family gatherings they were expected to be quiet and do little more than answer questions as briefly as possible without expressing opinions. What was the payoff? Once a year, you get this red envelope of money to buy your silence.

Lonnie wasn't a kid but she was still a child. You remained a child until you were married. That's when the red envelopes stop and you can say whatever the hell you want at dinner.

AFTER PUTTING MY shoes back on and endlessly promising that, yes, I would come back to "play" again, as Chinese people like to phrase nonbusiness meetings, I went down the stairs to the street.

In the light rain, the Manhattan South guys were inside their plain sedan. It was a lousy disguise. Having the only tinted windows on the block made the car stand out. Someone in the backseat rolled down the window and spat out of it.

That pissed me off. If I was going to allow these guys to lean on my girlfriend, I was going to make sure they did so in a respectful way.

I came up from behind the car and knocked on the right rear window with my knuckles. Nothing happened, so I slammed my hand on the roof. The front passenger door opened.

"Hey, Chow, knock it off!" said BB Gun, a Manhattan South guy. He had made a name for himself in buy-and-bust drug stings. He was good at making people talk after.

"Keep your spit in your mouth when you come to Chinatown," I said.

"What're you talking about? Chinese people spit all the time!"

"They're not just spitting. We have a cultural belief that we have to get rid of bad fluids in our systems."

"Pizza Man had to get rid of bad fluids, too."

The rear window rolled down. Next to Pete I saw Bad Boy, who held a dull metal flask with both hands in his lap as if it were a prayer book.

"What are you two doing here?" I asked Pete.

"We're acting like the local guides to Manhattan South. They need us to show them the short cuts."

"How about I show you a quick way on to Internal Affairs? Drinking on the job!" The universally reviled rat patrol only grew by adding members of service who had disgraced themselves.

"We're not on the job, but if you want to make a stink out of it, these guys could take it out on your dearly beloved."

BB Gun said, "I might have to cuff her father, too. I think I saw him make a threatening move toward me."

I stood straight up and crossed my arms.

"Hey listen, Chow," said Bad Boy. "Don't take it too hard. You don't have a gold shield yet, but by the time you do, you'll know how it is. All we have here is a bad situation. These guys know Lonnie is innocent. They're just doing their job. You don't have to give them shit over it."

"Their job is finding the murderer!"

"Don't you know by now how good it looks in the report that they've been staking out the only apparent suspect? C'mon, now. Something else is bound to turn up and then they won't have to do this anymore. They're not going to be here forever. Say, how about a few nips of this?"

"I don't drink anymore. I'm sober now."

"Goddamn, I didn't know. I thought you just had it under control."

I looked at Pete.

"Sorry I had to spit," he said. "I had to get rid of the gum."

I nodded.

"Aw, hey, he's all right. Everyone's all right," said BB Gun. He patted my elbow and shut his door. I walked off and heard the rear window shriek as Pete wound it back up.

I WENT TO see Izzy again. He was so preoccupied he wouldn't even sit back down after letting me into his office.

"I know you're getting fed up with how long this is taking," he said. "You can't fight how this works by coming over here." Izzy picked up a folder from his desk and thumbed through it.

"I happened to come across your detectives last night," I said. "They were associating with two members of the Fifth Precinct squad."

"Are you trying to interfere with the official investigation, Chow?"

"No."

"These boundaries were drawn up before we were born and you're going to respect it. We don't go on your turf and you stay out of Manhattan South cases. You don't contact the guys in the field. Ever. You want to help, you come to me.

"Now what were my guys doing with the Fifth Precinct guys?"

"They were drinking in the car."

He dropped the folder on his desk and sank into his seat. "All of 'em were drinking?"

"I'm only sure about our guys."

"Did you meet Plutarch?"

"Which one was he?"

"He's got bags under his eyes and a long face. He's the driver."

"I didn't meet him."

"Good. You make doubly sure to stay away from him. He's a sadistic son of a bitch. His specialty is breaking into the cars of suspects and spraying Mace into the ventilation system. When the car starts up, it's like a tear-gas raid."

We both had a laugh.

Izzy wiped his forehead. "He's not going to pull any dirty tricks on Lonnie."

"Apparently they all know she's innocent."

"It's not her they're watching, per se. They expect the real guy to swing by and observe. In theory, the actual murderer is a little miffed that someone else is taking the credit—and a woman at that. I know the Chinese culture looks down on women."

"It looks down on cops, too."

"Who doesn't?"

Izzy looked over his hands and talked to his knuckles. "Remember, don't let The Brow find out."

"There's no way that could possibly happen."

"You'd be surprised. These hard-boiled types gossip like girls at a sleepover when they get together."

"Izzy, are there any details left that I don't know about?"

"What else is there? Last seen walking out with Lonnie. The car voucher. Killed by blunt object close to midnight. Missing finger."

"Did Mr. Chen have any visitors at The Plaza?"

"No one ever visited him, apart from Lonnie. The last time he was seen alive he was walking out of the lobby with her. Mr. Chen never made any calls from his hotel room."

"Did he have any incoming calls?"

"None the entire stay."

"Were there fingerprints in the hotel room?"

"Nothing useful."

"What about Mr. Chen's effects?"

"Books and clothes and a jar of smelly medicine. We had a native Chinese speaker go through the entire thing and there was nothing for us."

"I stopped by the livery-cab office. They don't know who the driver is yet. When we find him the first thing he'll do is probably admit he added the extra line for the money, trust me."

"We'll see."

"The evidence isn't really coming together."

"Is Lonnie also looking like a better suspect to you, now?"

I smirked. "I'll find something out. I don't know how, but I will."

"I'm sure you will, too. Oh, and by the way. Everything you find belongs to us. I can't guarantee that you get credit for any of this."

"I'm not just doing this for credit."

"That girl better marry you and carry your sons. You like sons, right?"

ON TOP OF figuring out who had stuffed those guns into the apartment mailbox on Henry Street, I was supposed to be making a case on some gang kids who were extorting merchants. They would show up at a store with one of those little trees in a pot as a present and then ask the owner to give them some "lucky money" or "tea money" in return.

This scam works best on newly opened businesses. A guy with a new restaurant doesn't want any trouble right off the bat, so he'll pay up, hoping they won't come back. But they always do.

The average Chinese merchant is a frightened and superstitious creature. He thinks that the merchant association, family association, and region association that he belongs to can and will handle all the problems he has. After all, he did get loan references through them to start up his business. But if he complains about the fact that he has to make these monthly payments, he'll be met with amusement and veiled threats.

"Don't you know that's the price of doing business? You pay even less than the guy before you! Hey, if you think this is bad, you know how much you'd have to pay in Hong Kong? If you tell to the police, the white people are going to send an inspector from the Department of Buildings and condemn your property! You want that?"

I talked it over with English and convinced him that I would have to use a substantial amount of time trying to dig up evidence to clear Lonnie or at least come up with another suspect.

He was cool about it because he knew how hopeless my caseload was. I also think he felt bad that Pete piled this dead-end work on me.

I told him I would always be on the prowl for merchants who would step forward and tell their story, but of course, I would probably have to threaten them with extortion to get them to testify that they were victims of extortion.

I told him I wasn't even going to put in for overtime until I had Lonnie off the hook. For the first time ever I saw the look of surprise on his face. A cop not taking overtime was like skipping seconds at a buffet.

It was assumed that Vandyne would be with me on a lot of the work because he was my old partner. They often say that partners couldn't be closer if they were married. You spend more time with each other, that's for sure, and whether you love or hate the other person, you understand each other and that understanding goes beyond emotions that are subject to change. At the funerals the ex-partner cries as hard as the widow because they both lost a part of themselves.

Of course, this investigation wasn't going to end with a funeral. Not for the good guys, anyway.

I SPREAD OUT a subway-route map on top of a bus-route map already on my desk. I traced my finger from The Plaza Hotel at the southeast corner of Central Park all the way down to Sara Roosevelt Park. I couldn't make sense of it.

Even a seasoned New Yorker would have been foolhardy to take public transportation that late at night. A newcomer to the city wouldn't have been able to negotiate the late-night track work that rerouted the subways.

Nor would he have been able to manage the multiple bus transfers to get down to Chinatown. If that had been his choice of transportation, he would still be waiting for a transfer.

Maybe Mr. Chen never did go to Chinatown. Maybe he was killed close to his hotel. He had left the lobby without a coat and didn't return. Did assassins get him as he left? Or maybe he did himself in on his own by trying the F. Scott Fitzgerald thing and jumped in the fountain but he cracked his head?

No, that was a terrible idea. I scratched my face and stretched out my legs. It was a little after 0200. I was in the squad room on my own time. Bad Boy was at his desk talking in a low voice to someone on the phone. He was a seasoned detective with a lot of good work under his belt. If he were me, what would he be looking for in this case?

I looked back to the maps. It probably wasn't too hard to have gotten Mr. Chen at his hotel. It would have had to be planned, though. But then why was his corpse lugged all the way to China-town and then dumped? Maybe the killer was trying to send some sort of message.

What exactly was the message, though? Surely, it was nothing personal against Mr. Chen. It was meant as a warning to Li Na. Yet the meaning wasn't entirely clear.

Was this move against Li Na meant to target her for being her mother's daughter and thereby an accomplice to the Gang of Four? Or maybe it was an anti-Mao job. The killer or killers may have even been trying to send a shocking and confusing message to sow chaos on the mainland. In that case, were they KMT agents or Communist agents?

I yawned and crossed my arms. I looked over at Bad Boy again. He was still talking with no expression on his face, eyes dead. I couldn't hear a word of what he was saying.

It was so unfair that he could simply do his job in Chinatown and not take personally all the political crap. But as an Italian American, he had other stuff to deal with. Both of those *Godfather* movies had enforced the image of lawless Italians upon the consciousness of the country. I enjoyed them and I know Lonnie did, too. But if someone non-Chinese came up and told me how much they loved Charlie Chan and Fu Manchu films, I'd probably be pretty annoyed.

Bad Boy hated the two movies. He complained when a Mid-town revival theater showed them as a double feature. That was actually the run that Lonnie and I had caught. Bad Boy had given money to an Italian American organization to fight the stereo-types in the films, and when a cop gives money to something, it's a cause that he would want to die for.

Pizza Man, who was also Italian American, actually liked the movies and he told Bad Boy that they proved that criminals get theirs in the end. Besides, there was no sense in getting worked up about it because there could never be a *Godfather: Part III*.

For me, the *Godfather* movies were about family. Maybe Chinese people read family themes into everything they do.

Did Mr. Chen have family in Chinatown?

No. He had a wife and kids in Beijing. He apparently was able to rise in the political machine precisely because he didn't have any family abroad, least of all in Taiwan or America.

I turned back to the subway-route map and smoothed out the folds. I patted the area where The Plaza was.

I closed my eyes and tried to picture him leaving the hotel with Lonnie and what he did after her car left. I had seen psychics do this on *In Search Of . . .* to much success.

Could he have gone to a diner? No. If he was hungry, he could have ordered room service.

Maybe he wanted to see what Central Park was like at night. Highly unlikely. He wouldn't have gone into a park that had an international reputation for being prime mugging grounds.

Porn. Mr. Chen had heard of capitalist New York's decadent reputation and he wanted to see live strippers. Or maybe even a pross house in Chinatown. This idea was also shot down by the food argument. He could have had room service. I don't care that it was a really nice hotel. That only means the freight elevator operator brings up the girls from the loading dock so they don't have to go through the lobby.

Mr. Chen knew that he was risking a lot politically by strolling out of the hotel, so it must have been something he had wanted to do pretty badly, perhaps desperately.

When I thought about it, there's nowhere else in the city a Chinese guy would want to go to apart from Chinatown, and Mr. Chen was no exception.

Why and how, though?

Maybe he had hailed a cab. But if he did he couldn't have explained in detail where he wanted to go. He would have said, "Chinatown," and been dropped off somewhere on Canal. Mr. Chen didn't know Chinatown, though, so it doesn't make sense that he would come all the way down to wander around in the streets. Maybe that is what happened, and a mugger got him.

Mr. Chen couldn't have come here to admire the architecture and the metal pagoda hats on the public telephones, though. Something in particular made him come down, a person or a group of people. If his trip was planned out, Mr. Chen could have given a cabbie a piece of paper with an address on it.

But that didn't make sense, either. Most of Chinatown was already closed. If he and his unknown party had gone to a twenty-four-hour restaurant, Mr. Chen's appearance would have caused a ruckus. Also, if an association or person had really wanted to see him, they would have simply come up to The Plaza and Mr. Chen could have cleared them.

It had to be a party who didn't want to see Mr. Chen! That's why he had to go to Chinatown to find him or her or them!

I'll bet that someone at the meeting with the Department of the State may have slipped Mr. Chen an address or something. Possibly a second rendezvous for asylum talks. But not for Li Na—for him!

I looked back and forth at the two maps. I wasn't getting much else from them except a pair of tired eyes. I folded each of them up the wrong way and chucked them into the top drawer of my desk.

I sighed. I knew what I had to do. I had to go to Jade Palace and talk to Willie Gee. I'm sure that he had kept a close watch on Mr. Chen during the event. I should get Vandyne on this thing with me.

Why the fuck did you leave, Mr. Chen? Why couldn't you have just stayed in your goddamn hotel room? It would have been better for all of us.

JADE PALACE HAD never been busier. A certain grim fascination had taken ahold of Chinese living in the tri-state area and everyone and their newly born son wanted to eat where Mr. Chen had dined not so long ago.

Willie Gee had smartly brought back in the KMT flags to adorn the entrance and the main dining rooms. He knew those loyal to the Nationalists would want to have a celebratory feast where a representative of the mainland had had one of his last meals. Willie didn't worry about alienating Communist sympathizers. Commies never bought the expensive dishes or best liquor, anyway.

"Of course, I couldn't imagine that Mr. Chen would be murdered," said Willie. Vandyne and I were standing in his personal office, which had only one chair and it was for him. "I feel terrible for his family, friends, and supporters. But it was the best possible outcome I could have hoped for, in terms of my business. I had worried that there would be some short-term negative feelings about Jade Palace hosting the meeting. Now that's not a problem at all!"

"Mr. Gee," said Vandyne, "you seem almost happy that Mr. Chen was murdered."

Willie tilted his head and held up a finger to correct Vandyne. "Not happy about the actual murder, but happy about the benefits from it."

"You're a sick man, Willie," said Vandyne.

"I'm actually very healthy, physically and mentally," he said. "I just read an article in *The Harvard Business Review* about compartmentalizing. I'm able to separate my personal life from my work life. My emotions from my reasoning.

"You know from your own experience, Mr. Vandyne, that many Chinese are prejudiced against people of your color. But when I look at you, I don't think of muggers, murderers, and rapists! I think, 'Hey, here's a hungry customer and I can sell him some food.' In fact, in the last week alone, I had three black people eating here—and they loved it!" He crossed his arms and smiled.

"Willie," I said, "nobody here doubts your strong commitment to racial harmony. I just want to know if you noticed anything unusual during the meeting or if there were some suspicious people walking around."

He shrugged. "I've already told the other detectives everything I knew. The federal government was handling security, so they cleared everyone in attendance. Even all our staff that day was carefully screened."

"Did anything strange happen?"

"The whole thing was strange! There were armed men at every entrance and every window. You saw that protest outside, too? It made me feel like I was inside a castle while some barbarians were trying to break in!"

Vandyne asked, "Where were you during the meeting?"

"I was on my feet the entire time, walking around, making sure everything was perfect from the food to the service. I told all the FBI men that they could come back anytime and bring their family and friends and I would give them the business rate. There were even some black ones, too!"

"On behalf of all Chinese people, I apologize for his behavior," I told Vandyne.

"You don't have to be sorry," said Vandyne. "Willie is his own man."

"Did I say something rude?" Willie asked, his eyes wide-open and questioning.

"Nothing more than usual," I said. "Let's get back to that day, Willie. Did you receive any threatening phone calls?"

"In the days leading up to the event, yes I did. But I unplugged the phone the day before. It got pretty bad."

"You didn't tell the police about it," said Vandyne.

"You know why I didn't? There wasn't anything you could or would do. Were you going to trace phone calls because people call my staff and yell at them for being Commies or fascists? What would you charge them with, even if you did catch them? It was better to simply take the phone off the hook. It made the restaurant seem busier, anyway."

"Any calls since?" I asked.

"No, the only calls now are for reservations. This is the hot restaurant right now. It will probably remain so as long as the murder and the subsequent trial stay in the news. You are going to find the guy, right?"

"We'll find him," I said.

"I understand your girlfriend, Lonnie, was the last one to have seen Mr. Chen alive."

"Except for the murderer, of course."

"Of course. You know, you should really be asking her questions instead of me. I'm sure she must know quite a bit." Willie rose. "If you'll excuse me, I need to get back downstairs. People tend to slip up when they're not being watched."

He came around his giant rosewood desk to our side and opened the private elevator with a key. We all stepped in. As the doors were closing, Willie asked, "Have you all eaten?"

"Not yet," said Vandyne.

"I'd like to offer both of you lunch at the business rate," said Willie.

"We'd take it too personally to eat here for business," I said.

The door opened, and Vandyne and I left Willie, who looked like he was trying to figure out if he should be offended or not.

I HAD HEARD about David Ong and saw him in the Chinese newspapers before meeting him. I understood that this rookie was in a way my replacement to handle community celebrations and dinners. He was the new token NYPD face for Chinatown.

It was a part of my life I wasn't too proud of when my life as a whole was nothing to be proud of. I would shine up my shield, nurse my alcoholism at the dinners, and make a little smile for the cameras. David was doing a good job of it.

I'm not really complimenting him. If you just showed up and got through the evening without pissing your pants, you'd be doing a good job of it.

David came up to the squad room to see me and introduced himself.

"I heard you don't speak Chinese," I said.

"You heard right." He closed his eyes and smiled.

"Isn't that a bit of an impediment to the job?"

"Not so much. Frankly, if I can find just a few people to talk to, usually the younger people, I do just fine. It's the kids who tell me who's who and what's going on."

I looked David over carefully. He was tall, about six feet, and sort of storklike. Those gangly arms were meant to cradle books, not women. The kid had a sweet face, though.

"Do you like what you do?" I asked him.

"You mean the job?"

"What I mean is that you have the job and then going to banquets and stuff is extra work. That could be a major pain."

"What's so tough about sitting around and eating? It doesn't seem like extra work to me. It's like being at my relatives' houses. I just relax and daydream a little. It's a good time."

"So, basically, you wanted to be a cop to have a good time."

"No. I wasn't sure what to expect."

"I'll bet you're happy with it now, though."

"Should I be unhappy? What are you getting at?"

I came in close to him. "Let me tell you, David, I've heard some of the other guys calling you 'Ong Kong Phooey,' and it pisses me off."

"Why should you be pissed off?"

"They're making fun of you, man, and it's racist!"

"They're just joking around, Robert. I don't take it as racism. People have funny nicknames for each other."

"You don't mind being compared with a dog that does bullshit kung-fu and karate moves?"

"It's a nickname. It doesn't even matter."

"It does matter, and if you don't stop it now, it's just going to get worse. You're going to be 'Fu Manchu' next."

"I'm new to the job and I know you've been through a lot. But even I know it takes a sense of humor to get through the day. When was the last time you had a laugh?"

"When was the last time people had a laugh at your expense?"

He shook his head. "You are really something. The Brow warned me about you. I think I can see why."

"He warned you that I was a no-good alcoholic, right?"

"Naw. He told me you'd try to make me feel bad about myself for helping out the community."

"Let me tell you, man. These people you're eating with, they don't give a damn about you. They just want a picture with you."

"That part is true. Almost everyone I meet doesn't exactly have the nicest things to say about you. They say they're glad that you're gone."

"The feeling's mutual."

"Still, though, you gave up the easiest job in the world."

"NOBODY HATES MEETINGS more than me," English said to everyone in the squad room. "So I'll just call this a series of announcements. When you're typing up reports, remember to punch hard. You've got to get through to the carbon duplicate. We don't have a budget for fancy electric typewriters, so put some manly muscle into it. Some of you are typing too soft. We're dropping letters and sometimes even whole words. Nobody wants to read, 'Found out the murderer is garble garble.'

"No names now, but Vandyne, you got a light touch."

I couldn't help snickering and neither could Pete or Bad Boy.

"I'm not a secretary," said Vandyne.

"Then don't type like you wear a skirt! Get mad if you have to."

"I'm getting there right now. Anyway, it's not my fault. The stupid springs are old or something else needs to be adjusted. If you could dig out the manual, I'd fix it myself."

"The manuals are gone," said Bad Boy. "I think they needed to burn them for fuel in World War Two."

We heard boots in the stairwell.

"The struggle makes you stronger, Vandyne. Next. When you bring someone in who has pissed their pants, you don't have to pull him all the way up here and lock him in the squad cell. You can leave him downstairs in one of the common cells. Pete, you ruined my lunch the other day."

Someone was stomping down the hall to the squad room.

"Last . . . Yes, sir!" English stood at attention as The Brow walked into the room. All four of us stood up.

"At ease," The Brow called out. He was a small man and he looked up hatefully at everyone else in the room. His pretty blue eyes, windows into his glacier soul, sparkled above his indignant frown, which grew deeper with each step as he paced.

The commanding officer's real name was Sean Ahern, but because of a bare patch in his right eyebrow, everyone called him The Brow. Not to his face, of course, and not even to his back. He was in his late fifties and was thin and mean.

His hair was short, reddish brown, and looked like moss, the kind that liked to grow on tundra rock.

Izzy and The Brow had a major falling-out years ago, back when they were both in the academy. Over the years, Izzy rose through the ranks of Manhattan South, which oversaw the Fifth Precinct, among others. Izzy was my pal now, so I wasn't as frightened as I used to be by The Brow's scare tactics.

The Brow favored heavy boots that he liked to stomp for emphasis, sometimes for every word he said. On top of that, he'd pound his fists into his hands while focusing the hate beams from his eyes at you.

"I understand that some of you have been associating with the fine boys of Manhattan South," he said.

I tried to look at an interesting spot on my forehead close to the hairline. All of us had had direct contact with Manhattan South except for Vandyne.

"Manhattan South is investigating a case under their jurisdiction that happens to be in our precinct territory. I can understand how you may be confused by the situation. You probably think that you can hang out in their cars when they're doing a stakeout or that you can even help with the investigation."

He stomped his right foot and the entire building seemed to shake.

"Let's get something straight! You stay away from this case as if it were a whore stricken with oozing lesions! Do you understand that?"

The Brow pointed the second and third fingers of his left hand at Pete and Bad Boy and said, "I don't care how senior you are."

He pointed at me and said, "I don't care how new you are."

Finally he pointed at Vandyne and said, "I don't care how black you are." He turned to face us all head-on, fists shaking at his sides. "You're going to obey me or I'll have you walking a beat on the Manhattan Bridge on a cold and icy night."

Nobody said anything as The Brow stomped out of the room.

"Hope you enjoyed the floor show, folks," said English.

Vandyne and I absently shuffled into the kitchen.

"You are getting it good tonight," I said.

"That little bastard," muttered Vandyne. "I don't miss the patrolman days."

I rinsed out a cold pot of coffee and changed the filter.

"He's not going to last," I said. "Dictators never do. He's done like Castro's going to be done."

"Castro's not done yet."

"It couldn't possibly be much longer."

The coffee machine lurched into action. We took two seats at the table.

"Are we going to keep messing around with Mr. Chen's case?" asked Vandyne.

"The Brow's not going to stop us. He couldn't hate me any more, and anyway if he could have fucked me over, he would have by now. I've got Izzy in my corner."

Pete strolled in. "White guys allowed in the kitchenette?"

"Never," I said. He sat down with us at the table.

"I don't think he knows how corny he is with that stomping act. He's a real live Napoleon," said Pete.

"That guy used to make my life hell," I said.

"We could take him down. All of us."

Vandyne said, "I'd rather see him trip over his own laces."

English poked his head in. "Who poured out the cold coffee?"

"Me," I said.

"Goddammit, I was saving it."

"Then pour it into a mug next time," said Pete. "Where'd Bad Boy go?"

"Went to Happy's," said English. "I think."

"I'm going, too, then. How about you two?" Vandyne and I both passed.

English walked over to the sink and stared at the drain. "Goddammit," he said again.

I WENT TO break up an illegal protest that amazingly was not at Jade Palace. It was at the midget's toy store.

A group of mothers were staging an impromptu siege against the midget's store. Apparently they were locking arms and blocking the entrance. But none of them were tall enough to cover up the GIMME JIMMY poster in the window.

The midget should have known better. Or maybe he didn't care. The fact that his store was solidly within the boundaries of pro-KMT Chinatown meant that he was in the middle of Gerald Ford Land. Hell, he was in the middle of Joe McCarthy Land.

Sure, Ford had gone to the People's Republic. He had shaken hands with Mao just like Nixon had. But Mao was dead, and so was any implicit agreement made with the handshake. Mainly, though, the pro-KMT Chinese remembered Ford's most recent actions. How he thundered against the International Olympics Committee after they barred Taiwan from competing in the 1976 Summer Olympics in Montreal.

Well, they weren't exactly barred from the games. Taiwan had wanted to compete once more as "The Republic of China," but ended up boycotting the games when they were told they had to compete as "Taiwan." The People's Republic was boycotting the Montreal games because it was still pissed off that Taiwan had been allowed to compete in 1972 as "The Republic of China."

When the next games came in 1980 Ford was going to stand up again for the Republic of China, which the United States recognized officially as the legitimate ruler of all of China. It was a given that Ford was going to maintain those ties. One more disastrous cultural revolution on the mainland might even give the KMT a chance for a sneak attack, backed by U.S. dollars and aid. The Ford Motor Company had built B-24 bombers in World War II. Surely a President Ford would lend some aircraft for the purpose of recovering the mainland.

Carter, on the other hand, was a pinko. KMT supporters had three firm pieces of evidence to prove that. One, he was a farmer.

Two, his family had practiced integration in the South and treating everybody as equals is the first step in brainwashing. The final straw was that he gave an interview to *Playboy*, a decadent magazine that was offensive to all upstanding people.

BY THE TIME I got to the toy store, the linked arms of the five ladies had slipped to holding hands. Their chanting remained spirited, though.

"Mao's dead!"

"Don't buy toys from bandits!"

"Little red book! Little red man!"

"Hello, there," I said. "I hate to tell you this, but you have to stop this right now."

"Oh, yeah?" said a five-five toughie with a smelly perm. She seemed to be the leader. The woman pointed a calloused finger at my right eye and said, "You are a Communist, too!"

"I'm a cop. This is an illegal gathering and it's gonna stop."

"I'm not going to stop until this store is out of business!"

"Is this all you understand?" I rattled loudly the handcuffs on my belt.

"You don't scare me!" said the woman, but the four behind her backed away.

"You're not going to leave, huh?" I broke open my handcuffs and the woman with the perm moved away so fast she was in danger of straightening her hair all over.

A little boy and two girls came over to me and smiled.

"You want to go in now?" I asked them. "Let's all go." They didn't say anything, but I pushed the door open and let them in first.

The midget was in front of the counter, testing the drawer on a tiny beat-up desk.

"Are you insane, putting up the Carter campaign poster in your window?" I asked him.

"Freedom of speech, baby," he said without looking up. He put his chin on the top of the desk and reached under with his right arm. "A little tangled up back there," he muttered to himself.

"Isn't it a little risky taking a political stance? Particularly an unpopular one on this block?"

The midget stood up and brushed off the dust from his shirt and pants. He glanced at me before heading back to his side of the counter.

"I have to think about my young customers," he said. "I don't want them to grow up thinking they can't say what they really think. I don't want them to be scared to speak up for what they believe in. That's what America's about."

"But that's not what Chinatown's about," I said.

"But it's what Chinatown *could* be about. I'll even go so far as to say that it's what Chinatown *should* be about." He disappeared and then popped back up with a pair of pliers. He snapped them a few times and grunted.

"No way, man. Conflict is in our blood."

"Conflicts don't have to be taken so personally," said the midget as he made his way back to the desk project. "Civilized people talk out their differences and make a better world for the next generation. They don't have kids just to carry on the same grudges they had."

"You can't stop the way people raise their kids with your toys and free-speech propaganda."

"Oh, I'm not going to have nearly as big a role as American schools and television. These kids don't even speak Chinese!" He pointed at the three kids who came in with me.

"Hey," I said to the boy in English. "You don't speak Chinese?"

He put on a sad little face and said, "No, sir."

To the midget I said, "This is ridiculous. I grew up speaking Chinese, so it can't be that hard."

He went under the desk and slammed something with the pliers. "You were such a good little boy, Robert. I guarantee you something. Your kids aren't going to speak Chinese. They won't even like Chinese food."

"They won't like it, but they'll eat it."

"How I wish you were my dad." The midget pulled himself out from under the desk. He took a deep breath and grabbed the drawer and pulled it out. "Success! Yes!"

"It's not that hard to get a drawer open."

He slammed the drawer shut. I heard some springs snap back. "Give it a shot, pal."

I walked over and stuck my hand under the drawer. "Aw, I get it. There are a few different switches you can pull. Only five, actually."

"How many combinations are there?"

"Five. No, wait. Ten?"

"Kids," the midget called in English. "Something funny!"

I struggled with the drawer. The wood looked as delicate as a graham cracker but there were metal reinforcements in it that held it strong. I kept jerking the drawer hard. The kids came over and laughed at me for not being able to open it.

"Anyone ever tell you that you have a very expressive face, Robert?" asked the midget.

"What's the combination?" I asked.

"One and four," he said.

"I was just about to try that one, anyway." The drawer slid open smoothly. The kids gave me a round of applause.

"You like that?" asked the midget. "It's an old cash register I found in the storage space. Pretty ingenious, isn't it? Have to admire those Chinese people."

"Tell me this, though. What good is this fancy combination lock if someone has a gun to your head?"

"Feel those little leather loops down there?"

"Yeah?"

"That's where you keep a knife or a pistol."

FOR A BREAK, the midget and I went to a cramped dumpling house that had opened in the arcade that connected Elizabeth with the Bowery in the middle of the block.

"It's a shame about Mr. Chen, isn't it?" asked the midget. "The whole thing."

"Yes, it is," I said. "I was actually contributing to the investigation when The Brow warned me—all of us, actually—to stay away."

"Still, it's a pressing matter, isn't it?"

"It's embarrassing for the U.S. that we haven't apprehended the suspect yet. The only reason why it's not an ugly international incident is that the People's Republic has decided not to make it an issue."

"They don't want to make it an issue! They want the U.S. to speed up the process of establishing formal diplomatic relations. They start complaining about it, then the resentment against China starts setting in."

"Anyway, I'm sure the mainland was not the biggest supporter of Mr. Chen."

"You want to know something? They probably wanted something bad to happen to him as a lesson to the folks at home."

"I know."

"What a sad and strange thing to have happened. Remember what happened to Lin Piao? He was the guy who tried to overthrow Mao. The plot hits a snag so he jumps into a plane and tries to flee to the Soviet Union. Then, pow! Lin's plane crashes into a mountain. Sometimes it seems like the Communists can make bad things happen by just wishing for them."

"The North Vietnamese got their wish. Now they have all of Vietnam."

"It's interesting isn't it?" asked the midget, his eyes trying to read something in the hot-sauce streaks on his plate. "With the mainland as a permanent member of the United Nations' Security Council, I don't think the rest of the world can delay membership for Vietnam for too long."

"You know what the problem with that is? North Korea is going to take that as a cue that if they overrun South Korea and unite that whole peninsula, then they, too, can be a legitimate state."

"China would never allow that."

"It allowed the Vietnam War."

"That's completely different. If you haven't noticed, China and Vietnam aren't buddies. China and North Korea are as close as lips and teeth, as they say, and China needs Korea to remain divided and in a state of uncertainty to have an edge over the U.S."

"Well, that doesn't make any sense. Uncertainty cuts both ways. How is China more secure with it than the U.S.?"

"Who has more people who know the Korean language and culture, the U.S. government or the Chinese government?"

"I see."

The midget wove his fingers together, pushed his hands away from his body, and cracked his knuckles.

"So, how's Lonnie holding up?" he asked.

"Hanging in there."

"She's a strong woman. She'll be fine in the end. As long as you do your part."

"Jesus, I'm trying as hard as I can! You think it's easy finding a murderer?"

"Looks easy on TV."

"One problem is that there are so many motivations to kill Mr. Chen. It could be seen as a pro-Communist move or an anti-Communist move."

"It could also be a pro-feminist move, taking out this older man who is in a position of power."

"You're forgetting that he was acting on behalf of Li Na, who is a woman."

"But Li Na also represents her father, Mao Tse-tung. That's one reason why she was purged from the Communist party."

"There was another reason?"

"Her mother was Jiang Qing. You know her, right? Mao's last wife and also the leader of the Gang of Four? If your mother was branded as a leader of a counterrevolutionary clique, then you probably don't have much of a political future."

"That poor kid," I said.

"Li Na? She's not a poor kid. She'll live out her life in a gilded cage. Lonnie is the poor kid!"

Izzy called me at home. "The Brow had his shitfit."

"Sorry about that, but I was being as careful as possible."

"It wasn't you, you know? It was those idiots drinking in the car. The Brow tailed Pizza Man and Bad Boy. Saw you come up to the car later, but he knew you weren't a member of the party."

"So my cover wasn't blown. I can still look into Mr. Chen."

"That's what I was thinking. The best thing is that when you meet up with Chinese people, you can say it's personal, not business."

Barbara called me at the station and told me that a Mr. Wilson Yi of the New York outpost of the Republic of China's embassy wanted to talk to me about the murder of Mr. Chen. I was wary of how the KMT diplomat would try to spin me politically, but decided to go anyway because it couldn't hurt and also because it would make Barbara look good.

She had already helped me with an old classmate in addition to finding Paul an internship and Lonnie her job, so I owed Barbara two or three favors. But she had also dumped me a while ago, so that cut into the favors-owed column.

The R.O.C. embassy was inside a skyscraper close to Rockefeller Center. Ten Taiwan flags stood on floor bases on either side of the passageway to the elevators, representing the 10-10 of the October 10 anniversary date of the founding of the Kuomintang Party.

When I got to the right floor Barbara and another woman were waiting for me outside the embassy entrance.

"Hello, Robert," said Barbara in Mandarin, "this is Mr. Yi's secretary, Ms. Kung."

"Hello," I said to the short woman. She was about five feet tall and on the heavier side. She had a sweet face behind her horn-rimmed black glasses, though.

"Wow, you look American! You're so big!"

"Thank you."

"Mr. Yi is very anxious to see you." With that, she led us into the offices. She took us around the corner and past a section of furiously loud typists to a giant rosewood desk, presumably Ms. Kung's. She bent over her desk awkwardly and tried to reach the intercom button. Ms. Kung had to climb up the side a little bit, like a pug climbing onto a bed. I chuckled a little and Barbara punched me in the arm.

Ms. Kung finally reached the button and screeched, "They're here!"

The wooden double doors in the wall swung open and a man stepped out. He was in his late thirties, about five foot five, and his black hair was in permed curls. Like a lot of men who had grown up in Taiwan under the tropical sun, he had dark brown skin. The girls would avoid the sun so they wouldn't be confused with the lower classes who had to work outdoors.

"Please come in!" Mr. Yi called in perfect English.

I took a seat facing Mr. Yi across his modest table while Barbara sat on the right wing.

"Thank you so much for taking the time to see me," Mr. Yi told me.

"I'm glad to visit, as long as there is useful information you have for me. If Barbara says it's important, it's good enough for me."

Ms. Kung waddled in with a cheap bamboo tray that held a clay teapot and three cups. She set it down on Mr. Yi's desk and pushed it to an area equidistant from and just slightly inconvenient for each of us. She left quietly.

Barbara reached for the teapot, but Mr. Yi waved her off.

"Just a little bit longer," he said, smiling. "You have to give the tea leaves a chance to unfold."

"I had the feeling this wasn't going to be restaurant tea," I said.

"I have my own personal favorite," said Mr. Yi. "It's not very expensive, but the taste is so subtle, it's precious."

"I'd still take coffee over tea any day," said Barbara.

"When I was young I drank mostly coffee, too. When I got older, I learned to appreciate the, ah, *ambiguity* the better teas have." Turning to me, Mr. Yi said, "Well, I've known Barbara for some time now, but you and I don't know each other."

"Gee, where should I start?"

"I think you've misunderstood! Barbara has told me all about you already. Let me tell you about myself!

"My family has been in Taiwan since the 1700s. They came over from Fujian province. I'm one of the highest-ranking native Taiwanese in the KMT, maybe *the* highest. For the most part, the KMT is run by Chinese who fled the mainland after losing the civil war in 1949."

"I thought the KMT's platform represented something most native Taiwanese don't go for."

"That Taiwan is a part of China? I'll tell you, my father sure didn't like it at first. He was very conflicted about joining the KMT, even though as the oldest son of a family that owned plastics factories, he would have been forced to join the party or lose his business. If he wanted to, he could have fought the KMT tooth and nail. But he went to a temple to ask for guidance and a monk told him to go through our family's records.

"He came upon an old journal from the early 1800s that said something to the effect that the family longed to return to China after the 'barbarians' were eliminated. That journal was referring to the Manchus who rode in and toppled the Ming Dynasty and established the Qing Dynasty, but my father took it as a sign, since the KMT referred to the Communists as 'barbarians.' So he joined."

"Mr. Yi, what is your personal story?"

"You want to know why I speak English so well, huh? I grew up with private tutors and came here to the States for college, undergrad at Stanford and Ph.D. from Harvard. That's where I met Barbara." Mr. Yi stood up and reached awkwardly for the teapot. He gathered the three teacups to him.

"You didn't tell me you knew each other from school," I told Barbara.

"Of course, everybody knew who Barbara was," he said, chuckling. Mr. Yi poured out tea for Barbara and me, and pushed the teacups as far as he could to us. He then poured his own tea. "Such an attractive woman is more famous on campus than the best-known professors."

Barbara sniffed the steam from her tea while shaking her head.

"What did you study, Mr. Yi?" I asked him.

"Chemistry. I don't recommend it."

"I guess you were being groomed for the family business."

"I hate plastics. I hate the way they smell. I can't even use a plastic umbrella. There's no future in plastics. Not for me, anyway. My father was pretty disappointed, to say the least, but he had the connections to hear of a vacancy in this office and once they heard 'Harvard Ph.D.,' I was in. I enjoy what I do, but it was rather unfortunate how I got this job."

"There's no shame in using family connections," I said.

"Well, the position was vacant because my predecessor left. When the People's Republic took the Republic of China's U.N. seat, he saw the writing on the wall and flew back to Taiwan. After he got home he hanged himself."

I drank some tea. "That's awful," I said.

"Yes."

"There is a perceived diminished value to this office as well. The American diplomat to the Republic of China, Leonard Unger, was in New York a few months ago. We had set up a dinner banquet for him in Midtown—not some crappy Jade Palace joint. Mr. Unger sent an assistant in his place. He didn't even have the courtesy to call to tell us in advance."

I looked at Mr. Yi's phone. It seemed that the only important call he would get would be to come home because it was all over.

"Can we get to the matter at hand?" asked Barbara. "I don't mean to rush you, Mr. Yi, but I have to stick to my schedule."

"Yes, yes, of course. Well, Robert, I wanted to discuss a sensitive matter about poor Mr. Chen with you. There are fringe elements, the extreme right wing of the KMT, who are outraged by his murder. They believed that Mr. Chen was killed because he and Li Na were embarrassing the mainland. Mao's daughter could never be assassinated, so Mr. Chen became the scapegoat.

"What's very problematic is that these KMT extremists are convinced that Communist elements in Chinatown are responsible for killing Mr. Chen."

"It's possible," I said.

Mr. Yi took a big swig of tea. "The extremists have criminal connections. In the past, a number of critics of the KMT and

Chiang Kai-shek have been killed all around the world. I would think that the same fate would befall anyone suspected of having a part in killing Mr. Chen."

"I see. These men are pretty ruthless, I take it."

"Yes, they are. Mainly though, I wanted to tell you that they often disguise themselves with R.O.C. diplomatic IDs and license plates. If you are ever approached by people claiming to be from this office, and if I didn't tell you they were coming, they are not to be trusted."

"Won't I be able to tell from their IDs? I can spot fake documents."

"They don't use fake documents. Everything they use is authentic. There are high-ranking KMT officers who lean to the far right and provide the necessary materials for these squads to work with."

I knew exactly whom Mr. Yi was referring to. There were branches of the KMT that didn't go to Taiwan after the civil war. They instead withdrew into the jungles of Thailand and established militarized bases financed with drugs. It was like printing money. They apparently had roving death squads in Asia that killed high-ranking Communists in the surrounding countries, along with critics of Chiang Kai-shek and the KMT.

But they hadn't carried out assassinations in the United States. Yet.

"I don't quite know what to say, Mr. Yi."

"Don't give out any information to anyone claiming to be from agencies of the R.O.C. Lives may depend upon it."

"You understand that my girlfriend is implicated in the investigation of Mr. Chen's death."

"I know, but she couldn't have done it. Any fool can see that."

"The problem is, I'm having trouble finding the responsible parties."

"So are these squads."

"I don't even have jurisdiction here. Manhattan South is handling the case."

"Yet you're still making inquiries, so I imagine that you are involved in some capacity with the investigation. Even unofficially. Honestly, Robert, if that was my girlfriend, I'd be doing my damnedest to find the real killer."

"But I'm not the only one looking, right?"

"No, you're not the only one."

"Mr. Yi, I understand that it was private Taiwanese citizens who helped Mr. Chen fly into New York."

"That is true, although they didn't work alone. A number of Hong Kong businessmen were involved, too. The whole thing was an incredibly naïve operation, that's for sure. It's a nice idea that Mr. Chen is an advocate for Li Na, but surely, wouldn't such a powerful man also harbor his own intentions and push for his own interests?"

WHEN WE WERE done, Mr. Yi buzzed in Ms. Kung, who showed us the way to the elevators. I was a little shaken up, imagining that gunmen were walking the same streets, looking for the same man as me.

Tipping me off was pretty risky and I had to give Mr. Yi credit. He seemed like an all-right guy.

As we waited at the elevator bank, I asked Barbara if she ever dated Mr. Yi.

"Oh, please, he's like ten years older than me!" she said.

"He didn't ask you?"

"No! He's been married since he was twenty. He already has two kids, too."

"I didn't know he was a family man! Still seems pretty happy."

"Having a family doesn't mean you're going to be unhappy."

DAVID ONG CAME into the squad room and found me. I looked up and saw he was worried, maybe scared.

"Robert, I think I saw some people with outstanding warrants."

"You think?"

"I'm pretty sure."

"By 'people,' do you mean gang kids?"

"No, older."

"How old?"

"Mid-twenties."

"How many?"

"Three."

"Where are they?"

"They're in the tunnels under Doyers Street. I think they were shaking down a merchant for money. I know them because I've been looking through the mug books regularly. I mean, the ones of prior convicts."

I stared at him hard. "Listen, David. We *only* have mug books of prior convicts. Understand?"

"Yeah, that's what we have."

"You just saw them now?" asked Vandyne.

"Yeah, I just ran back here."

Vandyne and I shook on our coats. "Next time," said Vandyne, "use your radio and call it in."

"The goddamn thing wouldn't work underground."

"Welcome to the job," I said.

Doyers Street has a bad reputation that is well deserved. In the 1800s, it was the favorite site of the so-called hatchet men to waylay enemies of their tong. You could probably hide a football team in the shadow of the elbow of the sharp turn.

At the turn of the century, shoot-outs with pistols were common in the "bloody angle." I have met old men who, as kids, used to collect the round little bullets and play with them like marbles.

Later on someone cleaned out the grain storage areas that were beneath Doyers, because the entire street itself used to be the private drive of a long-gone farmhouse. An entire underground chamber now ran roughly along Doyers, connecting Bowery, Mott, and Pell. It was far bigger than the tunnel Mr. Chen used to get into Jade Palace, and it was filled with twists and turns.

Not surprisingly, as space never goes to waste in Chinatown, it also was the home to many mom-and-pop stores and restaurants. The stupid gang kids would be especially bold when hitting the underground businesses for money because they felt emboldened hidden from the street.

Their cockiness was somewhat justified. If they were minors, there wasn't really much we could do to them if they were apprehended. They wouldn't even get a tough talking-to from the judge. But once they turned eighteen, they could be tried as adults, and the protection racket was a game for kids.

When we got close to Pell Street, Vandyne said, "We're going to come at them from different directions. Are you sure you're up for this, David?"

"I am. This is the first real action I'm going to be a part of."

"Watch yourself, David," I said. "Rounding up these assholes is not a dinner party. They have lousy aim, but they'll make up for it in shots fired."

David nodded. "So we split up?"

"Let's meet up in the food court on the second level. I'm gonna take the Bowery entrance," I said.

"I'll take Pell," said Vandyne. "David, you're all right with Mott?"

He put his hands on his belt and nodded. I quickly cut across Pell and made a right on Bowery. I entered the bank on the corner and took the stairs down to the underground area.

The fluorescent lighting through discolored plastic shades gave everybody and everything a pus-colored glow. The fish struggling in the gloomy water in the aquarium store came off the worst. I heard some shouting from around a turn, but it was only a woman with a baby trying to get her money back for a toy that broke after less than a week. I thought I recognized the woman, so I turned my head until I was safely past the store.

I lifted a low-hanging towel in front of a housewares store and eased by battery-operated toy cars driving around in circles on the floor.

Everything seemed to be normal, if a little chaotic. Those guys David had seen were probably long gone. The older ones liked to work through the young recruits, anyway.

I went down to the second level and it was more of the same. The air was humid thanks to the numerous stands boiling dumplings and noodles. I went around a wonderfully smelly fried-dough joint with half a mind to get a stick. It didn't seem safe to have an open flame in this area. I wondered how it had passed safety inspections. But then I realized this little underground world probably wasn't even on the radar.

When I passed the sticky-rice stand, I saw Vandyne across the way giving me a meaningful look. He tipped his head to the northeast. I slowly looked over and saw the three scumbags sitting at the only spot they could find free. It was a kids-sized folding table and they were all on plastic step stools with their knees up at their shoulders. They looked like they had crashed a little girl's tea party.

I saw this guy Marcus who liked wearing paisley shirts. He had missed a court date a few months ago for robbery. I don't say "alleged," because Vandyne had caught him in the act.

Another guy had a face like a cat with a small nose and eyes that were too close together. I called him Catwoman, and he had also missed a court date, for assault and battery on a store owner.

The third guy I wasn't too sure about until I saw a big red blotch on his left arm when he raised his rice bowl. It was Sherman, who had been mixed up in heroin. He had grown out his hair but there was no getting rid of that ugly birthmark.

"Robert," whispered David, who was crouching by my right elbow. "That's them!"

"I know," I said without turning my head. "So you stay back here while—" He sauntered in front of me and strolled down to the three assholes. "Aw, fuck." I followed close behind. I was sure Vandyne was behind me.

"All right, freeze!" David yelled at the three, gun drawn.

Marcus ignored the command and threw more noodles into his mouth.

"Hey, you fucking asshole, I'm talking to you!"

I was impressed to hear that harsh voice and tone coming out of David. Problem was, it was the wrong language.

When you confront someone, you need to establish authority quickly. Sometimes you can do it by acting loud and mean, sometimes quietly. A white or black cop would almost automatically have the upper hand on a Chinese suspect because those cops would already represent a sort of status quo authority figure.

But an Asian guy speaking English would be seen as a lightweight, some jackass who didn't even know what he was.

So I shouldn't have been surprised when Marcus calmly put down his chopsticks and reached under his seat.

"Get your hands up, asshole!" I yelled in Cantonese at Marcus. He stared at the barrel of my gun and let his hands float to the ceiling. Quietly, other diners picked up their bowls and stepped out of the line of fire.

Vandyne said behind me, "Stand up slowly, all you motherfuckers, and get up against the wall!"

I kicked their legs out and frisked them all. None of them had anything on them, apart from Sherman, who had a paring knife.

"It's for fruit, man!" he said.

"Should have used your fingernails, Sherm," I said. I didn't know if the concealed weapon thing would stick with him. Unlike the other two, there wasn't a warrant out for him.

When Vandyne and I had them all cuffed, I said, "David, go over and see what Marcus had under his seat."

"It's a bag," David said.

"Look in the bag but don't touch anything. What do you see?"

"A small gun. And a book."

"Bring it over here."

It was a cheap-shit .25 caliber gun that we called a Saturday night special. "Hey, Marcus, how come you're still using the same gun you had when you were twelve?" He spat on the ground. "David, these are good collars. You did a real good job. David?"

His face was falling apart. Tears and snot were all over the place.

"David, c'mon, man! It's all right!"

Vandyne called out, "Dave, we've got it all together now. We're going home."

"He was going to shoot me," he gasped. "I had my gun drawn. He was going to shoot me anyway."

Marcus snickered.

"Watch your step, Marcus," I said, dragging him to the right. "I'd hate it if you slipped and hit the ground with your face a few times." In English, I said to David, "You have to stop that, now. You want them to start calling you 'Ong Kong Boo Hooey'?"

"I'm just kinda shook up," he said, wiping off his face with the backs of his hands.

"Let's book these guys. I'm giving you primary credit, too. The Brow is going to love you for this."

THE BROW HAD me in his office and as these things usually go, he was yelling at me as soon as I stepped into the room. It was to be expected. There were only two reasons why you'd be in there. You were either in trouble or you were in big trouble.

"Why the hell have you put my boy in harm's way?" he yelled. I closed the door behind me and took two steps toward his desk.

"Sir, David Ong came to me after spotting suspects with warrants out."

"How the hell would he know them on sight?"

"Sir, he looks through our mug books in the squad room. It's good that he did."

"Who the hell told him to look through the blasted mug books?"

"Sir, probably someone at the academy."

"Mr. Chow, did you know that Mr. Ong was very nearly shot dead yesterday?"

"Sir, John Vandyne and I were both there. We were looking out for David."

"Why couldn't you and the fine Mr. Vandyne have handled it yourselves?"

"Sir, there are three exits to the Doyers underground complex. There's no way to cover it with only two people. If you would read the report—"

"I've read the entire bloody report! I almost went blind because the typing was barely legible! Did you type that report?" Vandyne had typed it up.

"Yes, sir, and I apologize for the typing job. I'll do better next time."

"You could have taken along anybody else besides Mr. Ong. Anybody! Even Peepshow Geller! If you ever use Mr. Ong again on any dangerous case, I'll send you to the goddamn firing squad!"

"Understood, sir."

"He's my golden boy, and you don't get to cloud his mind!"

By the time he dismissed me my ears were ringing, but I shook it off.

Poor Peepshow. He was a guy who was going to walk a beat his entire career. If you get branded as incompetent early on, your career is pretty much dead. Sure, you'll get the union-mandated raises and cost-of-living increases, but promotions? Forget about it.

There was no way Peepshow was ever going to pass the sergeant's exam to go up the supervisor track.

If he had wanted to become a detective, it was even tougher because it was discretionary. Someone higher up would have had to take a liking to him and toss him some investigative work.

But nobody was ever going to hand Peepshow an assignment, much less a cup of coffee. He was going to be forever the overweight and goofy white guy whose only pair of jeans had a rip in the lower-ass area. The ultimate insult was that not even the C.O. would use his real first name anymore. In fact, everyone had forgotten it.

VANDYNE CAME OVER to have dinner with Paul and me.

"That fucking Brow," I said.

"Cheer up, man. It's guys' night," said Vandyne. "I know I shouldn't have, but I went ahead and splurged." He held up a box from Dunkin' Donuts.

"Did you get any éclairs?" asked Paul.

"Hey!" I said. "The first words I want to hear out of your mouth are 'Thank you'!"

"Thank you," said Paul.

"That's all right, Paul," said Vandyne. "It wasn't much trouble at all and, hell, I even used a coupon! Actually, I should be thanking you, little man, because I know Chow didn't have much of a hand in cooking."

"You're wrong there, partner," I said. "I stirred in the tomato sauce and I added in a secret ingredient."

Paul and I had prepared Sloppy Joe filling from the package directions, but it didn't have enough taste, so I put in some crushed red pepper—not a lot. It was definitely a meal for guys. The sides came out of chip bags and we drank soda out of the cans.

"This is what Saturday night has come down to, Chow," said Vandyne. "Sloppy Joe night with Paul."

"Are you having a bad time?" asked Paul.

"Oh, no no no! I'm worried we're boring *you*! You're still in the prime of your life with a great future ahead. It's a shame you have to spend a weekend night with two crazy vets."

"One more doesn't make a difference."

We all laughed at that. Paul was growing up into a pretty decent ballbuster. Vandyne pushed his chair over to the window and cracked it open.

"You guys don't mind if I smoke, do you?" he asked.

"Go ahead," I said.

Vandyne touched a lit match to his cigarette. He blew out the flame, dropped the match in his empty soda can, and said, "Paul, don't you ever dare start smoking. It's a dirty and disgusting habit and the industry that backs it is racist against men of color. All colors."

"I've already tried smoking," said Paul. "I didn't like it."

"Don't ever start again," said Vandyne.

"And don't ever drink, Paul," I added.

"Okay, don't smoke and don't drink," said Paul. "Anything else I should remember?"

"Study hard and get into a decent school," I said. Suddenly I noticed that I had a Sloppy Joe blotch on the arm of my shirt. I stuck it in my mouth and sucked on it.

"Chow tells me you have a shot at Columbia," Vandyne said to Paul.

"I work there now."

"What do you do?"

"I do a lot of things. I help catalog sea-floor sample cores and do some computer-card programming. I'm starting to build a database that will take years to finish."

"That's smart," I said. "You fix it so that you're the only one who understands how to use it and then they have to keep you around to work on it. I'm thinking this will make you a shoo-in for college at Columbia when it's time."

Paul shrugged. "What I do isn't that hard. They could probably train someone else to work on it."

"That's why you have to develop some sort of filing system that no one else can figure out," said Vandyne. "Then no one else can learn it."

"But the value of the core database is so that anyone can use it. What's the point of collecting information if only a few people know what's going on? You guys read newspapers. How would you like it if they held back on the news they were giving you?"

"Tell me something, Paul," said Vandyne. "What sort of application is there to knowing the sea cores?"

"There are a few. We can determine climate conditions in the past, evolution of marine life, and we can also determine stratification. That's important for oil discoveries."

"Now *that's* where the money is," I said.

"Yes!" said Vandyne. "That is the kind of information worth keeping from others! You could get rich from that!"

Paul sighed. "The main thing, though, isn't where the oil deposits are, of course. A lot of them are known. The big problem is getting the oil out."

"You just stick a straw in there," I said.

"Great," said Paul.

"You could study that when you get to college," suggested Vandyne.

"I could," said Paul. "Say, Mr. Vandyne?"

"Please call me John."

"John, you play guitar, right?"

Vandyne exhaled heavily and dropped his cigarette into his soda can. "From time to time."

"I saw you play at that ceremony for Robert a few months ago. You're really good."

"Thank you very much."

"Do you think you could teach me how to play?"

"Wait a second," I cut in. "Aren't you busy enough with school and work?"

"I want to learn how to play for fun. I'm allowed to have some fun, right?"

"In all honesty," said Vandyne, "if you're just looking to mess around for fun, you're not going to get far on the guitar. It's a serious instrument that men and women have signed away their souls to."

"You looked like you were having fun playing," said Paul.

"I've been playing for fifteen years, Paul. I'm just starting to have fun now. My mother forced me to learn it to keep me off the streets. I only had about a week to learn each song and she didn't know how to play guitar. I had to teach myself so maybe I wouldn't be a good teacher."

"How did you get that guitar?"

"It was my father's."

Vandyne looked like he was going to reach for another cigarette when Paul said, "Do you want to hear the Ramones?"

"I've heard of them, but I haven't heard them. Do you like them?"

"Paul," I said, "Vandyne doesn't have time to listen to that crap.
That stuff is for degenerates."

"The Nazis called art degenerate, too."

"I'm not a Nazi. Look at this album. They dress like degenerates
and name their songs 'Now I Wanna Sniff Some Glue'? There's no
socially redeeming value to it."

"You know what?" asked Vandyne. "I think I *do* want to hear
it. A little bit, anyway."

"You're in for a treat," I said. "Paul got this record from some
wacko college liberal coworker."

"I got it from my boss," he said. "She's a doctoral candidate in
environmental engineering."

The opening chords blasted out of the speakers and Vandyne
flinched. But he was tapping his foot during the second song. Paul
studied his face, but there wasn't much to read.

"Had enough?" I asked Vandyne. "I think I have."

"For now, that's enough," he said. "You know, Chow, it's not
great but it's not as bad as you think it is. Comes across something
like Chuck Berry without the guitar solos or leads. A lot of chords
packed in there—a lot of the same ones."

"I want to play like that," said Paul.

"No, you don't," I said. "That's not even playing a guitar. That's
just sliding a cheese grater across the strings."

"I could hear a blues progression," said Vandyne. "It's not that
hard to learn to play. Do you have a guitar, Paul?"

"Yeah," he said.

"You do?" I asked.

Paul took a padded guitar bag out of the closet, laid it flat on the ground, and unzipped it. Inside was an acoustic guitar that was a little scraped up but still in decent shape.

"Where the hell did you get that from?" I asked.

"My boss said she didn't need this one anymore. She has three more and this one is a beginner model."

Vandyne picked up the guitar and looked it over. He strummed it a little and frowned. "It's missing two strings and the ones left need to be tuned, but that's not a big deal at all. Neck is straight and all the tuning pegs are still there."

"How are you going to pay for it?" I asked Paul.

"She gave it to me. She was going to give it to one of the Goodwill stores, but I said I would take it."

"This thing is only worth about fifteen bucks," said Vandyne.

"That's still money," I said. "Paul, you have to give your boss something."

"I pick up groceries for her in Chinatown so I'm helping her out."

"I have extra strings at home that would work on this," said Vandyne. "I could get this thing back into good shape."

"Do you have time to teach Paul how to play?" I asked.

Vandyne smiled. "Sure."

"Paul, when you play, I don't want to hear chainsaws going off."

"It's an acoustic guitar, Robert. It's not that loud."

"It won't be bad, Chow," added Vandyne. "Paul won't be anywhere near as loud as that record."

"So then this is good news to me," I said. "But Paul, if your grades or your work start to suffer, you're going to give this thing up."

"Let me handle it, Robert!"

"Jesus, this better not start you off on a path of smoking dope and then dropping out of school before you get to college."

Vandyne said, "I'll make sure he only plays the clean-cut notes."

"Worst comes to worst," said Paul, "I'll just be a cop."

"That's it," I said. "Vandyne, you get his legs!" I pinned Paul's arms behind his back and he yelled like he was at summer camp.

I MET MY mother in a small teahouse on Baxter. A booth that sold ching-chong crap near the entrance was obnoxious enough to practically block the teahouse door with a stack of fake hair queues attached to skullcaps.

A middle-aged hostess with her hair in a bun seated us in a booth near the back and dealt us menus.

"Pardon me," I told her. "You should tell the guy out front to move his stand back a few feet. That old buzzard's hurting your business."

"That's my father!" she said.

"He looks good," I said. The hostess glared at me and then slowly slipped away from our table.

My mother kicked me under the table. I knew what she was going to say, but I was going to have to wait a while before hearing it.

My mother lived by herself in a brownstone apartment past Bay Ridge in Brooklyn in a suburban Little Italy. She moved out there from Chinatown not too long after my father died by falling from a roof to the street. He had been drinking.

My mother never drank, and studied whenever she could. Because she had learned English so well, she had gotten a job sorting eighty-column cards in Midtown while my father was still waiting tables. Now she supervised the department.

She took off her huge shades and unwrapped her scarf. Mom kept trying for that Jackie O look.

Her face was calm as she scanned the menu, but she was good at covering up how she felt. In fact her face was as smooth as a scoop of Breyers vanilla, and her skin was about the same color with fewer black flecks. My mother was in her late forties and the only time wrinkles appeared on her face was when she was telling me what I was doing wrong with my life.

"You insulted that woman," she said under her breath and without looking at me.

"I knew you were going to say that. But I insulted her father, not her."

"If you insult her father, it's an insult to her, too! If someone insulted you, it would also be an insult to me!" She looked at me directly. Her brown eyes were on fire, but they had lost quite a few flames after I had discovered a rather uncomfortable fact or two about my family a few months ago.

"I'm sorry, I forgot," I said. "We're all the same person."

Still nearly whispering, my mother said, "I heard that Lonnie was the last person to see Mr. Chen. Everybody I know read that interview, but I don't dare to tell my friends I know her or that she is my son's fiancée."

"Girlfriend!"

"Whatever you call it!"

"Neither of us is ready to get married, Mom." I was annoyed at myself for also speaking softly.

"You're never going to be ready to marry a murderer!"

"She's not a murderer!"

"How do you know she didn't kill that man?"

"Because I know her!"

"These girls from Hong Kong. You don't know what they're like!"

"She came over when she was six!"

"That doesn't mean anything. Look at how she was raised. Look at the parents. Her father divorced his wife! What a shame that is."

"So her parents got divorced. That makes her a killer?"

"All criminals come from bad families! You know how many people in jail had divorced parents?"

"We're in America, Mom! Every other marriage ends in divorce."

"You see? That's why there's so much crime in this country."

I sat back in my seat and noticed that a waitress had sidled up to us. I didn't know how long she had been there.

"Should I come back?" she asked. The uniform here was a dark blue polo and slacks, and it looked good on her. The girl would be attractive when she was older and all the acne cleared up.

"We're ready," I said. We got a pot of decent black tea, sandwiches, and coconut-covered toast.

"Maybe it's time to find someone else," my mother continued in her hushed voice.

"You're talking crazy, Mom."

"Don't you understand? Her parents are divorced!"

"You think they should have stayed together?"

"Of course! If you want your children to turn out okay."

"You would have never divorced Dad? You two weren't happy together."

"We would have stayed together to the end. That's the duty of parents. Sometimes, I think . . ." She stopped and her eyes began to water. "I think if he were still here you would have turned out better."

I took in a deep breath and let it out. "Mom, he didn't die until I was already an adult. The war was what really screwed me up and, honestly, all my drinking." I thought a little bit. "You didn't do anything wrong," I lied.

The waitress came back holding our teapot and cups in one hand while the other carried against her waist a beat-up metal tray with our food. She put down the teapot with an awkward thud and shakily transferred each dish to the table from her tray.

The teahouse's training program was clearly slipping. Actually, they probably didn't have a training program and they probably weren't paying this girl shit.

"Thank you," I said. She did a micro-curtsy with her head down and left.

"Do you think she's good enough for you?" my mother asked, her voice a little closer to normal.

"She's not the greatest server, but maybe, in time, we could grow to love each other."

"Not the waitress! Lonnie! Don't you think you could find someone better?"

"I did find someone better."

I cut the coconut toast in half and glanced at my mother to catch her annoyed face, which suddenly turned into a look of alarm. I looked where she was looking and I saw that the guy who ran the souvenir booth was standing next to me.

"How are you doing, sir?" I asked.

"I heard you had some comments about my business." When he was done talking, he jutted out his jaw and wrapped his bottom lip over it.

"I was just saying that it was a shame that a man of your stature had to work such long hours in the cold."

"That's not what I heard you said!"

"Honestly, that is what I think!"

"You young people have no manners. You think you can say anything you want without consequences. I'm going to remember your little insult and so will my entire family!"

It helps to know that saying "sorry" is useless in Chinese culture. Forgiveness isn't seen as a value. We pray for good luck, money, long life, and happiness, but we don't pray for those who have caused us injury. No way. We're not even dumb enough to pray that others forgive us.

I don't even think that Chinese Christians believe in forgiveness. They probably think the expression "turn the other cheek" means "try to hit your enemy with your cheek."

If Chinese people forgave each other, it would shatter the plot of every kung-fu movie.

Despite knowing all of this, I said, "I'm sorry."

"Just you wait," the old man muttered before leaving.

"You never think about your reputation, do you, Robert?" asked my mother.

"*My* reputation? He was insulting you, as well!"

"We can never come back here. Not until this place closes and someone else takes over."

I looked at the pimply waitress serving another table as if the ground were moving.

"It might not be long, Mom."

I WALKED BY a dark brown Buick Regal sedan parked on the west side of Bowery. It was in front of a fire hydrant but what really got my attention were the Bicentennial diplomatic plates from Washington, D.C. That meant Taiwan because they were from the Republic of China embassy.

If the diplomatic plates were New York, that would have indicated the United Nations mission of the People's Republic.

The windows were tinted and the only things I could see through the right rear passenger's window were what looked like a tissue box on the backseat and a suit bag hung over the other rear passenger's door.

It was after eleven at night. All the places that serve decent food had closed hours ago. What was left open was unfit for even the lowest-ranked foreign official.

I came around and looked through the driver's window at the seat. I wasn't able to glean much more except that the steering wheel was sheathed in leather. Why couldn't people place their identification on their seats when they left their cars?

"Excuse me, sir," asked a woman's voice in Mandarin. I stepped back from the car and saw in the window a reflection of an attractive woman in a camel-hair coat. I turned to look at her and realized that the glass had distorted the woman's face. She was ordinary looking, in her mid-sixties, with shiny coal eyes and a dull red mouth with smudges along the bottom lip. It was tough to tell what her hair looked like but it must have been on the short side to fit up inside her beaten brown leather cap.

"What do you want?" I said.

"Oh, I just wanted to tell you something." No man had probably ever spoken to her roughly before. She pouted a little. "But I want to know first if you are a policeman or not."

"I am a policeman."

"Here's what I have to tell you. I was coming down the block when I saw two men looking at you. One of them said to the other that you were a cop and they ducked into an establishment near the intersection with Pell."

"An establishment?"

"Yes. I believe it's a gambling parlor. So maybe you want to go over there and look for them."

"Oh, so that's the pitch."

"What's a pitch?"

"Let's go back a little. As you were coming out of the gambling parlor, you noticed two guys who were looking at me and talking."

Her face flushed. "I wasn't gambling."

"I'm not here to bust you or anything. Tell me more about these two guys."

"They both were holding little leather bags, like what doctors used to carry. It seemed a little suspicious."

"And they ducked into New Tang Dynasty."

She crossed her arms. "Yes."

"What did these guys look like?"

"They were both tall. Taller than you. Both of them were sort of built. Dark-skinned army guys. You know what I mean?"

"I do."

They were either Taiwanese or ethnic Chinese from the Golden Triangle in Thailand loyal to the KMT government.

Taiwan had a mandatory two-year military service for all men and you had to do it before you could get your college degree. Most of them served out their time on one of two offshore islands held by the KMT that were close to the mainland. If the People's

Republic wanted to launch a takeover of Taiwan, those two islands would be invaded first. Such an operation didn't seem imminent but that didn't stop China from pounding the islands with mortar shells for the hell of it.

If the woman's description was right, these guys could be a hit squad sent here to find Mr. Chen's murderer. I sure hoped they were from Taiwan, because if they were from Thailand they were probably a lot more ruthless and wouldn't hesitate to shoot a cop.

I crouched to get a good up-close look at the car's rear license plate. It seemed to be real, and as I recalled from my talk with Mr. Yi, it likely was real.

If I went into the gambling parlor, I'd be taking a big risk. We'd been warned to stay out of illegal gambling sites not only because it would implicate us as taking bribes, but it would also jeopardize any sting operations in place.

If I waited by the car, those two men could slip away for good, leaving the car, which could be driven away later by a Taiwanese official with no penalty. Not even Peepshow was dumb enough to ticket a car with diplomatic plates.

"I'm going to go into New Tang Dynasty," I told the woman. "I think you should go home."

"I'm going to hide inside this doorway in case they double-back and come out before you," she said. "I love the detective shows."

"If you're going to stick around, then stay out of sight. Seriously."

"I won't even move," she promised.

NEW TANG DYNASTY, like all illegal establishments in China-town, was sweating it out in a huge way. In the November election, New Jersey was going to vote on whether or not to allow Atlantic City to open gaming casinos and hotels in a bid to revive the area.

As I understood it, the town was in such crappy shape, a couple blocks of pawn shops would improve the city center.

The Chinatown underworld fought back by improving the gambling experience. New furniture and carpeting was brought in, along with better booze and free packs of cigarettes for big-time losers.

The street-level outer entrance was open, but just down the hall two skinny guys stood on either side of the main entrance to New Tang Dynasty. I walked down to the end, the too-bright fluorescent lighting buzzing like a swarm of flies over my head.

The skinny guys looked me over and the one with spiky hair touched the one with a crew cut and said, "He's a fucking cop!"

"Relax, guys," I said. I recognized the one who spoke as one of the guards who had stood outside of Together Chinese a week ago. "I'm here for pleasure, not for business."

"You can't take your gun in," said Spiky Hair.

"I was told it wouldn't be a problem."

"That's bullshit," said Crew Cut.

"Wait," said Spiky Hair. "He knows Mr. Song."

"Who's Mr. Song?"

"The big Commie!"

"So what?" said Crew Cut. "Maybe we should we ask Little Uncle?"

"Go get him. I'll tell him how extremely disrespectful the both of you were."

"Hey, don't be annoyed." said Spiky Hair. "We weren't told of any special guests tonight." Still, he wasn't sure what to do.

I opened my wallet and took out two fives. "One for each of you," I said. "Buy something to eat."

"He's all right," said Crew Cut.

"He is," said Spiky Hair.

"Say, did you two happen to notice a pair of guys who came in here probably five minutes ago?"

"What did they look like?" asked Crew Cut.

"Shut up," said Spiky Hair. "We don't see anybody. We don't even see this cop coming in. Understand?"

They opened the door for me. What idiots. No wonder these stupid kids shot each other all the time over nothing. I wished I had my camera to take their pictures for "Happy Memories."

I FOUND A waiting area with a small bar and three couches. Somewhere deeper inside were the gambling tables, accessible only if you checked out all right, and there's no way I would.

Heavy curtains covered the three walls. One man flailed his way through a part to my left and entered the room. There was a door back there, but to what? Pai Gow, chuck-a-luck tables, blackjack? A blackjack to the head?

I should have remembered that entering the gambling parlor would likely put me in close contact with alcohol. Here it was, right in my face. About a dozen men of all ages, including under eighteen, sat or stood around, nursing drinks. None of them had the disciplined look of soldiers. They were on the way out and judging by the lack of conversation, they were all losers.

The smell of the cheap liquor made the roots of my hair sizzle and I could feel my scalp begin to sweat. Microscopic droplets of watered-down whiskey drifted through the air every time an old man let out an uncovered cough.

I lost track of my thoughts. I tried to breathe through my mouth and leaned against the side of the bar to give my knees a chance to steady themselves. I leaned over and gasped.

"Are you all right?" asked the bartender, the only authority figure in the room. He looked like a nice guy. He was in his mid-forties, and stood at about five feet three with kind eyes that offered sympathy and gratitude to the gambler for keeping the boss fat and rich. "How about a drink?"

"No!" I barked.

"Buddy, take it easy. I know you had it rough, but luck don't come to negative thinkers. I was gonna offer you one on the house."

"Two dark-skinned men, soldier types."

"Huh?"

"Have you seen two men? With dark skin. Could be soldiers."

He shrugged. "Sounds like it could be anybody."

"They would have just come through. Right before me."

"Buddy, I don't know. I don't have a good mind for details."

"Over there, where that guy came in . . . what does that door go to?"

"The can."

"How about I go over there?"

"It's locked. You need to be buzzed in."

"Then buzz me in."

He put his elbows up against the counter. I could see the bottom of the tattoo of something on the top of his right wrist slide out from under his shirtsleeves. "Buddy, we're not going to have a misunderstanding, are we? You don't go through that door."

I marched straight for it. I heard a chirp of white noise from a walkie-talkie behind me.

I reached the wall and tore the curtain aside. The wall was made of cinder blocks encrusted with cement. The metal door was solid steel with only a handle on it. I pulled on it but it was like trying to tug a battleship onto dry land. I gave it all I had and I felt something in my back come apart.

The bartender was on me with his right hand on my shoulder. I could tell that he'd been working on his grip.

"Chow, is it?" he asked me. "Do you want to walk out on your own or do you want a booster kick?"

Another idea had entered my head.

That woman outside was their lookout! She had gotten rid of me so that they could hop in their car unseen and get away!

And who said there were two men? There could have been four or just one.

I broke away from the bartender's grip and stomped through the door I had come in from.

"Good night, boys," I said to Spiky Hair and Crew Cut on the way out.

"Come again," said Spiky Hair.

On the street, I saw that I had been right. The car was gone and so was the woman. I walked up to the spot by the hydrant where it had been and cursed myself for not writing down the plate number.

I heard some sobbing from the shadows.

I followed the sound to a stairwell leading to a below-the-sidewalk store entrance and saw a homeless person curled up at the bottom.

It was the middle-aged woman who had spoken with me earlier.

"They pushed me down here!" she wailed. "They kicked me!"

I helped her up the stairs. She wasn't hurt badly but was extremely shaken up. There wasn't even any blood and she was more dirty than bruised.

"They told me to mind my own business."

"Let me take you to the precinct," I said.

"No no no."

"At least let me get you to a hospital so they can check you out."

"No hospital. I need to go home. I've learned my lesson."

"There were two men?" I asked her.

"There was nobody. I didn't see anything."

I watched her scurry away. It was an unsettling sight. Now I knew I could be dealing with men who wouldn't hesitate to rough up an old lady.

DAVID ONG HAD tipped me off that Mr. Yi, the Taiwanese official in New York, was going to be at a dinner banquet thrown by the Greater China Association. I ambushed Mr. Yi by the escalators to the Ocean Harmony restaurant and I rode up backward and slouched to get face-to-face with him. Other members of his staff leaned on either side from behind him to get a look at me. It was a long ride for an escalator, three flights.

"Mr. Yi, I think we had visitors from Taiwan two nights ago," I said. "They had diplomatic license plates from Washington." I acknowledged one frowning face behind Mr. Yi. "Hello, Ms. Kung. How are you? See, I'm Robert Chow, not some maniac. Well, Mr. Yi, what do you have to say?"

"I don't know anything about any car from D.C. coming in," he said.

"These guys roughed up an old lady for just being a bystander."

"I'm sorry to hear that. She should report it to the police."

"They scared her off that."

The first floor, crowded with loud parents and running children, slowly slipped by. In any other restaurant or building, this would be the second floor, but then that would make the top floor the fourth floor, and four was a bad number for Chinese people. So the fourth floor was Ocean Harmony's third, and the ground floor didn't have a name.

"Robert," said Mr. Yi, "I don't know what to say. If she didn't report it, then how did you know about it?"

"I was there and I talked to her about it."

"Did you witness the assault?"

I felt my face flush up. "No, I didn't."

"Then we're talking about something that's theoretical in nature and unsubstantiated."

"Try this on for a theory: You could tell your man in Washington that there could be a situation in which he and his island country are extremely embarrassed. Say, a Chinatown shoot-out in which bad men carrying Republic of China identities are killed."

"I don't tell Washington anything, all right? I can't warn them or advise them on what to do. It's a one-way communication line and I'm the one taking orders."

The second floor, which was either rehearsing or staging a wedding, drifted by.

"Have you heard anything about Republic of China agents driving around Chinatown?" I asked.

"You're the first one to tell me, but I'm not surprised."

"Apparently, they were spending some time gambling." Mr. Yi shook his head sadly.

"The most rational and efficient people, unfazed by guns or torture, lose their minds and get sloppy when you dangle cards and chips in front of their faces."

We hit the third floor, and I stepped aside. Mr. Yi slipped around to continue our private conversation and signaled his entourage to stay back.

"Robert, they don't even tell me the full details of the dinners that I go to. In that sense, I'm in the same boat that you used to be."

"Barbara told you about those days, I guess."

"Well, I've also seen your face and your expressions in pictures in the Chinese newspapers. They help me to remember to keep a big smile on."

"Then I did some good after all."

"Listen. If it does come down to a shoot-out, I hope you get those guys. It would be for the best. For the future."

Mr. Yi left me and rejoined his group. Before he entered the dining room, I saw him bow three times to a portrait of Sun Yat-sen, the claimed father of both the People's Republic and the Republic of China.

THE CONFUCIUS PLAZA complex is a gigantic housing complex that sits at the intersection of three different gangs' turfs. When the project was being built several years ago there were massive protests organized by college-educated Asian Americans to force the contractor to hire Asians. The contractor caved and the plaza was built.

The buildings of the complex sat on a triangular plot of land bounded by Bowery, Division Street, and the Manhattan Bridge approach, while Pell Street ran into Bowery from the west and pointed right at the entrance to Confucius Plaza.

Bowery, which ran northeast and southwest, had a lot of restaurants, the dirtiest of which were open twenty-four hours a day to cater to Chinese cabbies and everyone else who worked night shifts.

Division, which ran east and west, was crowded during the day with mobile stands of fruits and vegetables and the odd clothing hawker.

Pell Street, just to the north of Division, was home to businesses including travel agencies, insurance brokers, barbershops, and some more restaurants.

Bowery had a number of tourists walking up and down it because it had a wide sidewalk and was marked as being the eastern end of Chinatown in the woefully outdated tourist maps.

Only white people who were lost walked down Pell, with its forebodingly dark, narrow, and slanted walkways, or Division, with its crowds of noisy open-mouth-chewing Chinese people.

Which was fine for the gangs who considered Pell, west of Bowery, and Division, east of Bowery, as fighting grounds for territory.

Retailers on the ground level had to choose the association they wanted to be affiliated with while the kids who grew up in Confucius Plaza had to choose what gang they wanted to be affiliated with.

Kids were typically recruited by being jumped and beaten into submission. Parents were no help to kids because they were probably working sixteen-hour days and were too tired to do anything but eat and sleep. Teachers and principals were no help because they'd tell the kids to try "talking" to the "bullies." The police were no help because the police were no help. Believe me, by the time a kid resorts to asking a cop for help, he's been beaten up by a gang because he belonged to a rival gang.

The girls only held the guns for the boys, but they could fight better hand-to-hand. It was true that girls couldn't throw baseballs, but they could throw punches and land them hard.

The joint-precinct Asian gang task force that was supposed to launch was put on the back burner for some bullshit administrative reason. I think the adjoining Seventh Precinct needed to replace some copier machines and some squad cars. Holding a press conference to announce that we would form a task force was deemed to be enough to address the problem for now.

I didn't think I'd ever be put in the position of saving a kid from the gangs again, but here I was. I had been waiting to hear something, anything about the Mr. Chen case, but nothing seemed to break. Those guns from the apartment mailbox weren't ready to talk to me, either.

So when the midget called and told me that Drew Bai had come into work at the toy store with a black eye and his face all puffy, it was something I felt I could address right away.

Drew lived in Confucius Plaza and had to cross Bowery near Pell to get to the midget's store. But he got jumped and was told to join the gang or next time he would get his face cut. He was talking about maybe making a list for me of all the kids who had assaulted him.

Of course, in the minutes it took for me to get to the store, he decided there wasn't a problem after all.

"I'm going to be all right," Drew said. "Don't worry about it."

"You're not going to be all right," I said.

"Do you really want to know the names of the kids?"

"Actually, that would be pretty useless because not only are they minors, but we'd have to establish that they were present."

"So it's a useless situation, isn't it?"

"Just stay prepared and be smart about where you go."

"The next time they come, I'm going to have some help with me."

"What kind of help?"

He didn't say anything.

"What kind of weapon are you going to carry?" I asked.

"I'm gonna have a gun!"

"That's great. Even if you managed to shoot someone, don't you think they'll come at you with two guns?"

"Then I'll join a rival gang."

"And then you'll end up jumping another kid to try to force him to join your gang!"

"What else can I do? I'm not going to be scared to walk around Chinatown. This is my home. At least when you're in a gang you have some protection. Somebody is watching your back."

"You remind me of a young man who thought he had no other option than being another stupid gang kid."

"Yeah, yeah, I know about Paul. He lives with you now and he's going to go to Columbia and everything. But you can only help one kid at a time, right?"

"That's right."

"So tell me what I'm supposed to do. I can't just fade into the background. I can't move in with relatives in California."

I looked at the midget. He was leaning against the front display case, his jaw set hard. We both knew the answer to the problem.

"Drew," I said, "you can't work here anymore."

"No!"

"Don't even cross Bowery after school unless you have friends with you."

"I need this job."

"You're a smart kid, you'll find something else. There's a lot of opportunity right now for a hard worker like you. Maybe you could work at school or work at a place within Confucius Plaza."

He was quiet because he knew I was right.

"Look, when you go to college, you're going to have the last laugh because these gang kids are going to be in jail, or in the hospital, or maybe dead."

"Take it from Robert," said the midget. "He was in a gang as a kid and he saw what a lousy life it was. Look at him now."

"I'm not so sure I'm a good example," I said.

"Yeah, you're sort of like the dented can in the supermarket, but you're all I've got right now to show the kid," said the midget. We chuckled a little bit. "Seriously, Drew, it seems like you don't have a lot of options right now, but if you play it smart, you'll see that you really can do anything."

Drew said, "They might come back at me."

"They might," I said.

"I was thinking about the guy from China who was killed: Mr. Chen."

"Why were you thinking about him?"

"He was probably ambushed like I was."

"I'm not so sure about that."

"I'm pretty certain about one thing, though."

"What?"

"If he had a gun, he'd still be alive or at least have a better chance of being alive."

"No, he wouldn't. He'd still be dead and there would be one more unlicensed firearm in the hands of criminals. Where would you get a gun from, anyway?"

"I heard about a guy who sells weapons."

"Who is this guy?"

"He works in this after-school program."

"Who?!"

"I don't want to tell you!"

"You want another black eye, wise ass?"

"Robert!" said the midget. "Enough!"

I THREW OPEN the door to the BDC After-School Program. The alarm went off again. I couldn't hear anything but I saw Lincoln at the far side of the room, looking over something on a conference table.

I didn't see Sunny Chu, who pushed a flat hand against my gut. For a middle-aged woman, she was tough. I pushed against her and Sunny began to shake from the effort of holding me back. Lincoln managed to cut the alarm.

As soon as it was quiet, Sunny asked me, "What do you mean by busting in here?"

"Oh, excuse me," I said. "I was just going to test the constitutional limits on free speech and the use of excessive force on Lincoln."

"What did I do?" asked Lincoln.

"Don't listen to him," Sunny told him. Then to me she said, "Get out! I'm filing a complaint about you!"

"You enjoy working that much with someone who sells guns to kids?"

"He sells what?"

"You heard me. Your cute little thing over there peddles firearms to children. You probably stash them in the apartment mailboxes up and down the street."

"This is a big misunderstanding," said Lincoln.

"What am I not understanding?"

"I tell the kids I sell weapons. When they come see me, I give them this." He reached inside his pocket.

"Slowly," I warned him. He pulled out a red plastic box and held it out to me. I didn't reach for it, so he turned it over. It was Mao's little red book. In English.

"Knowledge is a weapon," Lincoln said triumphantly.

"You're giving this to kids?" I asked. All I needed to read was the opening page.

WORKERS OF ALL COUNTRIES, UNITE!

"How the hell is this supposed to prepare our youth for today's job marketplace?" I asked.

"Once they are armed with the words of the Great Helmsman, nobody can stand in their way."

"Not even Mr. Chen, right?"

"Of course. He kind of got what he deserved. A traitor of the Revolution."

"Then why are you sitting in this crappy office with your crappy quasi-governmental job? Aren't you a fully indoctrinated Maoist? You haven't done shit with your life."

"I'm working on it."

"I know you're working on it. That's why I'm going to sic some people on your ass. You won't know what hit you."

"When *our* time comes, Robert, you'll be one of the first to know. You and all the running dogs of capitalism."

He actually made me laugh. "I'm a running dog of capitalism? I'm in a union, jackass. You're a manager. You're the big boss man."

"No, I'm not!"

"Of course you are. You work with kids because you like to boss them around and tell them what to think."

He yanked back his book. "You don't get to have one of these."

"Too bad you can't read Chinese," I said. "The book really loses a lot in translation."

VANDYNE AND I were sitting in a plain sedan across the street from Lincoln's apartment. I pulled the tab off a can of Coke. The fizzing sound of the soda broke the silence between us.

"You're kind of quiet tonight," Vandyne said.

"My goddamn back," I said. "I pulled something that night in the gambling parlor."

"Don't ever tell anybody you were there. It will be your ass."

"You're the only one I told."

"Good."

"Vandyne, I was just thinking. Right now, we're doing the same thing to Lincoln that those Manhattan South guys are doing to Lonnie. Sitting tight, waiting for them to do something to let us build a case against them."

"There's a difference, though. Lonnie is innocent."

"Of course she is. As much as Lincoln is dirty. But I can't help but think that, maybe, he didn't murder Mr. Chen."

"That's not your job! Leave that for the Justice Department to weigh in with their reasonable doubt."

I played with the soda tab a little bit in my right hand and patted the roof of the car with my left. "Is this it, man? I mean, is this really what being a detective is like? Being trapped all night in this coffin?"

"You have to suffer for your art, don't you know that, Chow?"

"I'm no artist." I turned to Vandyne. "But you are. I mean you could be one. You're a guitar player and you're really good!"

"Thank you for the compliment, but I'm just an all-right guy."

I punched him in the arm. "C'mon! I've heard you play, man!"

"In all honesty, I don't practice enough. The other cats who play for a living, they would eat me alive. You have to play every day, or else you just backslide. Just like what you said about learning to read Chinese."

"That's true. You skip a day and everything starts going gray. But wouldn't you rather be playing guitar than doing this?"

"It's too late to do anything else, partner! When they put a gun in my hand, it ruined me for almost anything else. I guess, except for being on the other side of the law." He pointed his hand like a gun and said, "Pow! Pow! Pow!" as he picked off imaginary targets in the street.

I laughed. "I know what you mean. I'm not going to teach kids how to sing or become, you know, a productive member of society."

"So now you're a part of the freaky fringe protecting decent folk from the sickos and crazies."

I played with the soda tab some more. "They should draft people to go through bullshit like this."

"Naw," said Vandyne. "I like being here, spending time with you." He sniffed. "Guess I'm not good enough company for you."

"I never said that." I flipped the tab onto the floor mat.

"Hey," chided Vandyne. "You're littering! You know, other people have to use this car. We're not the only ones."

"You polluted the air and the whole insides of the car," I said.

"Yeah, but at least I put the cigarette out in the ashtray. I didn't throw it on the floor."

"Just wait until Jimmy Carter takes office. He'll put an end to your smoking with his new clean-air laws. Oh, wait, you don't want him to win."

"He could win. Actually, after that stupidity of President Ford with Vernon Jordan, I can't back him anymore."

In some ads placed in black publications, Gerald Ford was pictured standing next to Jordan, the head of the National Urban League, and other black leaders. Jordan had demanded that the ad be removed, as it seemed like he was endorsing Ford when in reality he was backing Carter. The White House at first denied planting the ads, but later admitted it and put an end to them.

Vandyne said, "The second I saw that ad, with that opportunist Jesse Jackson in it, I knew it couldn't be genuine."

"That's the guy from Operation PUSH, right?"

"How do you know about PUSH? It's based in Chicago."

"Then why is he in New York all the time?"

"Exactly. Jackson does good things, but he's in it partly for the publicity."

A light went off in Lincoln's apartment. Even though neither of us had been looking directly at the window, we immediately shut up and focused on the building door, waiting for someone to come downstairs and pop out of it.

Lincoln came out, shivering in a surplus field coat.

"That motherfucker," I said.

"Dressing like he was in Nam," said Vandyne.

When Lincoln was farther down the block, Vandyne started up the engine and we rolled slowly toward him. Lincoln didn't go far. Soon, he was back in his favorite restaurant, sitting at a table with his pals.

"This is too much excitement for me for one night," I said. "I think I'd rather see an empty street than watch people sitting around."

"They have to break it up sooner or later, though," said Vandyne. "When they leave, we can split up and follow the top guys."

"Hope that happens soon."

"They're all guys. How long can they sit around and talk?"
Vandyne eased back his seat. "You'll see."

Two hours later, after both of us each had used our own empty
Thermos bottle, Lincoln and his friends were still at it. One guy
would write something on a piece of paper and pass it around,
leading to a round of arguing. Then the guy would cross out what
he'd written with exaggerated annoyance and write something
else. That led to more arguing.

"This is like watching the drafting committee of the Declara-
tion of Independence," I said.

"Then they should charge people to watch them and take
advantage of the bicentennial year," said Vandyne.

"These guys are Commies. They wouldn't go for touristy stuff."

"Just make them live up to 'All men are created equal.' Then
I don't have any problem with it." He paused. "Now that I think
about it, that phrase does have a Communist ring to it."

"We may all start in the same place, but we all take different
roads. Some people get handed the maps where everything is
marked out and labeled." Hearing no reaction, I turned to face
Vandyne directly. "You know, the map is already marked where
all the good and bad stuff is, so you know where to go and what
to avoid."

Vandyne turned to me. "I'm hungry," he said quietly.

"Me, too. What should we do?"

"We've got to tough this one out. I didn't think this would last
long, but here we are."

"You never hear about cops going hungry. Usually it's the other extreme."

"Oh, you don't need to tell me. It's not like you and me need it. We're in the best shape in the whole squad."

"You see the one with the mean face?" I asked.

"Yeah, with the wrinkled forehead."

"I've seen him at the livery-cab office, but I know him from somewhere else, too. I couldn't find him in our, uh, vacation photo albums." I hunched my shoulders and leaned forward to get a better look. I saw someone pull on a jacket. "Looks like it's breaking up."

In silence we watched the five men exit the restaurant. The mean-faced guy was a beacon with his orange knit cap on. He went in the opposite direction of Lincoln, who for some reason was headed away from home.

"Mean Face," said Vandyne, and pointed to himself. I nodded.

When they were all far away enough, Vandyne and I exited the car and closed our door with clicks quiet enough to have come from ballpoint pens.

I walked north as Vandyne headed west.

Lincoln walked quickly, sometimes hopping on his heels. When he reached a dark spot on the sidewalk between two dim streetlights he stopped and turned to the wall.

Should've gone back at the restaurant, pal, I thought. I could write you up now for public urination, but I want to save you. I want to see you swing for killing Mr. Chen.

He zipped himself up and kept going. His breath in the air looked like an empty thought bubble over his head.

I followed him as he stepped off the sidewalk onto the street.

I WAS SEARCHING my right pants pocket for a stick of gum when I felt someone tap me on the shoulder. I glanced back quickly and saw Teresa.

"You like watching guys pee?" she asked in bad Cantonese. I guess that's not fair to say because Cantonese, slangy by nature, disregards formal rules of grammar the same way that pedestrians ignore crossing lights in New York.

"It's my job too," I said. We didn't stop walking but we kept our voices low. "What are you doing here?"

"I'm following Lincoln. I think he's seeing someone else. Why are you following him?"

"Who says I am?"

"You want me to call out to him?"

"No!"

"You think he killed that Chinese official, don't you?"

"I didn't say that."

Lincoln turned a corner and Teresa and I both picked up the pace so we wouldn't lose him.

"He couldn't have killed Mr. Chen," she insisted.

"Where was he that night?"

"Honestly, I don't know. He could have been with someone else."

"Who?"

"I'm trying to find out now!"

"Then how do you know he isn't a murderer?"

"He doesn't have the guts. He only knows how to boss women around. Lincoln talks about socialism and equality, but he's a chauvinist. If he met the real Communists, they'd execute him with a firing squad of girls!"

"Let's keep it down, huh?" We watched Lincoln enter an apartment building on Canal Street.

"I guess that's what those two extra keys are for," said Teresa with a sigh.

I stopped and fished again for my gum.

"Why are you stopping?" she asked.

"I have to wait for him to come out," I said, putting the gum into my mouth. I rolled the wrapping paper between my fingers before tossing it into the street.

"I'll be damned if I'm stopping here!" She marched off to the building. I followed. I might not find a killer, but at the very least I could prevent a domestic assault.

Teresa was stronger than I thought. She ran up the building's front steps like she was storming a castle. When she reached the door she quickly pressed every apartment button in order two times through before someone got annoyed enough to buzz her in.

She held the door for me. "Are you coming?" she asked.

"I am," I said. "You're not carrying, are you? I don't want this to get messy."

"Carrying?"

"A weapon."

"No!"

Just on the remote chance that this was some kind of setup, I made sure always to keep Teresa in front of me.

The foyer was a typical Chinatown example, meaning that it probably didn't meet fire-safety codes.

The ceramic-tile floor was mostly pulverized, as if people worked out with free weights here and dropped them at the end of each set. Paint was peeling off the wallpaper that was peeling off the tin-sheet wall that was peeling off. At some point a chandelier had been hanging from the ceiling, but now only three curled wires were left, looking like the fingers of a dead witch.

"Where did he go?" Teresa asked as she looked up the stairs.

"You sound like a cop," I said.

That got to her. She took the stairs two steps at a time. The first door had a baby crying behind it. The second door was slightly open to create a breeze to help ventilate the apartment as someone cooked. Sounds of a news broadcast in Cantonese from the KMT-biased radio station came from the third door. The volume was turned up high, so it must have been elderly people listening.

"Try the next floor," I suggested. Again, I let Teresa take the lead. The heels of her cheap black shoes thundered in the stairwell. I felt a little bad for Lincoln.

The first door on this floor sounded like people were playing a game of air hockey. Someone was operating a sewing machine behind the second door. Soft jazz came out of the third door.

Teresa turned to me with a questioning expression on her face.

"There's only one thing soft jazz is good for," I said.

She moved to the third door and the doorknob turned in her hand. Teresa swung open the door. The music was coming from the bedroom. We tripped over some shoes in the hallway and we could hear people laughing.

Teresa yanked open the bedroom door. A wave of smoke came out and the smell brought me back to Nam. It was pot.

The lights were down low but we could make out four guys all circled around an impressive bong shaped like a standing Buddha.

"What the fuck is this?!" cried Teresa.

"What are *you* doing here?!" countered an indignant Lincoln. He knew it wasn't going to work.

"I work two jobs and you use my money to buy drugs!" She pointed at the other four Chinese men. "Do all of you work for a living? Or are you all gigolos and pimps, too?" She was met mostly with snickers.

"I have a job!" Lincoln declared.

"That's not a job! You play with kids all day! You don't know what real work is like!"

"I get paid for it, Teresa, so it must be a job!"

"Then why are you always asking me for money?"

"I get in a tight spot sometimes." He was backing off. You can't corner a man about his cash-flow problems in front of his friends without making him feel like a naked little boy. "Let's talk about this at home," Lincoln concluded.

"You're not going home! This policeman is here to arrest you all for drug abuse!"

"Hi, guys," I said, stepping out from behind Teresa. "Actually, the charge is drug possession, not abuse."

"Hey, what are *you* doing here?" asked Lincoln, now even more embarrassed. The only thing worse than getting a dress-down in front of your homeboys was getting dressed down in front of a man you don't know.

"I'm here to save your neck. Now let's break it up here. The party's over." I went to the stereo and switched it off. It was a nice amplifier. A lot nicer than mine.

The men stood up and groaned and grumbled. "Don't push me," I said. "If you don't want to leave on your own, I can call in escorts." I turned to Lincoln. "Whose place is this?"

"It's our place. We all split the rent on it. We keep the apartment to house friends who come in from out of town. Also, none of us wanted to keep the bong at our own apartments." With a sheepish look at me, he added, "We didn't want to get busted."

"You're lucky that I can't make a case out of this. I'm sure there are all sorts of privacy rights I'm violating by being here right now and I'm not going to try to fight it. But I'm putting you on notice. You work with kids. If I ever see you with drugs again, I won't rest until you're fired."

Teresa stepped in. "Get him fired from that stupid job so he can make some real money and be a real man!"

"You're not helping things," I told her.

"You see," Lincoln told Teresa, "even he's on my side!"

"I'm not on anyone's side!" I said. I eyed two stragglers in the hallway. "Let's go, let's go!"

When everyone had finally exited the apartment, I set the lock on the door and closed it behind me. I wasn't thankful for much that night, but I was glad they left the building quietly. Even Teresa and Lincoln walked quickly away, side by side. What was Teresa's problem?

I MET UP again with Vandyne at our usual rendezvous point—the stoop of the Fifth Precinct.

"We're not supposed to be sitting on the stoop of the House," said Vandyne as he walked up to me.

"I know. It looks bad. Cops loitering past midnight," I said. I stood up. Vandyne put one foot on the bottom step and looked up at me.

"You don't want The Brow to find out about this. He's ready to pounce on you for anything right now."

"He can pounce on this right here," I said. Vandyne laughed.

For a long time, before I started investigative assignments, I was sort of The Brow's little soldier boy. I used to go to all the community functions to represent the precinct and show that the

NYPD really cared about restaurant openings, school gradua-
tions, and stupid association banquets. When Izzy went over his
head to land me a spot in the detectives' squad room, The Brow
took it as a personal offense that my career had advanced. But now
he had a replacement for me.

"How long you think David Ong's gonna last?" asked Vandyne.

"You mean Ong Kong Phooey?"

"Don't make fun of him."

"Why not?"

"It's making fun of your own people."

"He is not one of my people, and besides, it is a good name for
him. Crying on the job and then I'm the one who takes shit from
The Brow for it."

"Maybe he is the right guy for that job with that timid
personality."

"Next time someone reaches for something under their seat at
one of those banquets, David's going to pull out his gun and start
shooting."

We shared a good laugh; then we got back to business. I told
him about the Lincoln-and-Teresa adventure. Vandyne told me
about how Mean Face simply went home—and also why he looked
familiar.

There had been a group affiliated with the Communists that
had been protesting the tour buses that came in and dropped off
tourists so they could act like ugly Americans in their own country.

These tourists would do obnoxious things such as sticking
cameras into people's faces and taking flash shots. They also
felt they had the right to touch the hair of little girls as if there
was a sign hanging from the lampposts that read: MOTT STREET
PETTING ZOO.

The KMT-affiliated tour company that operated the buses was incensed that the protest group would greet arriving buses with signs that read: GO BACK TO EUROPE! Naturally, these tourists were herded to patronize KMT-affiliated restaurants and gift shops, and if they felt unsafe, they wouldn't spend as much or come back.

The next time the Communists showed up to protest the buses, a pick-up group of KMT youths stormed in and a street fistfight broke out. In the confusion, one Communist kid was hit by a bus that was trying to back up. That kid was Mean Face.

"Vandyne, did he get broken or bruised ribs?"

"I don't remember, either. But the bus driver wasn't charged."

"Maybe we should call him 'Baby Bad Ribs.'"

"That's funny, but I like 'Mean Face' better. It's more to the point."

"Should we eat, man?"

Vandyne patted his stomach. "I still got it pretty bad. Let's make it quick. I want to get the paperwork done and hit the sack. I got a big day tomorrow."

"What's going on tomorrow?"

"Rose finally agreed to meet me for lunch."

"Wow, that's great news," I said, not inquiring further.

I MET MR. SONG at the ground-floor conference room at Together Chinese Kinship's office.

"What do you have to tell me?" he asked.

"I was just thinking," I said. "Are there any fringe Communist groups that would want Mr. Chen's killer dead?"

"Damn, you just come right out and say what's on your mind, don't you?" He shook his head. "I'd be lying if I said a great many Communists weren't relieved Mr. Chen is dead. There are a few who are very unhappy about it, but I doubt they would take any action."

"Are you sure?"

"I'm as sure as I could be, which is to say about ninety-five percent sure."

"Five percent is a pretty big margin of error."

"Look, Robert, the Communist Party is asking for your help in clearing their name in the murder. Why would they use their other hand to invalidate that work? If the Communists were implicated in killing the murderer, it would look like they were covering their tracks. We need that man brought in alive!"

"Are there Communist agents in Chinatown now?"

Mr. Song gave me a sour look. "And what constitutes a Communist *agent*, Senator McCarthy? We prefer the term 'comrade.' We have many comrades in Chinatown. Our numbers are less than those loyal to the KMT, but in a way we regard them as comrades as well. All Chinese are involved in class struggle, whether they know it or not. Even you, Robert."

"Look, I'm asking you about fringe groups because I know the other side has radicalized elements that are looking for someone's head. They regard Mr. Chen and Li Na as heroes for challenging the mainland."

Mr. Song tugged a handkerchief from his pants pocket and blew his nose. He folded the handkerchief and left it on the table-top. "Let me tell you about heroes, Robert. When privileged individuals in China worry that they will lose their status and seek to set themselves up in America, with a protected position, these people are not heroes. They are bandits. They are no different from the KMT soldiers who looted treasures from the museums of China as they made their cowardly retreat to Taiwan."

"You're forgetting that Li Na is the daughter of Mao."

"She is the daughter of evil Jiang Qing, too! She holds none of the Great Helmsman's cultured qualities. A mere blood relation to a great man has elevated her status for years. But now that Mao has passed away, a reckoning is on the way, and it will not be kind to Li Na."

"It wasn't kind to Mr. Chen, either."

"Mr. Chen has benefited from his ties to the Li Na clique. He would have also been reevaluated had he not had the misadventure of coming here.

"But make no mistake. He was not killed by a Communist. We are not brutes."

"Yes, you would have tortured him and sent him to a labor camp."

"Reeducation camp."

"What could he possibly learn there?"

Mr. Song smiled and stuffed his handkerchief back into his pocket. "The bitterness of life that we sometimes forget."

ROBERT, ARE YOU stupid?" the midget asked for a second time. We were crowded into his toy store's stockroom. He was halfway up a shelf on a ladder, so we were eye-level with each other.

"I already said that I wasn't."

"Then why the hell do you continue to visit Mr. Song?"

"I'm just looking for clues."

"You're not going to find any there! I also know you saw Mr. Yi at the Taiwanese office in Midtown."

"How did you know that?"

"I have sources all over. From running this store, I know all Chinese people who have kids. And all Chinese people have kids.

But listen, if I could find out where you've been, almost anybody could."

"I'm careful."

"No you're not! There are some ruthless people out there and they wouldn't think twice about killing a cop, especially a stupid one!"

"Stop calling me 'stupid'!"

"Then stop acting stupidly! Every time you step into and out of Together Chinese Kinship or the Taiwan office, you're telling the world, 'Hey, I support this political stance!' A Chinese cop on the wrong side would be worth more dead than alive in this propaganda war. Particularly now. You could be killed just to send a message, Robert.

"Both the Communists and the KMT are desperate. The Commies want that official diplomatic relationship with the U.S. and want Taiwan out right goddamned now. The KMT has threatened to join the Soviet Bloc if America severs ties and recognizes Beijing."

"No way in hell would that ever happen," I said. "Chiang Kai-shek founded the International Anti-Communist League!"

"You don't know your history, Robert! The KMT's early advisers included Russian revolutionaries. Chiang's own son lived there for many years and even married a Russian woman. Although the KMT did break ties with the Soviets, there is no one else apart from the U.S. who could feasibly offer Taiwan protection should the mainland attack."

"I still can't see that."

"Of course *you* can't," grumbled the midget.

"Will you give me a break? My Lonnie's neck is on the line here. I would pray to both Mao *and* Chiang if I thought it would help me with the case. But before it comes to that, if you could offer any thoughts, I would really appreciate it."

The midget came off the ladder and slapped his hands clean on his slacks. "This is what I think," he said. "I think whoever killed Mr. Chen is reckless. This was not a planned killing. You don't plan to murder somebody by bashing him in the head. Blood gets all over your clothes. If you really wanted to take somebody out, you use a gun from a distance."

"Wasn't that part of the message, though? That Mr. Chen wasn't even worth the cost of a bullet to kill?"

"I seriously doubt it. If the intention is to kill, there's no surer way. You don't know how hard heads are. You could pound somebody as hard as you could with a baseball bat and he might be able to run away, screaming bloody murder."

"What if your victim was restrained?"

"But Mr. Chen wasn't, was he?"

"No."

"I figured."

"Could his own guards have killed him?"

"They were contractors with the U.S. government. I seriously doubt they had the motives or initiative do so."

"Then who?"

"This was not a professional hit. It was a personal or political act. Maybe both. So keep an eye out on extremist groups and extremist people."

"The only one I've met so far is that guy Lincoln from the Union of the Three Armies."

"That stupid group? You know they've been recruiting kids to spray-paint their name all around Chinatown?"

"Could they be responsible for murder?"

"Do kids know how to swing a bat?"

STRANGELY, PAUL LOOKED distraught when I came home.

"Where were you?" he asked.

"I was at Great Adventure. They have this really cool water ride they only open up after midnight, and it's for cops only."

"Are you done?"

"Naw. I'll probably go tomorrow night, too."

Paul stared at me, frowning.

"Okay, stop it," I said. "You're killing me with that face."

"Lonnie wanted to talk with you. She's having a hard time at work."

"What's the problem?"

"Her editor is rejecting more of her stories. She used to write four or five short wire stories daily. Now she hasn't had a byline in two days."

I called Lonnie and she answered on the first ring.

"Yes?" she asked.

"Lonnie," I said.

"Robert, I think I'm going to lose my job! Instead of firing me directly, they can keep rejecting my stories so my editor can say I haven't been productive enough. I'm not a part of the union yet, so I don't have any support."

"Those motherfuckers."

"Have you found something out yet?"

"I sort of have a lead, I think. I'm trying as hard as I can. You know, I'm trying to top Manhattan South's best detectives and it's tough."

"I saw the Chinese U.N. representative in the hallway and he ran away to avoid me."

"It's a political issue, Lonnie. The People's Republic has a news blackout on Mr. Chen."

Lonnie sighed into the receiver. "I should go back to the bakery to work. Maybe the harassment would stop."

"No, you can't do that!"

"I guess I was never meant to leave Chinatown."

"You stay at the U.N., Lonnie!"

"You don't know what it feels like, Robert! I'm writing and rewriting stories all day that aren't published. I feel completely useless!"

"I promise you, I'm going to help put an end to this. I'm going to sic the detectives on this other guy instead of you."

"You already found a suspect?"

"I have this guy in mind."

"Do you think he did it?"

"I don't know. But he's a more likely suspect than you. He was protesting Mr. Chen at Jade Palace and he also said that he got what he deserved."

"That's a terrible thing to say. Mr. Chen was not a bad man."

"This suspect I have in mind—apart from being a loudmouth, he treats his girlfriend lousy."

"Do you think he did it, Robert?"

"He could have done it."

"I don't want you to switch the suspicion on to someone else who's innocent. I know how it feels and it's awful."

"I'd rather they focus on anybody else but you. Even me. But it won't be me."

"You have to find the killer, Robert. Do you understand?"

"I will."

Paul walked into the bedroom as soon as we were done talking.

"Paul, were you listening in or did you want advice on what to wear for Halloween?"

"I don't do that stuff anymore. Besides, Halloween is on a Sunday. That's a study night." He crossed his arms. "I'm worried about Lonnie."

"Everything's going to be fine."

"You're just saying that."

"I'm not just saying it. I believe it."

WORD HAD GOTTEN to us that the American Civil Liberties Union was preparing a lawsuit over our practice of taking Polaroids of suspected gang kids.

The detective squad hid the cameras in the highest kitchen-supply cabinets. We stashed the photo albums in our bottom drawers, pretending they were our personal photos. I realized that I didn't have many genuine pictures at all. I couldn't even fill up a single album.

Of course, I would be the most suspicious out of all of us for having these albums in my desk. A Chinese guy taking tour pictures in Chinatown? No way. Maybe the Upper East Side or Central Park.

With the cameras gone and access to the photo albums now shut down to the rest of the precinct, we had to readjust our operations to keep tabs on suspicious characters. The new methods were going to test our limits. English fished out a thesaurus from Lumpy's desk and gave it to me before we went out.

Because Vandyne was helping me out with tailing Lincoln, I backed him up on the latest crap assignment, which was writing down detailed descriptions of youths.

We sat on adjacent benches at Chatham Square, where Bowery, East Broadway, Worth, Division, and Mott all met up. Neither of us wore gloves so we could write with our bare hands. We each had a cup of hot coffee to pass between our fingers to keep warm.

The Kimlau Memorial Arch towered above the square. The arch itself didn't say what had happened to Lt. Benjamin Ralph Kimlau, a Chinese American who had fought in World War II, but I knew that the Japanese had shot him down. I'd be mad at Japanese people but I knew a lot of Americans of Japanese descent had also fought bravely in the war. Paul told me that groups of Japanese Americans were rounded up into internment camps for the duration of the war, but I didn't believe him entirely because I had never read about them anywhere.

Chatham Square was a good place to get a look at the kids walking around because it was close to Drew's home, Confucius Plaza, the biggest subsidized housing project in Chinatown. The project itself was to the north on Bowery above Division.

At the square we were close to the active gang boundaries near Confucius Plaza. On top of that, Bowery was the unofficial border between KMT-affiliated Chinatown, to the west, and Communist-affiliated Chinatown, to the east. More tourists were on the west side, but the growth was on the east side, where the liberal-minded and college-educated youth bought up Mao badges from the Cultural Revolution to wear to their comparative-literature classes.

There was usually a lot of action in this border zone. The Pagoda Theater nearby on Catherine saw shootings as regularly as the weekend matinee was changed. I also thought about poor Drew's face.

"The guy in the blue ski jacket," said Vandyne. "Would you say he has a skinny face?"

"Wait a second," I said, as I paged through the thesaurus. "I would actually use the word 'lean.' That seems like the right word. Chinese people have extra fat in their cheeks so I would never say that one had a 'skinny' face."

Vandyne measured up his guy against markings on a nearby streetlamp pole.

On Vandyne's suggestion we used pieces of duct tape to mark out heights of four, five, and six feet on poles, signposts, and building corners. Now we could get good approximations of height to go with our otherwise abysmal descriptions.

"There's Mean Face," I said, tipping my head in his direction.

"There he is," said Vandyne. We watched him push up his knit wool cap and scratch his forehead. "If anybody ever says a guy with a mean look on his face did something, we're going to swing by and pick him up."

"He drives a car, so we should call and make him pick us up."

"Exactly. Why should we waste the gas? Goddamn sixty-five cents a gallon."

"Whoa! I'm glad I don't have a car."

"If you did, then you could take Lonnie out for a weekend trip."

"A trip where?"

"Well, there are some really nice gardens to go see."

"Gardens?"

"Out in Pennsylvania, the guy who founded DuPont set up a huge garden that covers his estate. It's open to the public and it's a nice place to take a girl. I'm only mentioning it because I'm going to be taking Rose there."

I was so happy I nearly fell off my bench. "That's great, Vandyne. I guess lunch went pretty well?"

"Yeah, it did."

"So you guys are figuring on getting back together?"

"Maybe, man, maybe. We're just going to take it really slow. I think getting out of the city will help give us perspective."

I nodded. The last time I saw Rose it was a few months ago in a Chock Full o'Nuts and she was crying to me that she and Vandyne never talked anymore. Not too long after, she left Vandyne in Elmhurst, Queens, for her sister's home in Manhattan, a four-story brownstone with a view of the Hudson. The sister was married to a Chinese-American doctor who probably went to Midtown for Chinese food.

"You guys have already met up a few times in the city, right?" I asked.

"Few times. I think the best time was going to see Labelle in concert."

"That must have been great. I've heard those three girls go crazy onstage."

"You should have seen the outfits they had on, it was nuts."

I noticed that Lincoln was walking toward us from East Broadway. When he saw us, he picked up the pace.

"Aw, shit. This guy's gonna give us away," I said.

"Shit."

"Hey you guys," said Lincoln. "Thanks for following me around and harassing me."

"We're harassing you?" I asked. "You came running up to us. We're sitting here by ourselves minding our own business."

"I know what you're doing. You're taking pictures of kids. You've already convicted them in your minds just like how you're trying to set me up for the murder of Mr. Chen!"

"I'm also gonna pin a few more murders on you, Lincoln. All the cases I can't solve."

"There must be a lot of those."

"Go back to your bong, Lincoln."

He pointed to the thesaurus in my hands. "Reading on the job, huh?"

"It's a thesaurus."

"Find a synonym for 'pig.'"

Vandyne spoke up. "Listen, Lincoln. For your information, I want you to know that it's probably best not to give us grief. I'm a fairly rational person but my partner here can be provoked pretty easily."

"You're threatening me? We're both people of color being oppressed in a capitalist prison run by whites. You need to see things as they are, brother."

"Don't you 'brother' me!" snapped Vandyne. "Chow's my brother, not you!" Lincoln shook his head and walked away.

Hearing Vandyne say that made me feel good. I hoped as hard as I could that things would work out with Rose.

I sipped my coffee and looked for stupid gang kids that I could write lean descriptions of.

I THINK I'M going to have to find a new job, Robert," said Paul. We were at the Chatham Square Library. I was reading through back issues of Chinese-language newspapers to see if there was something I had missed that could be crucial to Mr. Chen's case.

"Why would you have to find a new job?"

"Think about it. If Carter wins, then there's going to be a big push into alternative energy. Solar energy, wind energy, and geo-thermal energy. We're going to cut way back on fossil fuels, and that means less money for oil exploration. That's going to zap the research funds for my department at the geological observatory."

"Don't be ridiculous. This country is always going to need oil like it needs doctors and lawyers. Your friendly local oilman isn't going to cut back on research. He's looking out for the next big oil patch." I felt something hit my foot. It was a toy car. I kicked it away.

"They won't stop their own internal research, but they'll cut the public research they fund. For the sake of public appearances, they'll reallocate those funds into solar-panel research and wind turbines. The oil companies will even take out big advertisements saying how they're actively researching renewable energy."

"You're paranoid, Paul. Nobody is ever going to think a big oil company is seriously looking into something that will make it extinct."

"If the political tide turns against your company or your entire business sector, you don't have to change what you do if you can change the public's perception of your company." He looked thoughtful. "Maybe I should be studying communications."

"Maybe you should be communicating less so that I can read in silence."

He made a face and opened another book. I wondered about Paul's generation. He and his friends could speak Cantonese fairly fluently, but I didn't know anybody his age who could read Chinese characters. In fact, I was the youngest person I knew who could. That meant that I was among the last of the Chinese Americans who could read the language of his ancestors.

I guess I could try to help Paul learn it, but I had been a lousy student and that probably made me an even worse teacher.

I read through several days' worth of the KMT-backed newspaper and got almost nothing new. The Communist-backed paper continued its blackout on Mr. Chen's death. The Hong

Kong–backed newspaper had news only about celebrities and businessmen, and Mr. Chen had been neither.

IT WAS EARLY morning and I was on my way to the precinct when I saw Mean Face a few yards ahead of me. It was too good a chance to pass up.

I followed him down to the corner and then came around to the exit of a three-level garage where the dispatch-car companies kept their Lincolns Continentals.

I tried not to smile. This was where my gang used to prowl, one of the best places to hack off "Continental" emblems. That was how we got our name, and collecting emblems was a way to solidify our collective identity.

We were all U.S.-born kids and when the immigration laws changed in the early 1960s, all these other kids came in from Hong Kong and tried to push us around. There was nothing like beating someone up and leaving a Continental emblem shoved in their belt.

The Hong Kong kids weren't stupid, though. They got in good with the associations and pretty soon they had nice clothes, nice hair, and guns. The Continentals faded away because we knew, as native English speakers, that we weren't going to be trapped in Chinatown the rest of our lives. These streets weren't worth a fight to the death for us.

I didn't want to kill anybody until I was in Nam.

I ducked into the parking garage and looked around. The stairwell was where I remembered it. My eyes fell upon Mean Face, who was sitting on a concrete bumper.

"Hey," I said. "Don't I know you from somewhere?"

"We don't have to pretend, Officer Chow. I know who you are. You know who I am."

"I know who you are but I don't know your name."

"Call me Lee."

"All right, Lee. Are you loitering here?"

"You want to play that game?" he asked, rising to his feet. "Fine with me. I won't tell you what I know."

"What do you know?"

"Well, I don't know where the guy with the mole is, the driver you're looking for, but I do know someone you might be looking for even more."

"Who?"

"I think I know who killed that diplomat guy from China."

"Who killed him?"

"You've been following him around! I'm surprised you haven't been able to shake it out of him. It's Lincoln!"

"How do you know? You were there with him?"

Lee shifted his weight and crossed his arms. "You keep pushing me like this, I can stop right now."

"Hey, I only said that because you're his second-in-command, aren't you? You play backup at the Union of the Three Armies."

He narrowed his eyes. "We're co-leaders of the group. Equals."

"Except you never killed anybody, right? The worst you ever did was throw snapper pops at tourists." Those were the China-town novelty toys, crystals wrapped in paper, that made loud popping sounds when they hit the ground. A tourist would think someone was firing a gun at their feet, trying to make them dance. "You drew an assault charge from that, didn't you, Lee?"

"It was dropped in exchange for an apology!" He crossed his arms. "After that, I stopped protesting the tourist buses and got a real job, driving cars."

"I wish more of our shiftless young men followed your example. So what were you going to tell me about Lincoln?"

"Well, it's just that after the killing, a few of the guys in the group were sort of wondering about Lincoln. Where he was that night."

"He wasn't with you?"

"We were waiting at the usual spot. OK Noodle. You know, where you were watching us."

"You saw me?"

"Naw, I didn't. Teresa told me about it."

"So you guys were all sitting around, eating and waiting."

"Yeah, mostly waiting because it was his turn to treat. Luckily we're regulars there, so they let us put it on a tab, but still . . ." Lee shook his head and dug his hands up into his armpits.

You don't screw over Chinese people when it comes to food or money, and certainly not both. You'll hear about it every day for the rest of your life.

"So Lincoln was AWOL," I said. "Then what did you guys do?"

"Everyone went home, but I was worried. This was probably two in the morning at this point. I stopped by his apartment and he wasn't there. Teresa said he hadn't been in all night."

"Then what?"

"I waited with Teresa because she was so worried. She was freaking out, man. And that motherfucker never came back."

"When was the next time you saw him?"

"Not until the next day, in the afternoon. He came to the food cart where I always get my lunch."

"Where's that?"

"Division and Bowery. The old woman who runs it has Hakka food like pork and fermented tofu."

"Yuck. Why do you want to eat Hakka food?"

Lee gave me a hard look. "Because I'm Hakka."

"Oh."

"And so is Lincoln, even though he can't speak Hakka."

"The Hakkas have a long and proud history. You people are really hard workers."

Hakkas were originally a migratory tribe in central China that later settled in the southeast and in Taiwan. Of course, the people already living in the areas that the Hakkas settled in regarded them as barbarians who only happened to know how to bathe and clothe themselves.

Hakkas seemed to have a knack for being at the forefront of political change. Sun Yat-sen and Madame Chiang Kai-shek were Hakkas. So was Mr. Chen.

The funny thing is that the casual Cantonese observer can't tell if someone is Hakka by appearance or even surname. Hakkas maintain their identity through their unique culture, which includes the Hakka dialect and their food. It is hidden like a secret power.

"You know what the problem is with Hakka food?" I said. "It's way too salty. That's bad for your health."

"It's salty because Hakkas were always manual laborers and you Cantonese forced us to live on the land that was hardest to farm on. We used to sweat so much we needed to eat salt to get it back into our system." Lee looked me in the face. "You *are* Cantonese, aren't you?"

"I consider myself Chinese American. But let's get back to your Hakka friend, Lincoln. You saw him at the salty food cart and then what?"

"I asked him if he had heard about Mr. Chen. By then, it was all over the place."

"How did he react?"

"Well, even before I asked him, he was looking terrible. His eyes were bloodshot and he was acting all jumpy. I asked him why he didn't come to the restaurant and he told me to tell everyone that he was sick and spent the night at my place."

"Did you tell him that you were over at his place? With Teresa?"

"I told him I stopped by. Let's get something straight right now. I would never mess around with Teresa."

"Because she's not Hakka?"

"No. A good Communist respects personal relationships. We don't sleep around like Chiang Kai-shek and other dissolute KMT officials."

I thought about all the rumors of Mao and illiterate peasant girls but I decided not to bring it up.

"Well," I asked, "what makes you think he killed Mr. Chen? Just because he didn't make it home doesn't mean he's a murderer."

"He has been saying over and over that Mr. Chen should be executed for being a traitor to the Communist cause."

"Talk's cheap."

"When I saw him he was wearing an outfit he kept at our little clubhouse. He must've changed clothes there."

"I see."

"And Teresa said her rolling pin was missing. Lincoln must have taken it. And used it. You should search our clubhouse. You might find some bloody clothes."

"I'm not sure I believe you. If I check with Teresa, is she going to say the same exact things as you?"

"She might not want to talk to you at all." Lee rubbed his hands. "You have a bad reputation."

"I wouldn't think cops would be too popular among you revolutionary youths."

"You know that Teresa works at a restaurant, don't you?"

"I didn't, but thanks for the information."

"She was a server at those big community banquets for a lot of years."

"Oh," I said. I stuck my hands in my coat pockets.

"She said that you barely seemed conscious, and your breath was practically flammable."

"That was a long time ago. I'm not that way anymore."

"Actually, she did say that when you dropped in on Lincoln you seemed like a new person."

"I'm going to check in on Teresa. Thanks for ratting on your friend."

"I'm betraying a man but I'm true to the cause. I draw the line at violence."

IT WAS ALMOST noon when Vandyne and I got to Teresa and Lincoln's apartment. She answered on the first ring and buzzed us up. When she opened the door, she said, "Oh! There are two of you!"

"Are you alone?" I asked. I used English because her Cantonese was as bad as my Mandarin. Also, I wanted Vandyne in on the act, too.

"Lincoln is at work," she said, spitting out the words like they were candy gone bad. "Lee told me you would be coming over, but I thought you'd be alone."

"We have a few questions about Lincoln," said Vandyne.

"You talked to Lee, also?" she asked Vandyne.

"Chow did," he said.

"You never thought Lincoln was cheating on you at all," I said. "You think he murdered Mr. Chen. But I can't figure out if you were really checking up on Lincoln or following me to warn him."

"What do you think?" she said.

"I just told you what I thought!"

"Oh. I did not think Lincoln killed Mr. Chen. Until Lee told me his story. Lincoln and his Hakka friends are out of control! They all think they are Sun Yat-sen, but they are really a bunch of irresponsible jerks!"

"Even Lee?"

"Lee is the least bad. At least he is in a job with some future. Someday he is going to own the car he drives and then the real money will come in."

"Something I wonder about you, Teresa."

"What?"

"Your English is really good, especially for someone who just works in a restaurant."

"Take that as a compliment," said Vandyne.

"I work hard," said Teresa. "I practiced English two hours every day when I got here. I listened to language tapes from the library instead of music." To Vandyne, she added, "I really like black music."

"What kind of black music?" he asked.

"The dancing kind!"

"Teresa," I interjected, "why didn't you come to us before? Lincoln wasn't in that night and your rolling pin was missing, right?"

"It is still missing!"

"How come you didn't tell me?"

"I was not sure! I wanted to make sure!"

"How were you going to make sure?"

"I was going to make Lincoln confess!"

Vandyne cleared his throat. "What if he tried to keep you quiet?"

"Nobody keeps me quiet!" she said.

"I mean, dead quiet," he added.

"Oh. He could not do that."

I THEN DID something I should have done even before seeing Teresa. I checked up with the Department of Motor Vehicles to see what kind of guy Lee was. After a confusing phone call, I hung up and looked at Pete, who was sitting at his desk cleaning out one of his ears with the eraser end of his pencil.

"Hey, Pizza Man."

"Chow."

"A funny thing happened when I called the DMV to check up on someone's driving record."

"What happened?"

"They told me to talk to you."

"Oh. Who was it about?"

"This Chinatown livery-cab driver named Lee. He has a number of outstanding parkers and movers—enough violations to lose his license, apparently."

"I gotta keep that guy driving, Chow. He gives me a lot of good info."

"What was the last thing he tipped you off about?"

"Mainly tells me about suspicious people he picks up and where he takes them to. I busted a smuggling operation that was sneaking in dried fungus and animal parts because of him."

"I remember that thing."

"Of course you do. Probably the first time ever that a dried tiger penis was shown at a press conference. Now, why are you looking into Lee?"

"Well, he told me something. I wanted to see what his record was like. I only knew about him protesting buses and harassing tourists."

"I got news for you. Back then he was one of my guys, too." Pete narrowed his eyes and tilted his head. "He told you something, huh?"

"Yeah. You know his pal Lincoln? They're both in the Union of the Three Armies, that fringe Commie group."

"I've heard of the group, of course, and I think I know who Lincoln is."

"Lee seems to think that Lincoln killed Mr. Chen. He told me some bloody clothes might have been stashed in the group's apartment."

Pete pushed his seat back and stood up. "Let's go get him now."

"We don't have a warrant."

"We don't need one because he's going to open the door and show us around."

"I guess he's never given you bad info."

He picked up his coat from the back of his chair and punched his arms through the sleeves. "Only one time, and then I showed him not to fuck with Pizza Man."

Pete told Lee on the phone to meet us at Bowery and Canal by the Manhattan Bridge on-ramp.

Lee brought Pete, me, and Vandyne back up to the apartment where I had met Lincoln and his bong buddies. I spoke some Cantonese with him, but because we were in mixed company, I told Lee to switch to half-decent English.

"Second time you come here, huh?" Lee asked me.

"Second time's the charm," I said.

"Why were you here before?" Pete asked me.

"I think I saved Lincoln's life that night. His girlfriend was ready to kill him. She thought he was stepping out on her. Turns out she never knew about the little boys' club they have here."

Vandyne went in first. "You don't still have marijuana in this apartment, do you?"

"Oh, no no no," insisted Lee. "Never have, never have."

I snorted. "Where are the bloody clothes?"

"I don't know where he hide. Somewhere inside."

We split into three teams. I took the kitchen. There was little but bottles of spices and beer in the refrigerator. Vandyne took the tiny bathroom and the hallway closet. Pete searched the bedroom.

We met up again in the living room.

"I got nothing," said Pizza Man.

"Same here," said Vandyne.

I threw up my hands.

"That means it has to be in the living room," said Pizza Man.

"There's nowhere to hide anything here," I said. "There aren't even any cabinets or drawers around."

The room held only a couch, a TV, a coffee table, and four befuddled men.

"He must hide in apartment," said Lee.

"You don't know where they are, do you?" Pizza Man asked him. Lee shook his head. "If you do, you're an accessory to murder."

Vandyne walked over to the couch and picked up a seat cushion. "This has a foldaway bed in it, right?"

"Yes," said Lee. "Maybe he hide there!"

When we had the couch open, we unfolded the first section and there was nothing. The second section also yielded nothing. Vandyne and I were folding the mattress back in when Pete spoke up.

"Hey, there's something down there!"

We pulled the couch away from the wall, revealing a cardboard box that had been shoved between the back of the couch and the wall.

Pete grabbed the box and opened it. It was stiff with dried blood. A rolling pin caked with blood fell to the floor with a thump. A watch was wound around it.

"You got him!" said Lee.

Pete closed in on him. "How do we know Lincoln hid them there and not you?"

"I don't hide! Lincoln hide!"

"Then we need you to testify in court to this."

"No! You say I don't go to court."

"I'm only kidding, buddy! This is real good work you did for us today. Let me ask you one more question. How come you went to Chow and not me with this?"

"Huh?"

"Why did you tell Robert Chow and not tell me to my face what was going on, my little sheep?"

"Huh?"

Pete punched Lee hard in the stomach, knocking him to the ground. "I told you that you only talk to me, you little fuck! Get it?"

"Hey, now!" said Vandyne.

"Hey, nothing! Don't take it personally, Chow. It's just that I've been cultivating this guy for years; I need for him to keep me in on the loop on things like this."

"If it helps at all, I was the one leaning on him for info," I said. Lee rose to his hands and knees and I wanted to give him more time before he could reasonably defend himself or run away.

"Bullshit, you pushed him! I'll let it go this time, Lee, but remember, 'When Lee see or hear something, he come to Pizza Man.' Get it?" Lee nodded. "Still, I might need you to testify in court. Then again, maybe I don't need you."

Pete got on his radio and notified Manhattan South of the situation. They were over in about fifteen minutes. I read the watch inscription for forensics. It was only a few hours later that they had a warrant to arrest Lincoln and they picked him up right off the street.

I heard that that punk acted like he had no idea what was going on.

THE RECOVERY OF Mr. Chen's watch, Lincoln's bloody clothes, and an unspecified weapon caused a sensation.

NYPD Commissioner Michael Codd held a press conference to say that a suspect had been apprehended in the murder of the Chinese official. The NYPD press office issued a correction the next day to say that Mr. Chen had come to the United States as a private citizen and was not an official of the People's Republic, nor was he acting in an official capacity.

When I read that Lincoln had been arrested but had been allowed to post bail, I got worried. Teresa had a restraining order on him, so he holed up at his co-manager Sunny Chu's apartment in Brooklyn.

I couldn't find out where that was exactly. I showed up at the BDC After-School Program office and told Sunny that Lincoln would be safer in jail, but she only gave me two stink eyes. I thought she didn't like him, but maybe she was one of those women who had a thing for murderers.

She complained to the Fifth Precinct, so I got another earwax-clearing lecture from The Brow about harassing the people we were supposed to be serving. I stared at nothing on the opposite wall and wondered if maybe Lincoln would be smart enough never to leave the house.

Lincoln must have known he was in trouble, too, because when they found him on the sidewalk, he had two layers of metal from bean-curd buckets wrapped around his chest and back. That would have worked fine against the crappy Saturday night specials that gang kids had, but it did nothing to stop the three .44 magnums that tore through him, probably fired from a rifle.

His improvised protective vest was probably worse than nothing because it meant more metal shards ripping through his organs. In any case, he wouldn't have survived, with or without it. His unknown assailants must have wanted to get him badly because they had gone all the way to Brooklyn to do so.

How the assassins found him, I wasn't sure. But bad guys get more and better info than police because they pay people to talk.

It's NOT A priority case when something unfortunate happens to a guy who has basically been convicted in the press. Put the cellophane wrap on that one because it's headed for the cold-case file. The murder of a murderer in Brooklyn? Yeah, they'll get right on it, ha-ha. The guy wasn't even good-looking, for crying out loud, and his girlfriend had that restraining order on him.

"You're sure he's the one who did it?" Lonnie asked me. We were sitting in a coffee shop at the United Nations eating warm and damp croissants.

"Based on what I know," I said, "Lincoln seems to have been our man."

"But you didn't have any witnesses to the murder!"

"I'm sure some people would have come forward after seeing his picture in the news. Anyway, I don't want you to worry one more second about this crap. It's over and you're cleared. Just get back to work."

"But I wanted to cover his trial for the newswire!"

"Look at all the important work you have to do here!"

"Another press conference about another pointless meeting where another useless agreement was or wasn't reached."

"Don't put down your work," I said, saying the words firmly so that I believed it as well. "Your job is important and there are people counting on you. What seems stupid to you could mean a lot to someone reading what you write."

"I know, I know, I should appreciate what I have." Lonnie wisely decided not to finish her lousy croissant and chose instead to tear it into pieces as she talked. "I could still be back at the bakery."

"That's my girl," I said.

I MET THE midget for dinner at a Buddhist food restaurant. Essentially the restaurant's clientele was composed of practicing Buddhists and regular people in mourning. Also, there were a few diners who had gone to a temple for help and were told to avoid eating meat for a week and to make a donation to the temple to make the prayers more effective.

The restaurant used tofu, wheat gluten, and other shudder-inducing ingredients to fashion meat substitutes. Mock ham fried rice. Mock beef chow fun. Mock duck.

"Wasn't Mock Duck one of the old Chinatown gangsters?" I asked the midget. "When I was a kid, there was a ghost story that you could hear his chain mail armor rattling around Doyers Street at midnight."

"I'll bet he was a real hero to you when you were in a gang, Robert." The midget paused to sip some tea and grimace. "Jesus, even the tea tastes fake."

"Why did you want to eat here?"

"I like a change of pace every now and then."

"From good food?"

"You don't have to eat here, you know."

"But I guess you do." The midget said nothing. "Seriously, can't you tell me what's going on?"

The midget dismissed me with a wave of his hand, but the waiter thought this meant we were ready and came to our table. He was wearing a plaid vest over a dirty Tshirt.

"How are you, my friend," he asked the midget.

"I'm healthy. Maybe too healthy to have to eat here."

"I'm assuming you'll want the usual."

"The usual?" I asked.

"Gluten spare ribs and bean-curd fish, with brown rice," said the waiter, smiling.

"Why is he eating here?" I asked.

"We have the best food. He's been coming in once a week. Oh, and what will you have?"

"I'll have the same," I said.

"You'll be sorry," muttered the midget.

The waiter smiled as his eyebrows shifted into a worried look. "May I suggest something else so that you can try a wider variety of the menu and share dishes?"

"No, I want the same thing as him," I said. The waiter nodded and left. "Tell me why you've been coming here! You obviously don't like the food. Is there a cute waitress or something?"

"I sort of lost a game," he said to the floor. This was big news. No one had ever beaten him at anything ever. The midget was the master at chess—both American and Chinese, checkers, board games, and, hell, even pinball, I'd bet.

"You goddamned lost at something!"

"No. I said, 'Sort of.' This kid who is actually a pretty good toy customer was bragging that he could beat me at Connect Four. I said he couldn't. So then he bet me a free dinner at his parents' restaurant every week for a month if I won. I said he could have a twenty-dollar gift certificate if he beat me. Really, I only agreed to play a game with him to get the boy away from the display case he was blocking."

"You should've asked him what restaurant his parents owned."

"Well, I was planning on just saying, 'Forget it,' you know? So after I won, I said, 'Forget it.' The kid was crying his eyes out. He had no idea he was going to lose. But he also said that a bet was a bet and if I didn't take him up on it, the win didn't count."

"What did you say?"

"I had to go with the spoils of the win, the kid was right. But now that I think about it, he had the inside angle all along. He knows the food sucks here. He's always got beef-jerky breath."

Our food swung in quickly.

"Well," I said. "You don't have to actually eat it, do you?"

"I'm not one to try to weasel my way out of life's tougher lessons. In any case this will probably prepare me for necessary humility the day when I really lose a game." He picked up a fork and began to flake up the bean curd that was shaped like a fish fil-let. We both began to take tentative bites.

"The guy who was shot in Brooklyn," said the midget. "Did he kill Mr. Chen?"

"I think so."

"How do you know?"

"We have the best kind of evidence—circumstantial."

"Humph. Seems pretty awkward to kill someone with a rolling pin. Especially out in the street."

"It might not have happened in the open."

"Then where?"

"Who knows? We haven't found the actual scene of the crime yet."

"Do you know who killed Lincoln?"

"Do you?"

"Yeah, John Wilkes Booth." For the first time that night I saw the midget's familiar smirk.

"You're so funny."

"No, you're the funny one. You think that because you now got Lonnie off the hook everything is fine. There are still a lot of unanswered questions."

"The Chinese government doesn't care. The Taiwanese government doesn't, either. Both the Chinatown KMT community leaders and the Communist groups are happy with Lincoln dead. In my mind, this means that the case is closed."

"What if Lincoln was innocent?"

"No way."

"He didn't even get to go to trial. You have no idea what would come out."

"It's better that way."

"What if it was Lonnie, Robert? What if she had been formally named as the murderer?"

"She wasn't because she was innocent and the accusation was going to come out in the wash, anyway."

"Not everyone has a cop boyfriend. That makes it easier to pull strings and get some residual benefits. You did an awful lot of investigating that you had no business doing."

"I acted out of concern for the wasting of taxpayer money. I didn't even draw any overtime."

"You mean you saved your girlfriend's neck for no charge? Wow!"

"Let's put a leash on it. This meal's already bad enough." I looked out at the street and noticed a boy who was about eight years old staring at us through the window.

"Damn kid even spies on me to make sure I hold up my end of the bet," muttered the midget.

"You should take him home. I think he likes you."

LATER, BACK AT my apartment, it was Paul's turn to hit me up with questions about the case.

"Something really bothers me," he said.

"What?"

"Well, I'm sure you thought about it, but how did Mr. Chen even get to Chinatown?"

"He probably had someone on his security detail call him a cab."

"No, he didn't tell any of them where he was going."

"Then he probably took the subway."

"He didn't know any English. How would he know how to buy a token and where to transfer and where to get out?"

"It doesn't matter how he got to Chinatown from Midtown. Hell, maybe he took a brisk seventy-block walk. It's the murder we're focused on, not his transportation choices."

"Beyond that, why did Mr. Chen come to Chinatown so late?"

"You know what I honestly think? He was probably trying to find some girly action."

"He could have just stayed in his hotel room for that."

"Mr. Chen probably would have wanted *Chinese* girly action."

Paul crossed his arms. "You know they send women up to Midtown, right?"

"All right. I don't know exactly how or why Mr. Chen came down to Chinatown. All I know is Lincoln runs into him on the street at random, something in his head snaps, and Lincoln beats Mr. Chen to death with a rolling pin."

"A rolling pin?"

"Aw, dammit, forget I said that! It wasn't disclosed to the public."

"Why would a guy walk around with a rolling pin?"

"He probably felt more comfortable having some protection on him."

"A rolling pin?"

The details of the case clearly weren't coming together. Things seemed even more confusing now. But it was over already, right? Who cared if the pieces didn't fit correctly? Lonnie was in the clear now, so I had no more personal interest in the case, which, for all intents and purposes, was closed now.

This city has more than four murders a day. I'll bet more than half of them are of criminals who may or may not have been previously caught. The public thinks so, too. The victims reap what they sow, so to hell with most of them. To hell with Lincoln, too.

What was annoying, though, was Lincoln's street address that I had written so long ago on the back of my left hand still hadn't come off yet. I used up the squad bathroom's Lava soap trying to get it off. Seeing the faded yet legible letters made me think of those heated discussions I had had with the guy and I couldn't help feeling bad for him. It was true that I didn't like him, but it was a horrible way for him to go, and he was young.

The pro-KMT newspaper tracked down his parents in Northern Jersey. They said it wasn't fair that someone of his scholarly lineage should have to die like a dog in the street. They told Lincoln to come home after posting bail but he had refused. He had such a good heart, he wanted to stay in New York and continue reaching out to the lowly Cantonese youth.

His mother added that Lincoln couldn't have killed Mr. Chen. The hands that played piano and the violin so well for so many years couldn't be capable of murder.

The parents were photographed sitting at their kitchen table, holding Lincoln's framed bachelor's and master's degrees.

ON MY DAY off, I asked Izzy if I could have a look through Mr. Chen's effects.

"There's nothing useful in there," he said. "But you can have first bid on it when we auction it off."

"I don't want to buy it. I just want to see it."

"What are you looking for?"

"I don't know."

"At this point, why the hell not?"

Mr. Chen's belongings were crammed into a stiff, medium-sized black-leather suitcase devoid of characteristic marks. It seemed like something a Communist would have. I knew they had had someone fluent in Chinese go through it already, but I had to see for myself.

The property clerk was a snide skinny guy with a spotty mustache. "Something in this thing smells funny," he said. "Well, maybe not to you."

"And why not to me?"

"Because you're probably accustomed to it. Are you not Chinese?"

I grunted and he handed me the clipboard to sign out the suitcase. "Aren't we going to open this thing up and go through everything for inventory?"

"No, it doesn't matter at this point. Maybe you should just take it. I won't tell."

The suitcase was on the heavier side. He had packed only two changes of clothing and only one pair of shoes, but Mr. Chen had jammed in as many books as he could fit. He might have been apprehensive about the long plane ride and being trapped with nothing to do. I understood because people get the same way about the subway. Platform newsstands that also sell books do very well.

Everything reeked of the camphor and menthol from Tiger Balm or a rip-off of Tiger Balm. It's a well-known panacea among Chinese people all over the world. When labeled for the U.S. market, the packaging states that it relieves sore muscles. But Chinese people use it for all sorts of things—including hemorrhoids and swallowing something to treat sore throats—that would repulse the Singapore-based company that made the official Tiger Balm. Americans are shocked when they see it for sale because they think it's made out of endangered tiger bones, but it's not. Anymore.

I lifted out a stack of paperback books that particularly stank and found a smashed glass container of Tiger Balm underneath. The books were boring Communist reports of overly optimistic urban planning and overly optimistic harvest reports. In the next stack of books, I found something odd. It was a New York Chinese telephone book. Mr. Chen couldn't have brought this book over from China. It was printed in New York and was thinner and smaller than what a cop would expect of a phone book. A non-cop Chinese interpreter might have missed it as a clue. Whoever packed up Mr. Chen's belongings from the hotel room probably glanced at the Chinese characters and thought it was just another one of his books.

I thumbed through the phone book and tried to look up Lincoln Chin. The listings included the entire three- or four-character Chinese name, by surname, along with the English name that the person went by, if any, and the street address.

There are a couple of characters that could be "Chin" as a family name. The most popular one was a compound character that has the entire character for "east" incorporated on the right side, and this compound character was the same as "Chen" in Mandarin, as in Mr. Chen. The second most popular was the character for "gold." Lincoln wasn't listed for either character. I was about to try yet another variant of "Chin" when I realized something.

Lincoln was a loafer. He probably didn't take care of the phone bill. Teresa did.

I looked up Teresa Lee, whose surname was a tree character on top of a child character. It's a popular name. One story says the very first Lee was born under a tree, surprise-surprise.

Teresa was listed in the book and her name was underlined.

Mr. Chen had known Teresa!

I patiently flipped through the thirty pages of the residential section and no other names were underlined.

Mr. Chen hadn't placed any calls from his hotel room because he didn't want to leave a record. He had to have left his room to call from a public pay phone.

I looked at Lincoln and Teresa's street address on the back of my hand.

Now there was an explanation for Mr. Chen's missing index finger. He had written down Teresa's phone number on it. Maybe her address, too. Teresa had wanted to destroy the evidence that literally fingered her as the killer.

My next stop was The Plaza Hotel.

I packed everything back into the suitcase and zipped it up. The property clerk looked dismayed when I handed it back.

"You're bringing that stinky thing back?"

"I sure am," I said. "Take deep breaths. Tiger Balm's good for opening up your nasal passages."

I TOOK THE subway to The Plaza at the southeast corner off Central Park.

At the front desk I showed my shield to a mousy white girl who looked like she was still in high school.

I asked her, "Do you have a Chinese phone book here?"

"Yes, we do," she said, stepping back. She fingered a button on her uniform and then crouched down, holding on to the edge of the desk for balance. I watched the flesh under her fingernails pulse white and pink. "That's funny," she called out. "It's not here."

"I thought it might be missing."

She popped back up and straightened out a skirt I couldn't see. "Why would anybody steal it?"

"It hasn't been stolen. It was borrowed and then mistakenly collected as evidence. Say, Mr. Chen—the Chinese official who was murdered—he didn't make any outgoing calls, did he?"

Her eyes widened for a second. "No, he didn't. That was one of the first things that you people—the police—asked. No calls were placed from his room over the three nights of his stay."

"And you've turned over the surveillance tapes of the lobby, as well?"

"That last night, yes."

"No, I meant his first and second nights, too!"

"I don't believe we have, but I also don't believe the police have asked for them."

"Do you have a pay phone in the lobby?"

"No, we don't. We try to keep people traffic to a minimum for the convenience of our guests."

"May I use your desk phone, please? This is official police business."

She brought me to the end of the counter and handed over a handset to me. I gave her the number to call, all the while suspecting that she wouldn't let me dial it myself because she thought I'd try calling Asia.

"Yeah?" said a gruff voice at the end of the line.

"Izzy. It's Robert Chow."

"Yeah?"

"I'm bringing more lobby tapes from the hotel."

"What! We already saw what we needed to."

"No, you haven't."

I PRACTICALLY RAN into the audio/visual room of Manhattan South to get to the videotape machine. It took a while for me to get used to the controls, but when I was able to find what I was looking for, I called up to Izzy's office and told him to come down.

"I thought he was under twenty-four-hour guard," said Izzy.

"They were in the next room with a panic-button setup," I said. "If he buzzed them, they'd kick the door in. But he didn't. It was meant to protect his privacy."

"Weren't the guards FBI?"

"They were contractors. Mr. Chen was a private citizen of a country that the U.S. doesn't officially believe exists."

We watched the playback of Mr. Chen calmly stepping out of The Plaza the first night close to midnight and returning half an hour later. The second night he did the same. It was creepy watching the image of a dead man walking around like everything was fine.

I WENT BACK to The Plaza at about midnight and circled the block. I wanted to see what Mr. Chen would have seen. Amazingly, or not, none of the street pay phones worked. The surrounding businesses across the street were upscale but had closed hours ago.

Then I noticed that the southwest corner, Fifty-eighth Street and Sixth Avenue, was a little scruffy. I saw a cheap newsstand on the diagonal corner and a little farther down the block was a diner.

There were too many mirrors and lights in the diner and as I walked in I had to shield my eyes from the glare. It was on the smaller side, with only about ten tables and a short counter. Only a few people were there. A family of tourists who were underdressed for the fall weather and a cabbie doing a crossword puzzle. I saw a wooden New York Telephone booth in the back and headed straight for it.

"You wanna seat for one?" the counterman asked me. He had on a wrinkled but clean white uniform with a T-shirt collar visible at his neck. He was about forty and some gray had crept into his crew cut black hair.

"I'm not gonna stay," I said. I got in the booth and shut the door, triggering a dim overhead light and a chugging fan. I couldn't see too well, but the phone number in the center of the dial was scratched off.

I picked up the handset and didn't hear a dial tone. I played with the cradle but it didn't help any. If the phone worked I could have easily asked the operator what number I was calling from.

The phone looked in good shape but who knew why it wasn't working.

I swung open the door and stepped out.

"It's broken. Broke this morning," said the counterman.

"You could have told me before I went in there," I said.

The right side of his mouth curled up. "I could've."

I slid on to a stool at the counter. "Can I ask you a favor, sir?"

"You sure can."

"What is the phone number to that booth?"

"I don't remember."

I sighed and reached for my wallet. I opened it up and laid it flat on the counter. I tapped on my shield and said, "Remember now?"

The counterman lost his smile. "The numbers kid doesn't come around here anymore, I swear to God."

"I'm not investigating bookies. I only want to know the phone number."

"I really don't remember. Previous owner warned me never to pick up that phone."

"I guess I can get the number later. One more pain-in-the-ass thing for me to do. Are you usually here this time of night, sir?"

"Call me Walt. I'm here sixteen hours a day, rain or shine."

"I'm Robert. Nice to meet you, Walt. You remember seeing an older Chinese guy using that phone around midnight for a couple nights?"

"How old?"

"In his late fifties, but probably looks younger than that to you."

"I can always tell, buddy," he said. "I got magic eyes. Yeah, some guy was using the phone."

"Have you heard on the news about a guy from China who was killed in Chinatown? He was named Mr. Chen."

"I did hear something about it. I guess I missed most of the story."

"I think that was Mr. Chen who was using the phone."

"No shit."

"Have a look at this picture. Was this the guy?"

He opened his mouth and licked his bottom lip. "I think so."

"Or did he look like this guy?"

"No, more like the first one."

"Now, how about this one?"

"Damn. I don't know."

"Are you sure? Use your magic eyes."

"It's either the first one or the third."

"That's not going to do it."

"Which one is right, though?"

"The right one was the first one. That's Mr. Chen. The second is a random government Chinese official. The third is an American World War Two veteran."

"You people fought in World War Two?"

"We sure did."

He leaned on the counter and whistled. This was mind-blowing for him. "That's great. Really."

"Now, about Mr. Chen."

"I did feel good about the first picture."

"Good enough to swear it was him?"

"Maybe not."

"The Chinese guy that you did see, was he alone or was there anyone with him?"

"No, he was definitely alone. He came in three times. The first two times, he used the phone and left, and the third, he sat alone in a booth and all he had was a cup of tea."

"You remember anything else?"

"When it's not too busy, I like to imagine stories about the customers. If someone looks sad, I'll make up some hard-luck story. That sort of stuff. Your guy sat there with a sort of blank look, trying not to look conspicuous. His eyes were excited, though, that third time, darting back and forth and everywhere.

"So I came up with a story about him. I know now that he's Chinese, but I imagined that he was a Japanese soldier, one of those who refused to surrender and stayed in the jungle for two decades. Then he comes out and becomes a cabbie in New York. One day this young Japanese guy gets in the cab and stares at him. The ex-soldier looks up in his rearview mirror and stares back. Then the young guy says, 'Dad?'"

"You have a mind for making movies."

"You like the rearview mirror thing? It's less confrontational than two people staring at each other. I took that from the mirrors in here. You wouldn't believe what people do when they don't think anyone's looking."

"You don't have to tell me," I said, standing up.

"I'm sure I don't! You've seen 'em all!"

"Can you make up a story about me?"

"I'm going to put you in the story I told you. You're the young Japanese passenger in the cab."

"I'm Chinese, too. It wouldn't work."

"Hey, it's moviemaking. We could pull it off with the right director."

IN THE EARLY afternoon I came to Vandyne in the squad room with the information I had from the diner the night before.

"So you probably want to get the phone number of the pay phone in the diner," he said. "That's easy."

"Yeah, that part is," I said. "But I also need a record of the outgoing calls from it. In a way that will stick in an affidavit."

"How sure are you that Mr. Chen used that phone?"

"I'm fifty-fifty. Maybe a little less."

"Aw, shit."

"What?" asked English, immediately on alert. He was on the phone and I had my back to him. "Do I want to know?"

I turned my head slightly to him and said, "No, you don't."

"Good."

"Bad Boy could help you on this," said Vandyne.

"Are we talking about using tools out of the black bag?"

I was referring to the extra-legal measures the old cops used to resort to.

"It's like dynamite," said Vandyne. "If you're careful with it, then everything will be all right."

I crossed my arms and looked up at nothing.

"This doesn't make you a dirty cop or anything," said Vandyne. "You're not doing this for money. You're doing this to cut red tape. If you find out Mr. Chen didn't use that phone, you just drop it. No harm done. But if it works, we are only helping along a happy coincidence."

"Okay," I said. "Where's Bad Boy?"

"Try Happy's."

I WALKED INTO Happy's on Baxter Street, one of the few non-Chinese restaurants south of Canal. It was run by Happy himself, a grossly overweight man who took little pleasure in anything, not in the food his restaurant served and certainly not in the company of others.

Happy would "greet" you with a sad little clown smile and talk about how he was going to die soon and nothing would fucking matter, anyway.

He was a little less jovial when he saw me, which meant that he looked thoroughly depressed.

"I'm looking for Bad Boy," I said.

Happy swept an arm back and pointed to a corner near the back. Then he disappeared as if he were swept out to sea. The place was crowded with elderly patrons who had been eating here since the block was a part of Little Italy. Coughing was louder than the conversation.

I eased my way to the back brick wall and through an arch to a small alcove that held a private booth. The curtain was usually closed, but Bad Boy wanted the smell of his cigar to waft out into the dining room.

He glanced up and tapped the cigar into his empty soup bowl. "Chow."

"Hey."

"Have a seat. I know you don't drink. Guess you want a steak."

"No, thanks."

"Don't thank me. It's on the house and so is anything else you want to drink. You know that, right?"

"Naw. I'm not hungry."

"You will be, though. Better eat now while the kitchen's open."

"I'll eat when I get hungry."

"That's a novel idea." Bad Boy smiled and puffed on his cigar. "So what's on your mind, kid?"

"I'm trying to get the outside numbers called on a pay phone."

"That's easy."

"But even if I could get them, I don't think I have enough to make it stick in an affidavit."

"Is that all?"

"It's enough of a problem."

"What condition was the phone in?"

"It was broken."

"Smashed up?"

"No, it's a phone booth inside a diner in Midtown. It looks fine except the line is down."

"It doesn't look fine."

"What?"

"Go back there and pry off the dial. The phone's been vandalized. Destruction of public property. You have to trace outgoing calls to help determine who could have committed such a crime. You can go through me to speed up the number retrieval. But don't let anyone in the Midtown precinct know. They might come after your ass for destruction of public property."

"You do things like this regularly?"

"No no no! This is kids' stuff, Chow. You get the bobcat badge for this one. You can even give me the phone number now so I can get a head start on it."

"I don't know the number, but the diner's on the corner of Fifty-eighth and Sixth."

He scratched his chin. "Funny. I think I know that place. A bookie was working that line, right?"

"That's what I heard. But I'm not after the bookie."

"Yeah, stay away from them. Could know a lot of people higher up, and a young guy like you hasn't got much cover. So are you looking for any particular number?"

"Just one over three nights. The murdered Chinese guy was using the phone, I think."

His mouth tightened. "Aw, fuck. Not that. Are you good with Izzy?"

"Yeah, I am."

"Okay. You scared me for a second. So. What am I going to get out of this?"

"You're going to get to give me a bobcat badge."

Bad Boy smiled. "I like you. I mean that. So, really, no steak for you?"

I was actually pretty hungry. It would have been so easy to sit down and put a napkin in my lap.

IT TOOK ME a while to get back to the diner because the train schedules were all messed up due to a track fire. I ate a Hostess apple pie while waiting on the subway platform, but it only made me a little hungrier and thirsty on top of that.

I was worried that the counter guy would want to chat again, but luckily, a guy I didn't know was behind the counter talking to two goofy girls in short skirts and big heels. In the phone booth, the dial came off surprisingly easy with just a cheap screwdriver. I shoved the dial in my jacket pocket.

I left and the guy didn't notice. I could've walked in with a flamethrower and he wouldn't have looked away from the girls.

Bad Boy had the list of calls for me the next morning; there was Teresa's number twice.

I gave what I had over to Izzy. I told him I was going to bring in a witness who could place Mr. Chen at the diner. Izzy looked at me and said I was going to get credit for working on the case. I said I wanted Vandyne on it, too, and he agreed.

"I DIDN'T THINK you had any white friends!" Vandyne said. He almost had to yell even though he was sitting next to me on a wooden bench against a wall.

"Anyone who will voluntarily take the time to head over to Manhattan South and make a statement is a friend of mine," I said. "Walt from the diner helped make us part of the investigation. Looked good for the affidavit, too. That arrest warrant should be here any second."

"Now you're going to officially get credit for your hard work!"

"This wasn't about work for me, man! It was personal!"

We looked around the room. Manhattan South's homicide bureau was as loud as a carnival that served booze. Phones were ringing everywhere. Down the hall, suspects who were locked up in temporary cells were screaming and banging themselves against the metal bars. The bureau was staffed with people who were hired based on how loud they could slam drawers and their ability to scream through layers of sound.

I didn't know how anyone could take it. My ears were ringing after about an hour. We had to wait for a warrant that could come any minute, hopefully before my hearing went.

Izzy stopped by and we huddled. "Everything cool, you two?"

Vandyne nodded and I gave a thumbs-up.

"That was good work, Chow."

"It was a lot of guesswork that paid off."

"Won't be long now."

"Any idea?" asked Vandyne.

"Ask Chow to guess." Izzy peeled off and did a cannonball into the teeming masses. Waves of people rippled away from him.

"I get it." I said.

"Get what?"

"This is what it's about. Being a detective. Having a gold shield. I used to think it would be just something for me, you know, what *I* would get out of it. Really, though, it's about being part of a larger organism."

"Let's see how you feel when you're figuring out your pension and you're not getting enough overtime in your last year to pad it out!"

"Vandyne, there aren't going to be pension funds left by the time we retire."

He smiled. "There's going to be pensions. Or there's going to be tensions."

I pounded the bench to show my approval. "Vandyne, I was wondering something."

"Shoot."

"What have you done that was out of the black bag?"

"I'll tell you. Someone broke a window in the backseat of a car and anonymously reported it to the police. I happened to be in the area so I responded. As I investigated the incident, I found an unregistered and loaded gun in the glove compartment. I arrested the car owner and that was the start of that heroin ring bust about a year ago."

"I thought the midget had fed you some tips for that case."

"He did, but it wasn't enough." Vandyne turned to me. "You can't tell me what I did was wrong. That was nothing compared with the shit you and I were doing in Nam and nobody stopped us there."

I nodded. Among other things, we had also each killed a little boy out there. Mine was holding a ball and wouldn't stop walking up to me. Vandyne's was inside a hollowed-out tree, shooting up a camp from inside the trunk.

I felt my kill was worse because the boy had nothing on him, but I never told Vandyne that.

"That case set you up for a gold shield, right?" I asked.

"Yeah, it did. If everything breaks the way it should in this case, it could do the same for you."

"Was that gun already in there?"

"It was there when I found it."

"Did you put it there?"

"No."

"Did someone else?"

"Yeah, someone else did. The suspect."

"Are you sure?"

"If I wasn't, I wouldn't have been able to type up that report."

"You can't type anyway, partner."

He shook his head.

I said, "Let's make a rule right now. Just you and me, Vandyne." I looked around. "We don't pull out the black bag for money."

"Absolutely."

"Otherwise we're no different from those scumbags Serpico wrote about."

"You're dead right."

We reached out to each other and shook hands. After making the promise I felt a little better.

"So, tell me how Paul is doing with the guitar."

"He's terrible!"

"Really?"

"Yeah."

"I think this could be the first thing he's having trouble learning."

"I don't think it's that. You have to suck at it for years until one day your experience pays off and you reach a point where you know what you're doing."

"It's like anything else, then, isn't it?"

On the other side of the room, Izzy held up a folded piece of paper that cut through the crowd like a shark fin headed for us.

"Looks like we've got action," I said.

I GENTLY PRESSED my finger to the apartment button. A wave of static shot back and the front door buzzed open. I looked back at Izzy and he nodded. We both went up.

When we got to Teresa's door, she looked shocked that we were there.

"Hi, Teresa. Have you met Izzy? He's one of the top guys at Manhattan South."

"Oh, what are you guys doing here?" she asked.

"Surprised?" asked Izzy. He pushed his way in and I followed.

"Yes," said Teresa. "I mean no. Have you found out more about who killed Lincoln?" She closed the door behind her and stepped into the living room. Teresa was wearing slacks and a blouse and no shoes.

"The thing is, Teresa," I said, "did you happen to speak to Mr. Chen at any time on the phone?" As I was talking, Izzy slowly walked along the walls of the rooms.

"Me? Why would I talk to Mr. Chen?"

"It seems that he had called here a couple times."

"He did?"

"Yeah, seemed pretty late at night, too. I think you would have been in, as you are now."

"How did you know he called here?"

"I talked to him."

"You talked to him?"

"Bodies always talk, don't you know that?"

Izzy stepped in from the kitchen. "Nice apartment," he said. "By the way, how did that blood splatter get on the wall? They never seem to come out completely, do they? I have the same problem in my house. Anyway, I think we can match some of your prints on the bloody rolling pin we've got."

"Why did you kill Mr. Chen?" I asked Teresa quietly.

Suddenly she was a blur. Teresa rushed out the door and ran up.

"We're covered, right?" asked Izzy.

"Oh, yeah." I said.

Two minutes later, Vandyne brought Teresa down in handcuffs with a Manhattan South detective behind.

"Why do people run up to the roof?" Vandyne growled. "Her feet are all cut up now."

"She wanted to say hi to Santa Claus," I said. We all laughed at her and her stupid bloody legs.

THE STORY CAME out that Mr. Chen had been calling Teresa from a pay phone. He could have called from his room, but he didn't want anyone to know that he was trying to reach his illegitimate daughter who had fled China years ago.

The lobby tapes had shown that Mr. Chen left the hotel temporarily the first two nights, coinciding with the phone calls at the pay-phone booth in the diner.

Teresa had grown up in near poverty with her mother, and Mr. Chen had sent them money only rarely. She saw his picture in the newspaper from time to time but didn't believe that he was her father until he visited very late at night on her tenth birthday. At the time, she had picked up a kitchen mallet and hit him on his arm as hard as she could with it.

He should have known not to come looking for her fifteen years later, after she had taken a train south and snuck into Hong Kong and then entered the United States through a sponsor family.

Teresa admitted that she had talked to Mr. Chen on the phone and even told him the cross streets of where she lived. He had come over and they were simply going to eat.

But then he had asked her if she could help bring his family over to America. After all, they were her family, too.

She thought about all those years of struggling with her mother while Mr. Chen and his wife and kids lived in luxury in condominiums built for provincial officials.

Her hands moved on their own and she hit him with whatever was handy. Repeatedly. When she saw her phone number and address on his finger, she took a Chinese kitchen knife and hacked it off.

Teresa insisted again and again that she acted absolutely alone and that Lee had been trying to cover for her with his story.

I MET VANDYNE next to where Mr. Chen's body was found in the park.

He turned the lapels up on his leather jacket and said, "If you're comfortable with Teresa being the murderer, then maybe this isn't necessary."

"I'm not. You know, Lonnie says that if I don't think a woman has the strength to carry a man, then I don't know how strong a woman can be."

"Teresa is a strong woman. I could tell she had a lot of upper-body strength when I was cuffing her."

We stepped over the tape and walked around. There could be something to tie Lee in with the murder.

"Still, though," I said. "I find it hard to believe that she could have dragged or carried a body six or seven blocks."

"I know that Chinese hardly ever call anything in, but a woman pulling a body in a shower curtain would have attracted some attention, right?"

"The guy with the mole is the key. He was actually the last person who spoke with Mr. Chen, not Lonnie."

"They probably put the body in his car and then dumped it off here," said Vandyne.

"But how do we find mole-man? Can't very well look through Heavenly Horse's employment records. They don't record the physical features of their drivers."

"What about the voucher Lonnie signed? Can't you track her driver from it?"

"The drivers are paid in cash when they turn in their vouchers and then they're alphabetized by the customer's last name. The desk clerk makes sure that the customer has signed but not that the slip is filled out completely. The driver's name was left blank, and that might be standard operating procedure in a largely cash business."

Vandyne nodded. "Looks like they pulled all the cigarette butts, soda cans, and needles from this area already."

"Yeah. So all this paper trash you see here is new. What makes people want to litter at a crime scene?"

"I think the wind could've blown all this into the area. Do you seriously think someone would have walked here to throw away a wig?"

"Where?"

"Right there, man. I thought it was a dead squirrel at first."

Vandyne's discovery made me think of something.

"What if there is no man with a mole?" I asked.

"What are you talking about?"

"What if that driver doesn't exist?"

"Didn't Lonnie say a man with a mole picked her up?"

"Yes."

"That means he's real, partner."

"The man is real, but the mole isn't!"

I SAW BAD BOY standing near the top of the stoop of the Fifth Precinct. He stood perfectly still while trying to read the minds of passersby. I went up the steps and stood on the opposite side of the door as him. Neither of us looked at each other.

"I've been thinking about something," I said.

"Trying something new, eh?"

"It's something that could get Pete mad."

"What do you mean 'mad'?"

"I mean this involves one of his guys."

"Which one?"

"Lee."

"Oh. He's gonna be pissed."

"Should I tell him what I think I got?"

"How bad is it?"

"Something to hang for."

"You better tell him now. His mood's only getting worse."

I ran into Pete in the squad room's kitchenette. He was sitting at the table. A paper plate in front of him held the skeletal crusts of what used to be three pizza slices.

"I thought you weren't working as the pizza man anymore," I said.

"Go fuck yourself, Chow!"

"What the hell's your problem?"

"This fucking scumbag reported me to the Civilian Complaint Review Board and they want to ask me some questions. He said I sprained his arm and neck. Motherfucker was resisting arrest!"

"Aw, shit."

"He's got all these bullshit medical bills and he's saying he missed work for a few months. Yeah, he missed standing on the corner and pushing junk on kids."

"Did he go to jail?"

"Suspended sentence. The trial was a complete sham. They brought up his traumatic childhood and lousy parents. Like that's an excuse. It only proves that it runs in the fucking family, if you ask me."

I thought about Paul. If he had stayed with his abusive father, where would he be now? I couldn't rule out selling drugs and getting arrested by a volatile cop.

"And anyway," said Pete, "this was two years ago, so fuck it!"

"Nothing's going to happen. The CCRB's got no teeth."

"You don't know, Chow. These things are so goddamn arbitrary. Yeah, most people, nothing happens to them. But if there's a cop they want to make an example out of, they stick it to him. I don't care if they go through my record with an infrared scanner. I've got nothing to hide."

"Speaking of which, I think someone's been holding back on you."

"What?"

"I think there's something about Lee."

"Is this still about the Chen murder thing? We got our man already. Uh, woman."

I told him what I suspected and what made sense to me. Pete didn't say anything or even interrupt to ask questions. When I was done, he rolled his head on his shoulders to crack his neck.

"Let's get a plain car and go for a little ride," he said. "Get Bad Boy, too."

"Right now?" I asked.

"Yes, right fucking now. I'll see you downstairs. There are some things I want to get first."

BAD BOY DROVE us out just east of Seward Park. I sat in the front passenger seat. Pete was in the back. He held up a small, old cushion that probably used to top a bar stool. It was thinned out by age.

"Remember this?" Pete asked Bad Boy.

"How could I forget the hot seat?"

"What's that?" I asked.

"You'll get to see it in action," said Pete.

"We're in the Seventh Precinct," I said. "Is this going to be a problem?"

"Naw," said Bad Boy. "They know he's our guy."

We found Lee outside a day-care center on Clinton Street.

Pete popped out of the door and walked up to him. "We gotta talk."

"My cousin's daughter—" started Lee.

"I know, I know. Now, this part is for your own good." Pete gave him a rough frisking, then pulled Lee's arms around and cuffed him in the back. "I don't want it to look like you're an informant."

Lee nodded. There wasn't much else he could do.

Pete opened the other back door.

Lee shifted nervously. He bent down and looked at us. "Hello," he said to me in Cantonese. "Do I have to get in?"

"We want to have some words with you," I said.

"Talking only, right? I can't leave here."

"We're not going anywhere." In English, I asked Pete and Bad Boy, "We're just going to talk to Lee in the car. We're not going to drive him somewhere, right?"

"We're staying right here," said Bad Boy. "We're going to keep him safe right in the car."

"See, look at this," said Pete. "I got this nice cushion for you to sit on because I don't want you to get hurt. I'm always looking out for you." Pete pushed Lee in, slammed the door, and came around to the other side. Bad Boy couldn't stifle a giggle.

As soon as Pete was in, Bad Boy tore the car away from the curb and did a U-turn against the one-way direction.

As we roared away, Lee cried out, "Robert, you said we weren't going anywhere!"

"Oh, well," I said. "You can't blame me. I'm only a passenger like you." It was true. I had no idea where we were going.

"What is going on here? Is something the matter?"

I said, "I was just thinking that it was good that we've picked up Teresa for the murder of Mr. Chen."

"That's a real shame."

"It sure is. But it made me wonder why you told me that bullshit story about you waiting with Teresa at her apartment the night Mr. Chen was murdered."

"I believe I made some sort of mistake," Lee said. Chinese people are good at smiling hard while talking. "I confused that night with another night that I couldn't find Lincoln. There were a lot of nights that he was missing, if you have to know."

"So it was all one big mistake, huh?"

"Something like that." He shifted uncomfortably in his seat. Pete watched Lee like a snake about to strike at a mouse but Bad Boy kept chuckling and glancing at the rearview mirror.

"Let me ask you about something else, Lee," I said. "There sure are a lot of drivers with moles on their faces, aren't there?"

"Quite a few, I guess. It's a natural thing. A lot of people have them."

"So how do you keep your mole from falling off?"

"My mole? I don't know what you're talking about."

"When you put on that fake mole, how do you keep it from falling off?"

"You're crazy, man!" At this point, Lee tried to lift his butt from the cushion, but with his hands cuffed behind his back it was impossible for his bent legs to sustain his weight.

"We got a wild bronco, here," said Pete. He put his arm around Lee's shoulders and forced him to stay still on the cushion. "Chow, I think you're saying something to upset this guy."

"Seat is a fire!" said Lee in English. He was so distraught, he stopped speaking Cantonese.

"Listen to this guy," said Pete.

"The guy who drove Lonnie home had a mole and a hat pulled down low. Sounds like a disguise for a guy who was up to no good," I said.

Lee said, "Help me! He hurting me! Hot! Hot!"

"Don't get Pete excited. If you just confess what you did, he won't get any madder."

"Let me out!"

"You were in the office when Lonnie came in and arranged for the car service back home from Midtown, right? She let it slip that she was doing an important interview. You figured out right away that she was going to see Mr. Chen. You grabbed that ticket as fast as you could but you didn't know yet how you would get to Mr. Chen."

"Maybe I only want to fucking your girl," said Lee. I reached back and punched him in the ribs. Pete took the cue and dove into Lee with an elbow.

"Bad Boy, you gotta watch those sharp turns!" he called out. "I almost took this guy's head off!"

"Hey, you know how rough these streets get," said Bad Boy. "I might have to hit some curbs, too."

"I get lawyer. Sue you. Police brutality," Lee managed to say.

I said, "You're going to need a lawyer when you explain in court how you decided to combine Teresa's motive to kill Mr. Chen with your idea to frame Lincoln for the crime. You wanted to be the sole leader of the Union of the Three Armies.

"You came to pick up Lonnie in disguise, hoping to find some way that you could get closer to Mr. Chen. You probably hoped that you could figure out some way that you could talk to one of his guards and convince them to let you take Mr. Chen for a ride to the airport or somewhere else in the city.

"When he came out with Lonnie and talked to you, you couldn't believe your luck. He asked you, probably in Mandarin, how to hire one of your cars and you replied in Hakka that you would come back to pick him up! You whipped out the Hakka dialect because you knew Mr. Chen would instantly trust a fellow Hakka.

"Lonnie doesn't know Mandarin that well and almost no Hakka, so she thought you guys might have been speaking some dialect of Mandarin the entire time! She had no idea what you guys were saying—and you counted on that!"

Lee stared at the back of Bad Boy's head and didn't say anything.

"You told Mr. Chen to wait in the diner for you to come back. Then, after you dropped off Lonnie, you changed the ticket to say there were two passengers. It was easy: you simply added another line to the character for 'one.' You figured that it would cause more confusion. You also alerted Teresa to get ready because you were going to be dropping off some fresh meat. You also probably got a shower curtain from your apartment and threw it in your trunk. You went back to pick up Mr. Chen and you pretended to need the address he was going to. You knew where he wanted to go, all right: Teresa's apartment."

Bad Boy eased the car into the entrance of a below-the-sidewalk garage and took us down two levels.

"I don't know when you went up to Teresa's apartment, before or after she killed Mr. Chen, but I'll bet you helped mash around Lincoln's shirt in Mr. Chen's blood. Then you wrapped up his body in the shower curtain and dumped it as Teresa cleaned up all the blood as best as she could."

We were idling in the shadows and the only things I could hear were my breathing and Lee's handcuffs clinking.

"How does it sound, Lee?" I asked. "Feel free to add in any extra details that I missed."

He was in tears from pain but he managed to chuckle a little and said, "You have nothing. Teresa say nothing."

"That's so brave of you to let this woman take the entire rap by herself. You're such a man."

"I am survivor. You don't know."

I felt the front door slam. Bad Boy had gotten out and left the engine running.

"Hey, where are you going?" I asked.

"I have to swing by to pick up some dry cleaning," he said. "It's just a few blocks from here."

Pete still had his arm around Lee's shoulders. Lee looked like he'd been through twenty rounds of boxing, fully panting and soaked in sweat.

"You're not looking too good," I told him. "I think a confession will help get this weight off your chest."

He shook his head hard.

"I don't think he's up for confessing," I said.

"I think we can do something about that," said Pete. "I know the guy who runs this garage. He'll swear none of us were around today when he's found on the third level."

"Who is found?" asked Lee.

"I get it," said Pete. "You understand a lot more English than you let on.

"Let me explain, Lee. When you get down to that level, your ears play tricks on you. You might think you hear screaming, but you're really only hearing noisy brakes and tire squeals." Pete reached down around his feet and came up with a crowbar. He rubbed the curved side of the hook across Lee's lips. "The teeth should be the first thing to go. Just to make sure they can't match up the dental records. You haven't missed any checkups lately, have you?

"Chow, I think you might need to give Bad Boy a hand with his dry cleaning. Make sure he doesn't strain himself."

"No!" said Lee. "He's going to kill me!"

I got out of the car and walked to the entrance. Bad Boy was leaning against a wall, drinking a cup of coffee from across the street. Nobody was around.

"Is it going to be rough for Lee?" I asked him.

"With Pete? Naw, Pete never really hurts anybody. The hot seat is the only thing he uses."

"What is the hot seat?"

"It's got Mace sprayed on it. When someone sits on it, the body temperature activates the Mace. Burns up your asshole and your balls." He chuckled. "I can laugh because I've been Maced by a suspect before and I know how bad that shit can be."

"It's not funny to me."

"What, you feel bad for Lee? He's a miserable fucking rat. He turns his friends in like poker chips."

"Oh, you got me wrong. I wouldn't give a shit if I picked up the paper tomorrow and saw that he'd been severed on railway tracks. This piece of shit fucked over my girlfriend in a big way."

"Then what's the problem?"

"The stuff pulled from the black bag."

"Aw, you got a problem with the hot seat? That is completely harmless compared to what they used to pull."

"Still. I don't feel real good about it. Honestly, I feel worse about the phone dial."

"You got the number you needed."

"Yeah, I did."

"It's not like that call was *not* placed from there, right?"

"That's true."

"And if it wasn't there, then nobody would have been hurt. Hell, nobody would've even noticed. And the hot seat is nothing, too. So there are some burning sensations. Nothing a few showers can't get rid of."

I looked across the street. Two little boys were throwing a red rubber ball to each other as they walked.

"Look at it this way," said Bad Boy. "Let's say there was going to be a soapbox derby. One team is allowed to use only what they have in their garage but the other is allowed to use an entire hardware store. Who has more options? Who do you think would win every time? Sometimes extra tools come in handy. We don't frame innocent people. We want to make sure the guilty get put away."

"A soapbox derby? It's been a lot of years since this was explained to you."

Bad Boy smiled. "Anyway, didn't I see you sneak in a punch on him?"

"I just poked him."

"Hey, it doesn't look that way to the CCRB. That's assault against a suspect in handcuffs."

"Speaking of which, isn't Pete worried about this with the CCRB thing coming up?"

"That thing is bullshit and Pete worries way too much about it."

Lee broke down. We took him back to the precinct and he made a confession. He could be tried together or separately from Teresa or maybe one could be turned against the other. I didn't worry about it because that wasn't my call.

We had Peepshow guard the plain car. We had to leave it on the street with the windows down to air out the piss smell.

As I WAS coming up the stairs, I heard Paul playing guitar. It stopped as I walked up to the door. When I came in, I found Paul sitting on the couch, reading a book. The guitar was already zipped up in its bag on the floor.

"I heard you playing," I said. "Why did you stop?"

"I didn't want to bother you."

"How are those lessons with Vandyne going?"

"I've only had two so far. It takes forever to get to Elmhurst and back."

"If you don't pay your dues, don't expect to get good at anything."

"It's harder than anything I've ever tried. I'm used to learning things in school quickly, but this isn't going to be one of them. Have you seen John play up close? That guy's a natural."

"He's not. His mother used to kick his ass if he didn't play right. You actually have an advantage over him because you have someone showing you how to play. He had to teach himself."

"I asked what kind of things I should listen to and he said to get forty-fives and play them at thirty-three revolutions per minute to figure out the guitar parts. He gave me some records to listen to."

I looked at a scratched-up Chuck Berry single on the turntable and wondered if it was one of the originals that Vandyne learned to play with. The Ramones album was gone.

"I see you got rid of that punk-rock record."

"I loaned it to John. He said he wanted to listen to it."

"I used to have a high opinion of his taste in music. What do you think of 'Rock and Roll Music,' Paul?"

"It's pretty tough. I'm having trouble with the chords."

"I meant do you like it?"

"I like it. You can see how it is an ancestor of what the Ramones do. Even the beat is about the same."

I put the needle on Chuck Berry and listened hard. The surface noise on the record made it sound even closer to the Ramones.

"Damn," I said. "I can hear it."

"So you're okay with the Ramones now, right?"

"No way. Chuck Berry was rock and roll. Comparing him to the Ramones is like saying La Choy is real Chinese food."

"Brilliant as usual."

"Are you keeping up in school and work?"

"Yeah."

"Can you expand a little bit on that?"

"Just wait for my report card to come in. You'll see I'm doing fine."

"You have any tests coming up?"

"What do you think I'm studying for?"

"So since you have to study, I guess you should go to the bedroom while I watch TV."

Paul grunted and left the room. I snapped on the television.

The Communist channel had a program about how much better life was for the people of Tibet province with improved access to education and health care.

The Taiwan channel was showing a concert with a squeaky clean, light-skinned man singing about a girl to a neutered version of "Rock and Roll Music."

The American channels gave me a choice of *$25,000 Pyramid*, *The Bobby Vinton Show*, and a repeat episode of *Adam-12*.

I thought about those goody-goody cops on *Adam-12*. No wonder they got canceled. They wouldn't have lasted a minute in New York City. They wouldn't have pulled out the hot seat, either.

I wasn't sure how I felt about it now. I didn't feel bad for Lee, but I wasn't laughing with Bad Boy, either. I think on the outside of it, I saw myself pushing around and beating Vietnamese to try to get answers out of them. I didn't feel anything about those memories, so I really shouldn't have been upset about the hot seat.

Yet it bothered me.

My eyes drifted to the guitar bag. I pulled it over and unzipped it.

The guitar had nylon and metal strings on it. I pulled the fattest one and two seconds later Paul yelled out, "Stay away from my guitar!"

I LOOKED THROUGH the mug books, something I should have been doing on a more regular basis. Then my phone rang and I didn't recognize the voice.

"Officer Chow?" asked an older man in English.

"Yes, that's right."

"My name is Byron Su. I've met you a few times already, although we never really had formal introductions done. We've never had tea."

"Where have we met?"

"Oh, pardon me. I first met you around Columbus Park a while back. I told you about my children. Later on, I met up with you late one night at a broken phone booth."

"Now I remember! How are you, Mr. Su?"

"Officer Chow, I was wondering if I could come in to see you for a little bit. I have a couple hours left in Chinatown before my daughter will pick me up, so I was wondering if I could come in and talk with you. I know something you may find interesting."

I looked at the mug books on my desk. "Do you know how to get to the precinct?"

"Yes, over on Elizabeth, right?"

"That's the one. It's the only one, as a matter of fact. When you get to the desk sergeant, tell him you're looking for me. He looks scary and his name is Rip, but he's a really nice guy."

I hung up and went to the kitchenette to wash out two mugs and to fix a pot of coffee. A few minutes later, the old man was in the squad room. I didn't bother to introduce him and nobody asked who he was.

"How do you take your coffee?" I asked.

"I don't. It's bad for my stomach and my heart. It's a case of two birds with one stone. My late wife once made me a cup of decaf and it hurt my stomach even more."

"You don't mind me drinking mine, do you? If the smell bothers you, I'll pour it out."

"Oh, for God's sake, please drink up. You're a young man. Now is when you should indulge because you can't later."

I looked at him and couldn't help smiling a little bit.

"You're giving me a pretty wide license there," I said. "But because of my profession, I can't fully give in to the permissiveness of the age we're in."

"That's very true! Moderation is probably the best track. The Taoists were right in a way." He looked down at the mug book open on my desk. "I'm not interrupting you, am I?"

"Not at all. I'm just staying abreast of some of the bad guys out there. This particular book features people who didn't bother to show up for court. We have warrants out for their arrest on sight. If I see them, I can take them in right off the street. Do you want to have a look?"

Mr. Su made a sheepish face and said, "Um, do you remember that I had something to tell you?"

"I do."

"Well, I saw a face in the Chinese newspaper that I recognized. It was the man who was arrested for his role in that awful killing. The Chinese official who had his head beat in."

"You recognized the photo of Mr. Chen?"

"No, the murderer. The driver. Do you know the restaurant that is by the broken phone booth?"

"Yeah?"

"Well, I was eating there with my kids late one night. I was in the restroom, brushing my teeth. I noticed that man go into one of the stalls. It was hard to miss—his face has such a tough expression.

"I brush my teeth for a long time. I'm very thorough—you have to be at my age—so I was still there when he came out. I saw that there was something very different about him." Mr. Su smiled. "He was now wearing a baseball cap and a mole on his face."

"How about that," I heard myself say.

"I was a little curious, maybe too curious, but I walked out of the restroom and saw the man get behind the wheel of a livery cab."

"Didn't you think that was strange?"

"Sure, I did. I was even thinking about going to the police with it, but an old friend from California was about to come and stay with me. I fully intended to tell somebody about it. You in particular because I had your card, Officer Chow. It's funny how I ran into you at the pay phone. I had wanted to tell you right there.

"But I also had the thought that there was the slightest chance that reporting it would interfere with my ability to host my visitor properly. We had many events planned out, you know. So I promised myself that I would tell you right after my friend left. And here I am. Coincidentally the man appeared in the newspaper today. So something tells me my timing was just right."

"Why the hell didn't you tell me when it happened?"

"It was strange, but I didn't think it was anything urgent. I didn't know that he was going to be a murder suspect."

"When you see someone changing their appearance, don't you think that person is going to be up to no good?"

"Or going to a costume party. Would you mind sitting back a little bit, Officer Chow? You're spitting right in my face."

I curled back into my seat.

"Because of you," I said, "my girlfriend had to go through hell as the default suspect."

"It's all right now, because you've got the right man anyway, right?"

I pounded my fist into my typewriter keys and the typebars mashed together in a bouquet of steel.

"By not reporting what you saw, you fucked her and me over, you lousy old man!"

"I never knew I did!"

"Let me tell you what's going to happen now," I said. "I'm going to fix my typewriter. Then I'm taking your sworn statement down. Then you're going to be a witness for the prosecution at the trial."

"Yes, of course I will."

I pulled back a few typebars and then I had another idea. Without wiping off my fingers, I dialed Lonnie at work. I handed the handset to Mr. Su.

"This is my girlfriend, Lonnie. You goddamn apologize to her right now!"

He took the handset and cradled it to his ear. I looked over at English and Bad Boy. They weren't looking directly at me but both were smiling.

I MET LONNIE for lunch the next day at the crappy U.N. coffee shop.

"Robert, you didn't have to make the guy call me," she said. "He sounded like he was terrified."

"He was actually racked with remorse. What a mess. You should have seen him."

"I'm so ashamed that I was fooled that easily. I should have known that my driver was wearing a disguise."

"You had no idea that someone would pull off something like that. You had the best intentions, too. You wanted to throw some business to a Chinatown company, so that the money would go to Chinese people. Look what you get."

"Chinese people aren't all bad."

"All people are bad, Lonnie. As bad as this roast beef. They should call this 'roach' beef."

She smiled and I watched orange soda creep up a straw into her mouth.

Lonnie didn't know how close she'd come to getting busted. The murder rap would never have stuck, but just out of spite the detectives would have found something on her. Maybe she had violated some antiquated law still on the book from the Un-American

Activities days. They would ruin Lonnie's journalism career to get back at her for all that wasted time.

Those Manhattan South guys are old, tired, and bitter. I know how they think. I was still pretty new at this but I was so sure that Lincoln was guilty I might have planted something to make certain that he was convicted.

It's terrifying that he turned out to be innocent.

I tried to smile and finished off my sandwich.

ENGLISH CALLED ME over to his desk. He opened up a box that had a gold shield wrapped in plastic.

"This isn't the actual one you're getting," he said. "But yours is going to look approximately like this. The Brow himself wants to get it to you as fast as possible. We have to figure out when a good time is, though. Like the way it looks?"

"It's not bad."

"Want to carry this one now? It's sort of a sample sale."

"I'll wait until after the ceremony."

I was going to play it cool and head for my desk without any fanfare, but English stopped me and shook my hand. Then I turned and shook hands with Bad Boy, Pete, and Vandyne. Pete slapped me hard on the back and said, "Welcome to third grade, motherfucker!"

BARBARA WAS BUGGING me every day until I agreed to meet with Wilson Yi one more time. He had wanted to congratulate me with a full banquet on the excellent job I had done, but I managed to knock that down to a lunch at the dining room in his office.

It was only the three of us—Mr. Yi, Barbara, and me—and we did the best job we could with the gigantic meat-only meal of beef, duck, and pork. Our table was lively as they asked me questions about the case, and I tried to be funny with my answers.

But there were other people eating in the room and the overall mood was quiet and somber. The stationed waiters and the clocks on the wall were silently counting the possible seconds to the inevitable time when the United States was going to switch full diplomatic recognition to Beijing from Taipei. I wondered how anybody in the building could focus on doing serious work at this point.

"What are your long-range plans?" Mr. Yi asked me.

"I guess to keep doing what I do as well as I can. That's all a cop can do. For twenty years, at least."

"I meant your personal life and when you're going to start a family."

"Oh, I don't know. Have to get married first, right?"

Barbara said, "His girlfriend is very, very pretty. She will make a beautiful mother someday." She threw me a questioning look.

I smiled. "Mr. Yi," I asked. "What are your plans for the future?"

"Right now my son is at Stanford University. He wants to study film of all things. I guess I didn't bring him up right. I indulged him with movies, and with my connections he met many famous actors and actresses." He shook his head but still looked pleased. "Maybe someday the Chinese will have films that are well regarded internationally. Someday."

Dropping his voice, he added, "My wife and I like this country very much. We are going to try to become American citizens soon." Barbara and I both nodded. There was no need for him to explain any more.

I washed up in the men's room. I think that once upon a time this had been a Fortune 500 company's headquarters building and that it would go back to being one. I looked at myself in the mirror. I looked like I needed more sleep. I got worried that I had some gray hairs, but it was only a shiny spot where the light was hitting my head.

I wished Mr. Yi the best and walked out with Barbara. The elevator was taking forever to come.

"What's next for you, Mr. Famous Detective?" she asked me.

"Nothing much, hopefully. I need to take it easy."

"Having that gold shield must help, right? Now you've reached a point where you can rest on your laurels a little bit."

"Like I told Mr. Yi, a gold shield doesn't necessarily mean I'm any better. It means I've done more time and not much else."

"The more time you spend investigating, the better you get, though, right?" She put her hand on my shoulder and leaned on me.

"In theory, but there are still things that puzzle me. Like how Artie's newspaper went up in flames. We actually thought it might be arson, so Vandyne and I staked it out, waiting for some dirtbag to show up and inspect the job he did. Funny thing is, you were the only one who came."

Barbara withdrew from me and pressed the already-lit down button a few more times.

"C'mon, dammit!" she muttered.

"I said it was funny how you were the only one who showed up after the fire, Barbara."

"Yeah, I heard you," she said. "You know that I never liked Artie. I think he's a lecherous bastard."

"I know."

"But you can't blame me for it. That fire was ruled accidental. A case of bad wiring."

"That's what the fire department and the insurance company both said."

"He was lucky he wasn't in the building," she said, shrugging. "Now he's got all that insurance money."

"Was he supposed to be in his office, Barbara?"

She laughed. "No one was supposed to be anywhere, okay, Robert? Could you not look at me like that? Listen to the things you say! You try to talk people into setting themselves up!"

The elevator finally came. It was packed. I let Barbara squeeze in by herself. I waved and watched the doors close over her.

ARTIE YI GAVE me a tour of a space on Pell Street that he was thinking of renting out as the new office for his English-language newspaper.

It was a tiny space and had most recently been a two-person travel office. The previous tenants had taken off without paying last month's rent, but they had left two large desks and file cabinets galore.

"What do you think?"

"Not bad."

"It's too bad Lonnie couldn't make it. I really wanted to show her the space."

"She is really busy catching up to her story quota."

"Ah, the life of a newswire reporter."

Artie and I sat on the two desks, facing each other.

"Artie, were you ever threatened by radical Chinese groups?" I asked.

"You mean like the Red Guard?"

"No, I mean here. Groups that are far-right and far-left wing. The kind that blow .44 bullets through people they don't like."

"Sure. I've been threatened by everyone. I don't give a shit. I've had my office broken into umpteen times, too. You people wouldn't do shit for me, either, thank you very much."

"Nothing of value was ever stolen, if I'm remembering correctly."

"That's right. Nothing of material value is in there. The most expensive thing I have is my typewriter and I carry that with me. All my confidential notes with my sources in them are locked in my desk at my regular job."

"There's never been an attempt on your life, right?"

"Not that I'm aware of. I mean, I may be doing an Inspector Clouseau sort of thing where I bend down to tie my shoe and a bullet whizzes by my head." He laughed hard. "But seriously, no. Sanchez, your boss, asked me before if I wanted to maybe think about getting licensed to carry a piece. I said no. There are enough guns in Chinatown already."

"Are you sure about starting your paper back up?"

"At this point it's a little up in the air. Landlords don't like me, but I do have all that insurance money, so I'm a safe bet as a paying tenant. There are always some willing to take a political risk by letting me sign a lease. But my insurance company wants to do a thorough inspection of any new space I rent. That kills my chances for finding a place in most of Chinatown, but I think this office could pass. Concrete everywhere!" He rubbed his hands together. "My paper was pretty damn good, wasn't it?"

"Yeah, it was a hell of a paper."

"I hate the thought that people will think I've given up, you know?"

"If the midget's taught me anything, it's that what you think about yourself is all that matters."

"Do you think people miss my newspaper? I'm going up against everything. People aren't going to want to read a newspaper when there's TV news with hot chicks, CB radios, and who knows what else is coming out. Serious news—print news—can't compete with entertainment."

"*The New York Times* seems to be holding up pretty well."

"I'm not the *Times*. For one thing, I've got more minorities on staff. How did you feel about Lonnie getting into the news business?"

"I felt good."

"But she's got that double handicap. She's a woman and a minority. No, she's got a triple handicap. She's also a foreigner."

"She's a U.S. citizen."

"Yeah, but they see her as a foreigner because of that accent."

"She doesn't have much of an accent."

"To me and you she doesn't because we're used to hearing English like that. But to News Editor Joe Blow from Peoria, she talks like she's singing Cantonese opera."

"She's doing really well at Presswire and they expect great things from her."

"Can I be honest with you, Robert?"

"No."

"Ha ha. I wish Lonnie were here, so I could have told her this, but listen. Newswires are for hacks, not professionals. It's not seen as serious journalism. When newspapers have room left over, they squeeze in AP, UPI, or Presswire stories so they don't have all that white space on the page."

"If you're in the paper, you're not a hack. Lonnie's interview with Mr. Chen ran all over the place."

"That is the exception, though. The general public won't see ninety-nine percent of her work. News from the United Nations? Give me a break, nobody reads that stuff, least of all newspaper editors! They put that in the paper so birds and dogs can shit on it."

"Let me make sure I've got this all down, Artie. My girlfriend, Lonnie, is an illiterate foreigner who does hack work for animals to shit on. Are there any more ways you can put her down?"

"I am not putting her down. I'm only saying that news is a tough business and she's facing all kinds of hurdles. Tell her not to stay too long at Presswire. While she's working there, she should freelance for as many newspapers as possible, if her editor will let her. Two years is the max she should stay at a newswire. Then stick it on the résumé and check out."

"Check out to where?"

"Some regional newspaper. New York's not where you climb the ladder. It's where you come to after you've learned the ropes in smaller cities. Lonnie will probably have to spend a few years in the Midwest or down South."

"Whoa! Wait, why can't she stay here in the city? There must be plenty of jobs at the *Times* or *Daily News* or *Post*."

"Of course there are plenty of them. But those are all dead ends for someone at Lonnie's low experience level. If you take one of those positions, you'll be stuck fact-checking stories and doing research for higher-ranking reporters. Your newspaper will also hire from the outside to fill in higher-paying positions. Being a low-level man or woman at a New York City paper is like being stuck walking a beat for years without a promotion."

I imagined Peepshow.

"You don't want that to happen to Lonnie, do you?" asked Artie.

"I don't, but there must be exceptions to the rule."

"There are. If Daddy owns the paper, you're on the fast track to promotion."

"You sound like you have a lot of personal issues tied into this."

"Maybe. I know someone who's been at *The New York Sun* for more than a decade."

"I've seen the *Sun* but I never pick it up. Is that a good place to work?"

"She started there as a researcher with the understanding that they would put her on a reporting track. That never happened."

"Is this woman Asian?"

"She's black, and she maintains the clips library, which means she cuts out stories done by reporters and catalogs it. Isn't that a shitty job?"

"That sounds better than my job, honestly. I'll bet people don't call her a fucking asshole to her face or shoot at her."

"Robert, it's a shitty job when you thought you were going to write that big Pulitzer Prize–winning series. She doesn't even get to work in the newsroom. She's on a different floor, next to the ad sales department."

"That doesn't sound like a bad deal."

"Journalists hate the business side because it's ideas and idealism that drives them."

"Artie," I said. "There's something I'm wondering."

"What's that?"

"How come you never left New York to get serious about journalism?"

"I had thought about it. If I were entirely serious about being a reporter, I would have. But I knew I didn't have the guts to, number one, really piss off my parents, and, number two, be willing to live in a small town for years as I built up my clips file."

"You already disappointed your parents enough by not going to medical school. Becoming a reporter would have driven a rail spike into their hearts."

"I can hear their voices complaining even now, God rest their souls. Yes, the paper had to be a hobby for me, but I was serious about it to the degree that I covered stories that nobody in the mainstream press did. I did have my fans, though. I would show you the letters I got, but, unfortunately, they were lost in the fire."

"Was the hate mail lost, too?"

"I never kept those. All the negativity was water off my back. But I did frame one letter that said I was guilty of sensationalizing all the bad things that happened in Chinatown to sell papers. That was lost in the fire, too, but do you know who sent it to me?"

"Who?"

"Mr. Tin! That guy who used to head the Greater China Association. Then the rumors got out that his son was retarded or insane, and he had to resign. The rest of the Greater China board thought that mental problems are hereditary and were wondering what was wrong with Mr. Tin."

"Not just them. Most of the community."

"That's true."

"I went to grade school with Don, his son."

"That makes sense. You guys are the same age."

"He wasn't slow or crazy. He needed serious medical attention and Mr. Tin was too afraid to let him go to a doctor. He thought word wouldn't get out, but it did anyway. I heard they all moved to London."

"That seems far enough away."

I CAME INTO the squad room with two hot-dog pastries in a bag. I saw Vandyne wearing a white-collared shirt and a dark-blue sports jacket.

"Whoa," I said. "Where's the job interview?"

Vandyne nodded. "I'm applying for my old position as partner in a marriage. I'm meeting up with Rose for that trip to Pennsylvania."

I admired the shirt's smooth look. "You even broke out the iron. That's dedication."

"I took it to the cleaners. I wasn't taking any chances on my physical appearance. I don't want her to think I've been slipping."

"I'm no expert on women, but don't you think you should look like you're in bad shape without her?"

"Naw, no way. A woman wants her man to look strong and sharp. Even if he has to fake it."

I put down the bag on my desk and shook off my wool coat.

"Getting chilly out there," I said, "and it'll probably be even colder out in Pennsylvania. You sure that garden will be open?"

"They'll be open. They're even open on Christmas Day. What's in the bag, Chow? I think I smell hot-dog pastries."

"They are."

"Didn't Lonnie forbid you from eating those anymore?"

"Yeah, but I figured one wouldn't hurt. We have to celebrate somehow. I brought one for you, too. I didn't know you were leaving early."

"I'm cutting out right now."

"You want one for the road?"

"I have to pass on that. I just got the car all cleaned out and that thing will stink it up." He held up an oversized dark-green trench coat and did two breaststrokes into it. He twirled a striped green scarf around his neck and popped an olive fedora onto his head.

"Vandyne, that is the ugliest scarf I've ever seen. No wonder you never wear it."

He buttoned up his coat. Without looking at me, he said, "It was a present from Rose."

"What I meant was that it doesn't go well with the rest of the outfit. It clashes with the hat, you know?"

Vandyne smiled. "I know it's ugly. But when you love someone, you accept everything about that person."

"But then you end up looking ugly, too."

"Isn't that the point?"

"You're going to wear that and you won't eat a hot-dog pastry?"

"I can't, partner, I can't. I have to save my appetite."

"All right. Hey, man, I wish you the best of luck." I shook his hand hard and clapped his back. "Both of you."

"I'll tell Rose you said, 'Hi.'"

After he left, I ate both hot-dog pastries by myself. I hadn't eaten them in months. The first one was great but eating the second was a horrible mistake.

November 2, 1976

LONNIE HAD WANTED to stay in the newsroom late to watch the presidential election but I told her she should watch it with me. We watched some of the early coverage together and I found myself getting into it. It looked like it was dead even between Ford and Carter.

I didn't feel strongly either way, but I thought Carter would win because the midget never picked losers.

We had dinner at a Spanish restaurant in the neighborhood. Chicken, pork, and black beans and yellow rice. We came back and the race was still neck and neck.

Paul was staying with the midget so we were alone in the apartment.

It was so close for so long, I had to open a bag of potato chips and eat because I was anxious and there wasn't anything else I could do. Lonnie was even more worked up than me but she wouldn't eat the chips. She said she didn't care who won because journalists were supposed to be objective, but I didn't believe her.

At midnight I turned off the TV and Lonnie screamed.

"Hey," I told her. "Save that for the bedroom."

AT SOME POINT in the night I woke up and saw Lonnie standing at the desk in my bedroom. She was holding something in the soft moonlight from the window.

Lonnie was naked. Her hair shone ghostlike in the dark. It was now past her shoulders and even though she'd been talking about having to get it cut, she still hadn't.

"What's that you've got over there?" I asked her.

"It's a telephone dial," she said. "Why is this on your desk? I don't remember it being here before."

"It's sort of a keepsake."

"Of what?"

"Something I had to do."

"Did you hurt someone?"

"No. Of course not."

"Did you do something wrong?"

I shook my head.

"Tell me what it was."

"It's cold, Lonnie. Come back to bed and I will. Wait. Leave that thing on the desk."

She got back in.

"So, what did you do?"

"Come here, let me hold you."

"Will you tell me?"

"It was nothing, really, in the end, anyway."

"Sure?"

"It was kind of a practical joke with Vandyne."

"A joke?"

"It's cop humor. Really inside stuff. You wouldn't get it."

"Please tell me."

"Well, it's part of a little story about a guy who thought that in the struggle against evil he would have to be extremely good. He thought that if he were even a little bad, that meant the bad guys won. But that isn't true. The good guys win as long as they do everything they can before resorting to being just a little bit bad.

"But you know what? This guy, our hero, promised he would always be after criminals, not money, and he made the promise with his best friend. That made everything all right."

She sighed.

"What's wrong?" I asked her.

"Falling asleep."

"Go to sleep, now, honey."

I traced the edge of her earlobe through her hair with my finger. It felt cold.

I sat up on my right elbow, looked through the torn mesh screen in my dirty window, and admired the quiet of the night.

Acknowledgments

DEEPER-THAN-THE-BENTHIC-ZONE LOVE FOR my universal partner and first reader, Cindy Cheung.

Sunyoung Lee started the ball rolling.

Kirby Kim and Eric Reid are playas.

Marcia Markland and Kat Brzozowski rock hard. Hector DeJean never sleeps.

John Schoenfelder has perfect pitch.

All respect to clans and extensions of Kaya, Cheng, Cheung, Kim, Lin, and Liu.

Detective Yu Sing Yee, NYPD (retired), and Detective Thomas Ong, NYPD (retired), thank you again for everything.

The Asian/Pacific/American Institute at New York University granted me access to their archives. You continue to be awesome and beautiful people: Jack Tchen, Laura Chen-Schultz, Alexandra Chang, and I-Ting Emily Chu.

Heavy bows and spicy noodles to Chez Ong, Corky Lee, Neela Banerjee, Karen Maeda Allman, Chris Bowe, Alan Chisholm,

Mario Diaz, Harvey Dong, Stuart Gersen, Maryelizabeth Hart, Eric Nakamura, Cate Park, Eugene Shih, Barbara Tom, Kristine Williams, and Martin Wong.

Epigraph from *A Dream of Red Mansions*, translated by Yang Hsien-yi and Gladys Yang.

About the Author

ED LIN, A native New Yorker of Taiwanese and Chinese descent, is the first author to win three Asian American Literary Awards and is an all-around standup kinda guy. His books include *Waylaid* and *This Is a Bust*, both published by Kaya Press in 2002 and 2007, respectively. *Snakes Can't Run* and *One Red Bastard*, which both continue the story of Robert Chow set in *This Is a Bust*, were published by Minotaur Books. His latest book, *Ghost Month*, a Taipei-based mystery, was published by Soho Crime in July 2014. Lin lives in Brooklyn with his wife, actress Cindy Cheung, and son.

www.edlinforpresident.com
www.facebook.com/edlinforpresident
www.twitter.com/robertchow
www.myspace.com/edlinforpresident

Discover great authors, exclusive offers, and more at hc.com.